"What would I do with a wife?"

Daniel stared out the window, awash in self-condemnation.

"You have a lot to offer," Karen said hesitantly. "And I'm sure many women would love living on the ranch."

He fixed his attention on her, scowling. "Oh, yeah? And what if I still lose the custody case? I wouldn't have the ranch then. I'd be down the road with nothing to call my own except a string of ponies. What woman would have me then? Who would marry a savage like me?"

Karen knew Daniel didn't expect a reply. But the temptation was too strong for her to resist. She took a deep breath and answered with her heart.

"I would."

D0048686

Dear Reader,

Welcome to Silhouette Special Edition...welcome to romance.

The lazy, hazy days and nights of August are perfect for romantic summer stories. These wonderful books are sure to take your mind off the heat but still warm your heart.

This month's THAT SPECIAL WOMAN! selection is by Rita Award-winner Cheryl Reavis. *One of Our Own* takes us to the hot plains of Northern Arizona for a tale of destiny and love, as a family comes together in the land of the Navajo.

And this month also features two exciting spin-offs from favorite authors. Erica Spindler returns with *Baby, Come Back,* her follow-up to *Baby Mine,* and Pamela Toth tells Daniel Sixkiller's story in *The Wedding Knot*—you first met Daniel in Pamela's last Silhouette Special Edition novel, *Walk Away, Joe.* And not to be missed are terrific books by Lucy Gordon, Patricia McLinn and Trisha Alexander.

I hope you enjoy this book, and the rest of the summer!

Sincerely,

Tara Gavin
Senior Editor

Please address questions and book requests to:
Silhouette Reader Service
U.S.: 3010 Walden Ave., P.O. Box 1325, Buffalo, NY 14269
Canadian: P.O. Box 609, Fort Erie, Ont. L2A 5X3

PAMELA TOTH
THE WEDDING KNOT

Silhouette®

SPECIAL EDITION®

Published by Silhouette Books
America's Publisher of Contemporary Romance

To Ann Sibley, who sat in front of me in homeroom about a
hundred years ago and has been a dear friend ever since.

Special thanks to Sandy Snider,
Colorado Wool Growers Association.

 SILHOUETTE BOOKS

ISBN 0-373-09905-3

THE WEDDING KNOT

Copyright © 1994 by Pamela Toth

Printed in U.S.A.

Books by Pamela Toth

Silhouette Special Edition

Thunderstruck #411
Dark Angel #515
Old Enough To Know Better #624
Two Sets of Footprints #729
A Warming Trend #760
Walk Away, Joe #850
The Wedding Knot #905

Silhouette Romance

Kissing Games #500
The Ladybug Lady #595

PAMELA TOTH

was born in Wisconsin, but grew up in Seattle, where she attended the University of Washington and majored in art. She still lives in Western Washington, and she enjoys reading, traveling and quilting when she isn't spending time with her two daughters and her Siamese cats. Two of her books, *Two Sets of Footprints* and *Walk Away, Joe,* have won the Romantic Times WISH Award, and she has been nominated for two *Romantic Times* Reviewer's Choice awards.

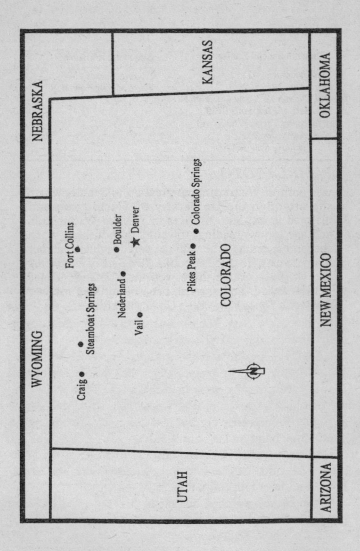

Prologue

The ringing of the telephone jarred Emma Sutter from a dreamless sleep. Her husband, Joe, whose body was curved behind hers, stirred and groaned. The phone rang again as he turned away from Emma and switched on the bedside lamp. Immediately she missed his warmth.

He hauled himself up and grabbed the receiver. "Blue Moon Ranch, Joe Sutter speaking." His deep voice stirred Emma's senses as she glanced at the clock. Then forboding shivered down her spine. Who would call a rancher this late at night? Apprehensively she slid closer to Joe and put a comforting hand on his bare shoulder.

He was listening intently. "Daniel Sixkiller is my foreman," he said. "I can take him a message in the bunkhouse and have him call you back in the morning."

While Emma watched anxiously, Joe took the pad and pen from the nightstand drawer. She felt him stiffen.

"Oh, my God," he muttered and closed his eyes. "How did it happen?"

"What is it?" Emma whispered. "Who's calling?"

He glanced up and shook his head.

"Are you sure?" he demanded after a moment. "There's no doubt?" Emma heard a tinny voice coming from the receiver.

"What about their little boy?" Joe asked, and icy dread chilled her. He had to be talking about Daniel's sister and her family, who raised sheep near Craig on the other side of the state.

Joe sighed as he rubbed his hand over his face. "I'll tell Daniel." His voice had deepened. "What's your number?" He picked up the pen and wrote on the pad while Emma tried to curb her fear and impatience. She liked Daniel. He had always treated her with courtesy. Even back when Joe had been fighting his feelings for her, Daniel had befriended her.

Now she blinked away sudden tears as Joe thanked the caller and hung up.

"What is it?" Emma demanded when she saw his harsh expression. "What's happened?"

Joe put his arm around her, pulling her close. "That was the state police. Daniel's sister and her husband were killed in a car accident tonight," he said as he buried his face in her hair.

"Oh, no." Emma choked out the words. It was much worse than she had feared. "Poor Daniel."

"Their little boy wasn't with them, thank God. He's at home with the housekeeper." Joe sighed and, for a moment, his arm tightened around Emma. Then he released her and slid out of bed. "I have to tell him."

"Do you want me to come with you?" Emma asked, starting to get up.

Joe was pulling on his jeans, his face taut with emotion. "No, honey. I'd better tell him alone. Why don't you make a pot of coffee instead?" He grabbed a shirt and pulled it on. "God, I hate like hell having to tell him this. I think Twyla and her son are his only family, and I have no idea how he's going to take the news."

Chapter One

"I won't and you can't make me!"

Karen Whitworth regarded the small boy who stood huddled by the classroom door. She sighed with mingled understanding and frustration. Jamie Powell had been such a sweet child at the beginning of the school year. He had loved kindergarten and gotten on well with the other children, his dark eyes usually crinkled with laughter.

Now, ever since the death of his parents two months before, Jamie's behavior had changed drastically. He no longer participated in class activities, no longer paid attention, either getting up and wandering around the room or arguing with the other students instead. He didn't smile, and he openly defied Karen, the teacher.

"Jamie, please come over with the rest of us and sit down," she requested in a patient voice. "You're making it hard for the others to pay attention."

He turned his back on her. "I don't care."

Several children giggled, looking at Karen to see what she would do next. Ignoring them, she walked over to Jamie, knowing she had to take back control of the classroom. He glared at her defiantly. When she saw his lower lip begin to tremble and his sad eyes fill with tears, her heart went out to him. She wished she could help. Slowly she pushed the straight black hair off his face.

"Come on, honey," she coaxed as he wiped his eyes on his sleeve. "I'm reading a story about horses. You like horses."

At first, she thought he was going to refuse. Then, with a deep breath, he nodded and took the hand she extended. For now, at least, the skirmish was over. They walked together to where the rest of the class waited, sitting in a circle on the floor. She would have to send another note home; if that didn't get a response from Jamie's uncle, she would phone him.

Karen finished reading the story and glanced up at the wall clock. It was time for the afternoon recess. Relieved, she instructed the other children to form their usual line and go outside.

"Jamie," she called, "would you come here for a minute?" Several students eyed him curiously as they filed out the door.

"Now," she said as soon as the last child had left, "why don't you tell me how things are going at home? Are you and your uncle getting along okay?"

He scowled and looked away, his small, bronze face obviously unhappy. "Uh-huh."

Karen remembered his parents from the fall open house. His mother, Twyla Powell, was a Native American, a lovely woman with hair that fell past her waist. His father, John, a sheep rancher, had intense blue eyes and a bald spot. Their happiness with each other and their son had been a tangible thing.

"I miss Mommy and Daddy," Jamie said now, as fresh tears trickled down his rounded cheeks. "I wish that Uncle Dani'l would go away again so they could come home."

"I'm not so sure that you're the best person to raise my nephew."

Daniel Sixkiller's hand tightened on the receiver as the voice of Ted Powell, Jamie's uncle on his father's side, droned on.

"My wife and I could give the boy a good home," Powell said.

"He has a home." Daniel glanced around impatiently. He was standing in the barn and he had work to do.

"You're a ranch hand, a drifter. What do you know about children?"

Daniel bit back his annoyance. Perhaps Ted did have only Jamie's best interests at heart. Still, deep down, Daniel didn't trust the man. Something in the smooth voice put him off. He didn't bother to point out that he had been the foreman on Joe Sutter's spread for nine years. Ted was some kind of real estate investor. He wouldn't be impressed.

"It was my sister's wish that I raise Jamie if anything happened to her," Daniel said instead. "You heard the will." That had been only the second time he'd met Ted and his wife, Dixie, even though they lived in Steamboat Springs. The first time had been at the funeral.

There was silence on the other end of the line. "Jamie will be home from school anytime now," Daniel added. "Do you want him to call you?"

"No, that's okay," Ted replied quickly. "I'm at the office. I'll talk to the boy later."

After he had hung up, Daniel walked back over to where he had been digging a ditch for a new water line in the near-frozen ground. A few minutes later, he heard the sound of the housekeeper's car returning from the school bus stop.

He stuck the blade of his shovel into the dirt and straightened, watching for Jamie. Up at the house a door slammed.
A small figure in jeans and a red parka slid on a patch of
snow as he crossed the yard. His breath made white puffs in
the air.

Daniel knew better than to hold out his arms. As likely as
not, Jamie would ignore the gesture.

"You look like an Indian," the boy said as he studied
Daniel, who had tied a bandanna around his head to keep
his long hair back.

"I am an Indian, mostly Comanche. So was your mom."

At the mention of his mother, Jamie's expression closed
up and Daniel silently cursed his loose tongue. He didn't
know what to say to make the boy feel any better.

"How was school?" he asked instead. After almost two
months, he hadn't been able to break through Jamie's reserve. Sometimes he still cried, especially at night, but he
refused to accept Daniel's comfort.

At the question about school, Jamie hung his head. His
black hair, the same color and texture as Daniel's own, was
short, but he needed a haircut. Perhaps Mary, the housekeeper, would take him into town to the barbershop. She
and the old shepherd, Cully, seemed to be the only ones Jamie didn't resent.

He scuffed his toe in the dirt and didn't answer Daniel's
question.

"What's wrong?" He squatted down so they were at eye
level. The two of them had always gotten along when Daniel came to visit.

Jamie thrust out his lower lip. "Nothin's wrong."

Daniel swallowed his sigh of impatience. How could he
help if the boy refused to let him? He didn't know much
about kids, and he hated to admit, even to himself, that he
was discouraged. The same little guy who used to beg for
piggyback rides now treated him like an intruder.

Daniel pulled off his work gloves while Jamie looked everywhere but at him. He had left a good job to come and manage the sheep ranch. To raise Jamie. There was nothing he would not do for his sister's child.

But nothing he did was right.

"How are things going at school?" Daniel persisted when his nephew remained stubbornly silent. He had meant to visit Jamie's kindergarten teacher to see if there had been any problems since the accident, but he'd been too busy trying to learn about the blasted sheep. Besides, Jamie always insisted that school was going fine. It had been easy for Daniel to put off the visit until more pressing issues were dealt with.

"School's okay." Jamie's voice was flat, colorless. Daniel remembered the sound of Jamie's childish laughter the last time Daniel had come to visit his sister. In his mind, he could picture Jamie's smiling face as Twyla scooped her son into a bear hug.

Daniel shut his eyes against the pain. So hard to accept that she and John were gone forever.

"I'm glad you're doing okay in school." He reached out to touch Jamie's thin shoulder in his heavy jacket. The boy flinched away and thrust out his chin. It was a miniature of his dad's sturdy jaw, but the rest of his face was pure Twyla. Daniel loved him as his own but had no idea how to reach him.

For once in his life, Daniel found himself wishing he had someone else to talk to.

Maybe he would call Joe Sutter, his former boss. Joe had taken in so many foster children at his cattle ranch, he must be an expert by now.

"Here," Jamie said, interrupting Daniel's thoughts as he tugged a crumpled piece of paper from his jeans pocket. "It's from Miss Whitworth. She wants to see you." He thrust the note at Daniel.

Miss Whitworth was Jamie's kindergarten teacher. According to him, she was old and wore her hair on top of her head. "Why does she want to see me?" Daniel asked as he unfolded the paper.

Jamie's shrug was deliberately vague. "I dunno."

From the pasture at the other side of the lambing shed, a sheep bleated. Another answered and then one of the dogs barked. It was getting colder. Abruptly Daniel tired of trying to make some meaningful contact with his nephew.

"Run back to the house and change into play clothes," he suggested. "Afterward, you can help me dig, if you want." He knew Jamie wouldn't come back. The boy avoided him as much as possible, but Daniel kept hoping he would begin to soften a little and share some small clue as to what he was feeling.

Jamie whirled and ran back to the house, thin arms pumping as he left Daniel to scan the wrinkled note.

"Jamie's behavior is getting more disruptive," it read. "We really need to discuss the situation. Please contact me at the school this week." It was signed "Karen Whitworth."

"Jamie!" Daniel shouted but Jamie had disappeared. They would have to talk about the note after supper.

He stared at the precise handwriting and wondered what Jamie's teacher wanted from him. Maybe she had just gotten too old to deal with active little boys. Ever since Joe had woken Daniel from a sound sleep one night to tell him about the accident, he had been doing his damnedest to cope—and making little progress.

Karen knew that Jamie's uncle had come to Craig to care for him and run the ranch, called White Ridge. She had heard from the school secretary, who was related to the housekeeper there, that he had been the foreman of a big cattle spread near Sterling. Rose said that White Ridge was being held in trust for Jamie and that the uncle was his guardian. Idly Karen wondered how he liked going from cowboy to sheep herder.

She had hoped he would take enough interest in Jamie to come by the school and introduce himself or to show up for the parent-teacher conferences. At the least, she had expected a reply to her first note. When none had been forthcoming, she decided that his priorities must be different than her own would have been under similar circumstances. Perhaps he had come here more for the chance to be the boss than for Jamie's well-being.

Jamie's behavior in the classroom was getting steadily worse. Yesterday, he had picked a fight on the school grounds. Any fighting was supposed to be reported to the principal, but Karen had put off discussing it with Mr. Appleby.

Now she glanced up from the new lesson plan spread before her to the round wall clock. Jamie's uncle had finally left a message with Rose that he would be here after school today. Karen hoped he'd show up.

A few minutes later, a knock drew her attention to the open doorway. A tall, lean man in jeans and a denim jacket stood there, a black Stetson pulled low over his face.

"Come in," Karen invited, rising. "You must be Jamie's uncle."

He came into the classroom and removed his hat. His sleek black hair was combed back and his skin was deeply tanned. His eyes—narrowed to slits and dark in color—were screened by thick, black lashes beneath slashing brows. High, sculpted cheekbones and a straight blade of a nose topped his unsmiling mouth.

"I'm Daniel Sixkiller." His voice was deep and soft, like black velvet. Karen guessed it might be the only soft thing about him. He glanced around. "I'm here to see Miss Whitworth."

Quickly she moved forward and extended her hand. "I'm Karen Whitworth, Jamie's teacher," she managed to say in an even voice, despite her momentary distraction. He towered over her as she looked up at him curiously.

His face was expressionless, but he shifted his hat from one hand to the other and clasped her fingers in a brief, strong grip. His gaze swept over her without so much as a flicker of reaction. Karen, who rarely fidgeted, had to stop herself from nervously patting her long, blond hair.

"I expected someone older."

She was used to that common misconception. "To a five-year-old, I'm ancient."

Understanding dawned on his face, but he didn't return her grin. Close up, she could see that his eyes were as dark as his nephew's. Pupil and iris merged together like pools of India ink. In them, she saw the tiny, twin reflections of her own image. No windows of the soul, this man's eyes revealed little more of himself than would a wall of black glass.

While he glanced around curiously, she stared, noticing that a tiny silver hoop pierced his earlobe.

"Did you get my message?" he asked.

Karen's preoccupation with his appearance was abruptly shattered. To cover her lapse in manners, she turned and gestured toward the front of the room.

"Yes. Please, come and have a seat." Keenly conscious of him following silently behind her, she tried to keep her hips still as she walked down one narrow aisle. Then she turned to face him as she perched on the edge of her desk.

He stopped in front of her and glanced at the small student desks hesitantly.

"Would you like to take my chair?" she asked.

"No, thank you." He sat gingerly down on a desktop. When it didn't collapse beneath him, he set his hat on one bent knee and folded his arms across his broad chest. He fixed Karen with an unwavering stare, apparently content to wait for her to begin.

She moistened suddenly dry lips and tried to decide where best to start, as he watched—silent and unmoving. As nervous as a new student on the first day of school, she happened to notice the decorative silver band on the Stetson he held. It was set with turquoise stones.

"That's lovely," she exclaimed without thinking. "Did you make it yourself?"

Daniel glanced at the hat and then back at her. "No. It's Navajo."

When he didn't elaborate, Karen wondered if she had offended him. His expression revealed nothing. Nervously she rose and circled her desk, sinking gratefully into the chair behind it. Somehow, she felt better with the wide barrier between them.

She was surprised to see the ghost of a grin on his hard face, as if he knew exactly why she had moved. "I'm glad to finally meet you," she said, determined to regain control of the situation.

His gaze remained steady on hers. "Finally?" he echoed. "I only got your note the other day."

"You missed parent-teacher conferences last month," she chided gently, "and I did send an earlier note. Didn't you receive it?"

Somewhere down the hall a door slammed. Footsteps sounded hollowly, growing fainter. Karen suppressed a shiver and willed herself to relax. Before her, Daniel Sixkiller uncoiled his body like a panther roused from sleep and got to his feet. Frowning, he went to the window and looked out. His straight black hair was gathered into a ponytail at his nape and bound with a leather thong. It gave him the look of a warrior.

"I know nothing of these conferences." He turned to face her. The softness had disappeared from his voice. "And no, I didn't get any other note."

"Sometimes the children fail to bring them home," she said hastily. "I didn't mean to imply that you were at fault."

"But you thought I might be."

Karen refused to keep apologizing. She stood, too, hackles rising. "It does happen on occasion," she said, refusing to become either defensive or submissive. "A parent or guardian who's too busy to get involved."

"You tried to contact me before?"

"That's right."

He scowled and, for a moment, she felt sorry for Jamie. "And you thought that I was ignoring your request?"

Karen hesitated. "I kept hoping that Jamie would begin to show some signs of adjustment," she said finally.

"But you think that he hasn't." A muscle twitched in Daniel's cheek and his eyes shifted away, becoming opaque.

Reluctantly Karen replied, "That's right. His behavior has become a problem." She wondered at the feelings this man must be keeping locked inside. Or did someone this self-contained permit himself to feel things?

"Have you any experience with children?" she asked.

His expression remained carefully blank but his nostrils flared. "Jamie and I share the same blood. Why do you ask?"

Karen hesitated and then pressed on. Jamie was too special for her to give up on him. "Perhaps your nephew needs some counseling," she said. "To help him get over—"

Something dangerous glittered in Daniel's eyes. "He has me. I'm family."

"Perhaps he needs more than that," she suggested gently. "Just for a little while. He's lost so much. Maybe it would help you both."

He seemed to be considering her idea, but then he made an abrupt gesture of dismissal. "What has the boy been doing wrong?" he asked.

Hesitantly Karen told him about Jamie's inattentiveness, his refusal to join in and the frequent arguments with other children. "He used to get along with everyone," she concluded, trying to gauge Daniel's reaction to what she had told him. "He was always smiling."

Jamie's uncle stared down at his hat. "He doesn't have much to smile about these days."

"I know," Karen said. "And I don't expect miracles."

"He's been telling me that school is going fine, no problems," the uncle muttered. Then he looked up and his gaze was steady again, his face an inscrutable mask. "I would have come sooner if I had gotten that first note or known about the conferences. I'll speak to Jamie."

Karen found that she believed him. Just as she believed instinctively that Daniel Sixkiller did care a great deal about his nephew.

"That doesn't matter now, but I am concerned about him," she confessed, and went on to tell Daniel about the fight on the playground.

"How do you know Jamie started it?" he demanded. "Just because he's Indian—"

Karen stiffened at his implication. "No. Just because there were several witnesses," she corrected. "And one of them is a Native American, like Jamie." She rubbed the back of her neck, which had begun to ache. "I do know that the other boy had been teasing Jamie about being an orphan," she admitted. "I spoke to him about that."

Daniel didn't look the least apologetic for his accusation. He shrugged. "I'll talk to Jamie," he repeated. "But what he needs is time to adjust."

"I'm sure you're trying very hard with him," she said quietly. "But you need to know that he's having real problems."

Daniel studied his nephew's teacher. When Jamie told him she was old, he had pictured a spinster with thick hose on her spindly legs and thinning gray hair pulled into a bun. This woman's hair was fastened into a smooth knot, but it was golden blonde. He wondered how long it was when it was loose. A thin fringe fell across her smooth forehead. He would have liked to brush it back from her eyes and study them. Were they gray as he had first thought, or green, as they seemed now? There was a sprinkling of freckles across her nose, and the color came and went in her cheeks, a barometer of her emotions. She would never be able to hide her feelings and it was obvious that she cared about Jamie. As for her legs, they were hidden by her slacks, but he would have bet they were neither spindly nor supported by thick hosiery.

"I appreciate your concern," Daniel told her, uncomfortable with his interest in her appearance. "And I'll take care of things. There will be no more fights at school. No more problems." He wished he felt as confident as he sounded. In truth, he had no idea how he was going to enlist Jamie's cooperation. For a moment, he was tempted to ask her advice. Then he pressed his lips together, reluctant to show any weakness. He was right; all Jamie needed was time.

She tipped her head to the side, studying him as openly as he had her. "It won't be easy. His life has been turned upside down."

"I know that."

"Yours, too," she murmured. "I'm very sorry about your sister and her husband. I met them at the fall open house, and they seemed very nice, very happy."

Daniel nodded, acknowledging her polite words. Pain burst inside him, filling his throat so he couldn't speak.

"Jamie's falling behind in his schoolwork," she continued. "He still hasn't learned his letter sounds, and he's behind in his social skills. It can be difficult to catch up later."

"I'll take care of it," Daniel said again, finding his voice. He wasn't sure what social skills a five-year-old was expected to master. What fork to use? How to make small talk? He watched the emotions parade across Miss Whitworth's expressive face: hesitation, indecision and then determination.

"Perhaps I'd better talk to the principal," she said finally. "The school district has a counselor on staff. It might be a good idea for Jamie to see her."

Daniel remembered Ted's words on the phone. What if someone decided that Daniel wasn't doing a good job with Jamie? Could they take the boy away from him, despite Twyla's wishes?

He didn't dare risk anyone from the school making a negative report.

"I'll take care of my nephew," he said.

"Do you think that will be enough?" Her concern seemed sincere.

"Of course." He had to be right.

Her eyes darkened with worry. "I wish you'd allow me to help."

He shook his head. If he was wrong about Jamie's only needing more time, then Daniel needed to find some way to reach the boy and he had to find it soon. For both their sakes.

"What about his schoolwork?" she persisted.

He thought for a moment. Jamie liked her, Daniel knew that he did. "If you think he's falling behind, then help him."

Her eyes widened. "What do you mean?"

He swallowed his pride and issued a challenge. "Come out to the ranch. Give him some one-on-one." The more Daniel considered the idea, the more he liked it. Let her see what Jamie's home was like. Perhaps then she would realize that the problem, if one really existed, was in her classroom.

"I don't know." She nibbled at her lip. "That's pretty unusual."

"You're a teacher. You say he's falling behind. So, teach him."

"All right, I will." Her sudden capitulation surprised Daniel. Her voice was hesitant, as if she were already having second thoughts. "I'll do it, if you really think visiting Jamie at home might help." She smiled, and Daniel was struck again by how pretty she was.

Was he doing the right thing? "I'm sure it will. Thank you." He slapped his hat onto his head and spun around, intent on leaving before she could change her mind.

"Next week?" he asked over his shoulder. "Could you come after school one day next week? What's a good day for you?"

She was almost skipping to keep up with him. "Wait a minute," she pleaded.

He slowed but didn't stop until he got to the open doorway. "Can you come on Tuesday?"

She looked distracted. "I guess Tuesday would be okay."

Daniel didn't trust the feeling of relief that went a long way toward calming his anxiety about Jamie. "I have to go," he said abruptly. "There's always a lot to do on a ranch."

Her expression was unreadable. "Thank you for taking the time to come in."

He glanced at her sharply but she seemed perfectly sincere. "No problem." He tried a smile.

She blinked. Her eyes were definitely more green than gray, and they tilted upward at the outer corners. Intriguing. "I'll be there on Tuesday," she said haltingly, and he realized he'd been staring.

"Good." He dredged up another smile, and noticed that her cheeks turned pink again. His own cheeks felt stiff from his efforts to appear relaxed.

He knew he'd pressured and manipulated her into agreeing to come out to the ranch. He didn't care. For Jamie, whatever it took, he would do. He might need her on his side.

"You'd better give me directions."

"I'll draw you a map," he said, the tension between his shoulders easing slightly as he fished in his pocket for paper and the stub of a pencil. Quickly he drew a diagram, explaining as he went.

"I know where that is," she exclaimed. "It's near the old Patterson place."

"That's right. Just past it." He handed her the map. His gaze met hers. "Tuesday," he said again.

"Okay."

Daniel extended his hand, though he really didn't want to. Her skin was too soft, too warm. And her scent, when he was this close, was distracting. She let her hand touch his briefly as he thanked her.

"I'm sure you'll be a big help to my nephew," he said.

"I hope you're right." She looked a little dazed, a little uncertain. Before she could say anything more, he turned and walked quickly from the room. All the way down the wide hall, he kept expecting to hear her voice calling him back, telling him she couldn't come out after all. Telling him she was going to talk to the principal or to the counselor.

Only when he had pushed his way past the reinforced glass front door and it had swung shut behind him did he relax.

Standing in the doorway of her classroom, Karen watched him leave. He moved with animal grace, his wide shoulders suggesting subtle male power. As the sound of the door shutting behind him echoed in the nearly empty building, she roused herself and went back inside. Had she made a mistake, agreeing to visit Jamie at home? Was she wrong about his problems? Did he only need some time? And was she getting more deeply involved for his sake, or because she wanted to see his handsome uncle again?

She gathered up her purse, her keys and her tote bag, then walked back to the door of her room. If talking to Jamie at home would help, she would be glad to do it. Even though her feminine survival instincts were doing their best to warn her that Daniel Sixkiller might very well be just about the most dangerous man she had ever met.

Tuesday was shaping up to be a bad day. When Daniel poked his head into Jamie's room to wake him, the boy turned over and groaned.

"I don't feel good. I want to stay home."

Daniel checked him over. Jamie's cheeks were flushed and his eyes slightly glazed. He didn't usually lie about not feeling well just to avoid school.

"Go back to sleep if you want," Daniel told him. "I'll have Mary bring you something to eat in a little while."

"Thanks," Jamie muttered, turning over and pulling the covers up so that only the top of his head was visible.

When Daniel came into the house later to see how he felt, Mary told him that Jamie probably only had some kind of bug. "Children get them," she said knowledgeably.

Relieved, he was pouring himself a cup of coffee when the doorbell rang.

"I'll get it," Mary said, hurrying from the kitchen. A few moments later, she called him. The mail carrier had a certified letter that Daniel needed to sign for.

After he had, he shut the door and examined the envelope. The return address was a law firm in Steamboat Springs. Impatiently he ripped open the envelope and glanced at the contents, his coffee forgotten.

"What is it?" Mary asked. She was used to being treated like one of the family, and now her moon-shaped face was creased with concern.

Daniel lifted his head, as a bleak sense of doom filled him. "It's from Ted's attorney. He's suing for custody of Jamie."

Chapter Two

Daniel read the lawyer's letter more carefully, with the faint hope that he had somehow misunderstood its contents.

He hadn't. It clearly stated that Ted and Dixie Powell, prompted by the certain knowledge that the minor child, James Powell, would be better off with them than with his present guardian, were petitioning the courts for sole and permanent custody.

"Bastard," Daniel growled. Fury ripped through him, but then, almost immediately, the burst of anger was replaced by the icy hand of fear upon his heart. He crumpled the letter and tossed it to the floor.

Mary bent down and picked up the wad of paper. Smoothing it out, she read silently, her lips moving as she did. "Oh, my," she exclaimed, brown eyes wide as she looked up at Daniel. "Can he do that?"

"He can try."

Daniel took the creased sheet of heavy cream paper from her unresisting fingers. "I don't want you to say anything about this to Jamie," he said, waving the letter. "Or to anyone else." He didn't want the boy more upset and he hated gossip.

"I won't breathe a word," Mary promised.

Daniel stalked into the small, crowded room that John had used as an office. He slammed the door shut behind him and sank into the worn leather chair. It squeaked in protest at his weight, but he barely noticed. He tossed the wrinkled letter onto the well-organized top of the old desk, feeling ill. His gut was doubled into a huge, hard knot.

He glared at the phone. He would have to call the lawyer who had taken care of the will. If Mr. Lu didn't handle custody cases, perhaps he could recommend someone who did. Someone who could help Daniel fulfill his sister's wishes.

He picked up Volume One of *Funk & Wagnall's Standard Desk Dictionary* and hefted it in his hand. Then he heaved it against the paneled wall, where it made a satisfying thud before it fell to the floor. He had no intentions of giving Jamie up, no matter what.

Daniel glanced at his watch as he rose to pick up the fallen dictionary. Right now he had sheep to deal with and stalls to clean. Tossing the letter into a desk drawer, he stormed back out to the mudroom, where he grabbed his hat and thrust his arms into the sleeves of his heavy jacket. Perhaps the cold outside air would take his mind off this new calamity.

What he really wanted to do was to call Ted Powell and ask what the hell he thought he was doing, but Daniel wasn't a man to move impulsively. Not when it came to something this important.

"Hey, mate," Cully said as he joined Daniel at the sheep pen, shifting the plug of tobacco from one grizzled cheek to the other and scratching absently at his elbow. "Looks like we're going to get some snow." The old herder had been with John since the beginning, living in a little house behind the outbuildings. He helped with the sheep, took care of the herd dogs and kept busy with odd jobs. Daniel was counting heavily on Cully's expertise to guide him through shearing and spring lambing.

Glancing at the sky, Daniel agreed with the old man's assessment of the weather. The feel of snow was in the air. "I hope you're wrong," he said. "It's late in the year for a storm." Without Cully's help these past weeks, Daniel had no idea what he would have done. He suspected, too, that Cully had been relieved to stay on at White Ridge after the accident. As far as Daniel knew, the old man had no family.

The two of them got on reasonably well together and Jamie treated Cully like a substitute grandparent. Only Mary appeared to have no use for him, rattling pots and pans alarmingly and slamming cupboard doors the one time that Cully had ventured into the kitchen with Daniel. From his muttered comments, Daniel guessed that Cully's opinion of the housekeeper was equally low. As a result, he avoided the main house and Mary strayed only as far as the small vegetable garden out back.

"You'll want the shearing crew to come in about two weeks," Cully announced, "before the ewes start dropping their lambs. You best be calling today to confirm the arrangements." He spit a stream of tobacco that barely missed Daniel's boot. Daniel had learned the hard way not to move his foot.

"Listen up," Cully continued, "or they might try to take advantage, you being green and not knowing what you're about yet."

Ignoring the old man's reference to his inexperience with sheep, Daniel listened closely while Cully told him what to say.

By the time Daniel went back into the house that afternoon, it was snowing lightly. He had called the leader of the shearing crew from the barn. When he hung up, Cully commented that, if he survived shearing and the lambing that would soon follow, he might just make a decent sheepman.

As he shed his hat and jacket in the mudroom, Daniel had an uneasy feeling that Cully hadn't been kidding.

"I'm glad you're back," Mary said when he walked into the kitchen. Her round face lacked its usual healthy color and her expression was strained.

A sense of foreboding shivered through Daniel. "Is Jamie worse?"

"No," she said softly. "I didn't mean to worry you. Jamie's feeling a little better. His temperature is down and he's sleeping." Mary squeezed her eyes shut as if the light was too bright.

"What's wrong?" Daniel asked, concerned.

She rubbed a work-worn hand across her forehead. "I have a migraine. It's very bad."

"Do you have something to take for it?" he asked, not sure what a migraine involved. He only knew it was a severe headache. Cookie's wife back on the Blue Moon used to get them.

Mary closed her eyes again. "I have medicine, but it works best if I sleep the headache off. That's the only thing that really makes it go away."

Awkwardly Daniel patted her plump shoulder. If he had a choice, he would rather milk a range cow than deal with a woman who didn't feel well. "Go ahead and lie down," he said uncomfortably. "I can manage." He hoped he was telling the truth.

"I left chicken soup on the stove for supper." Mary looked relieved. "I'll be better by tomorrow."

"No problem."

"I almost forgot," she added. "The cat's been restless all afternoon. I think she might be ready to have her kittens, so I made her up a box in the dining room. It's warm there and out of the way."

Playing midwife to a litter of kittens was all Daniel needed to round out his afternoon.

"Keep an eye on her so she doesn't have them on one of the beds."

He summoned a weak smile. "You bet." He felt a headache of his own working its way up the back of his neck. "Feel better soon," he urged her sincerely.

Mary lifted her hand in a limp wave as she walked down the hall toward her small sitting room, bedroom and private bath. When she disappeared behind the closed door, Daniel glanced out the window. It was snowing harder. He was thinking about pouring himself some coffee when he heard Jamie's voice from somewhere above him.

"Uncle Dan'il, come quick!"

He raced up the stairs, his heart in his throat. Jamie was standing in the bathroom doorway, wearing his plaid bathrobe. His eyes were wide and his feet were bare.

"Look!" he said, pointing. "There's water coming out of the cupboard."

Daniel stared at the growing puddle and groaned. Water was indeed seeping from under the closed door of the vanity cabinet below the sink. He opened the door and spotted the leak. Before he could examine it more closely, the doorbell peeled from the front hallway.

"Damn!" he muttered under his breath.

"Mary will answer the door," Jamie said, watching him. "How are we going to stop the water?" His tone held eager curiosity. Daniel didn't have the heart to admit that he hadn't figured that out.

"Mary went to bed with a headache," he explained instead. "I don't expect to see her again before morning."

There was a bath towel hanging on the shower curtain rod. Daniel grabbed it and tossed it over the growing puddle.

The doorbell sounded again.

"Jamie, can you spread this out on the water? I'll be right back." Without giving his nephew time to reply, Daniel hurried down the stairs, wondering who would be fool enough to come all the way out here in this weather.

Impatiently he yanked open the front door.

"Hello." Jamie's teacher, Karen Whitworth, stood on the porch, wrapped in a long quilted coat. There were snow-flakes on her curling lashes and in the blond hair pinned on top of her head. Her cheeks were pink and she looked even better than Daniel had remembered.

His expression must have revealed his surprise. Her smile faded abruptly. "Did you forget about our appointment?"

Tuesday! Today was Tuesday. Jamie had stayed home and Daniel hadn't given school another thought. Suddenly aware that he was staring, he opened the front door wider. "Of course not," he lied. "Come in!" He didn't need this. Not today.

"Thank you." Warily she wiped her booted feet on the welcome mat that Daniel would have liked to burn and slipped past him into the entry. "Is this a bad time?" she asked.

"Not at all." He was uncomfortably conscious of his muddy work clothes and damp, tangled hair. He probably smelled like one of his own sheep. In contrast, the scent of flowers wafted toward him like a gentle rebuke. Resigned, he stuck out his hand, only to notice the grime imbedded in his palm and yank it back again.

"Sorry," he muttered.

Jamie's teacher had already extended her own hand in response. Now she shifted direction and began unbuttoning her coat as if nothing awkward had happened. Daniel admired her quick reflexes and fast thinking. Remembering the manners his mother had drilled into him, he helped her slip the garment from her shoulders. He resisted the urge to lean closer and find out if that intoxicating scent of flowers came from her golden hair or the creamy skin of her throat.

Daniel gritted his teeth and swallowed a groan. Clearly he had been without a woman for too long.

"How's Jamie?" she asked. "We missed him at school today."

"He's not feeling well, but the housekeeper assured me that it's only a bug." Daniel's tone was blunt as he turned away to hang her coat on the oak coat tree. He had to remind himself that it wasn't her fault he had forgotten the appointment. At the very least, she deserved that he be civil.

"Perhaps I should have called first," she murmured.

"It's okay," he said quickly. "Jamie's up now. I think he feels better."

"I'm glad."

Daniel glanced at the stairs. "I was just checking out a leak in a bathroom pipe," he said, wondering how large the puddle was now.

"Heavens. I can look in on Jamie if you want to do that. Is he in his room?"

"He's keeping an eye on the water for me," Daniel said. "This way." He led her upstairs as Jamie came out of the bathroom. His hair was sticking up in untidy clumps and he was frowning.

"What's she doing here?" he demanded rudely.

Daniel returned his scowl with a warning look of his own, silently willing the boy to behave. "I invited her."

"Why?" Jamie's lower lip jutted out and his plump cheeks flushed.

"I thought it was a good idea." Daniel was uncomfortably aware of their visitor behind him.

"Didn't you tell him I was coming?" she whispered.

How could Daniel admit that he had forgotten all about the visit? "I meant to," he said instead, wondering just when he had lost control of the situation. Before or after Mary deserted him? For a moment, he wished he was back at the Blue Moon, with no more responsibilities than the management of a couple thousand head of cattle and a crew of itinerant cowboys. Compared to this, it sounded pretty easy.

"The water's wetting the carpet," Jamie announced.

"Aw, hell!"

"Why don't you let me talk to Jamie while you deal with your water problem?" she suggested. "It sounds as if you have enough to do right now." She had barely finished speaking when a loud meow came from somewhere downstairs.

Daniel allowed his shoulders to droop for a moment, then squared them again. "I forgot all about the damned cat." He brushed past her. "I don't suppose you know anything about having kittens?"

"I'm afraid not," the teacher murmured. "Tell me, is your life always this quiet?"

Daniel glanced over his shoulder to see humor dancing in her eyes. He might have smiled if he hadn't remembered the letter he'd gotten from Ted's attorney. Instead he growled, "You don't know the half of it."

While Daniel kept a watchful eye on the pregnant cat and tackled the plumbing problem, Karen coaxed Jamie back into bed, gave him a simplified explanation for her visit and read him several of the books she found in his room. By the end of the first one, his mood had improved.

From the bathroom, the occasional ring of metal against metal, punctuated with muffled exclamations, was interrupted by the sounds of Daniel's footsteps as he ran up and down the stairs. Apparently the cat was indeed in labor somewhere below.

At one point, while Jamie was choosing another book, Karen went down the hall to check on Daniel's progress. His head and wide shoulders were partially hidden by the open vanity cabinet beneath the sink. His lean torso and long legs were stretched across the bathroom floor, one knee bent, with his other foot in its battered Western boot extending into the hallway. A dark hand groped blindly toward her and a muttered curse sounded from the depths of the cabinet before his fingers, long and graceful, closed around a wrench on the floor. Then she heard a metallic scrape and an explicit oath.

Doing her best to ignore his sprawled masculine length, Karen silently tiptoed back to Jamie's bedroom. Finally the noise stopped altogether. Either the leak had been fixed and the cat had completed a successful delivery or else the water had washed Jamie's attractive uncle silently away, Karen concluded as she shut the last book. As she did so, Daniel appeared in the doorway. There was a bruise on his forehead and a smudge on his cheek. Prudently she made no comment.

"The pipe's patched until I can get to town and Muffy's had three kittens, who appear to be doing okay," he announced on a note of grim satisfaction. His gaze barely connected with Karen's before settling on Jamie, who had kicked off his covers. "Where are you going?" Daniel demanded. "You should be taking a nap."

Jamie hesitated. "Can I see the kittens first?"

One corner of Daniel's mouth lifted. "One fast peek and then it's right back to bed until dinner, okay?"

Karen realized this wasn't the time for a lesson. Not when Jamie didn't feel well and was distracted by the new family of kittens. She and his uncle would have to work out a different plan.

"Okay," Jamie agreed to Daniel's deal and hurried toward the stairs.

"Don't run," Daniel called after him. "Be careful and quiet or you'll scare them."

Immediately the rapid thudding of small feet slowed.

"He minds well," Karen remarked as she crossed to where Daniel waited in the doorway.

His expression turned wry. "Sometimes. Would you like to see the kittens, too?"

His offer pleased her. She liked cats, had even been thinking about getting one to keep her company in her apartment. She just hadn't taken the time to do anything about it yet. "I'd love to." She followed Daniel down the stairs, admiring the shift of masculine muscle in the snug, worn jeans. As she passed the open bathroom door, she saw that the floor had already been wiped up and the tools put away. The thought surfaced that not only was he ruggedly attractive and had great buns, but he was tidy, too. Good thing he never smiled or she might have been in real trouble.

In the dining room, she joined Jamie, who was kneeling on the floor peering into a box beneath a sideboard made of dark, polished wood. In the box was a black cat with white whiskers and watchful green eyes. Snuggled next to her were three tiny balls of damp fur.

"Look," Jamie said softly. "They're so small."

"They'll grow," Daniel assured him.

They watched the kittens nurse while Daniel patiently answered Jamie's numerous questions. Finally, though, Daniel got to his feet.

"It's time for your nap."

To Karen's surprise, Jamie didn't argue.

Instead he smiled at her. Apparently she had been forgiven for showing up unexpectedly. She was still kneeling when he gave her a hug.

"I'm as tall as you," he said. Then he looked up at Daniel. "I can put myself to bed."

His shrug was casual. "Okay, pal. I'll wake you for supper."

After Jamie had left, Daniel turned to Karen. "I'm sorry this visit didn't work out the way we planned."

"It wasn't your fault." She realized that it was time she left. Although the report on the radio had called for only a dusting of snow, she didn't want to be on the road alone too late. While she wondered if Daniel would ask her to visit Jamie again, he crossed to the window and pulled back the white lace curtain.

"Have you looked outside lately?"

She hadn't. The bathroom was windowless and Jamie's shades had been down. Now she gaped at the sight beyond the window—a swirling mass of white against the darkening sky.

"The weatherman said it wasn't going to stick," she protested. "I figured it would have stopped by now."

"Doesn't look like it."

Her eyes met Daniel's. "I have to go before it gets any worse."

He frowned. "It looks pretty bad out there."

Karen headed for the front hall and her coat. She was putting it on when Daniel caught up with her. He opened the door and looked out. Karen did, too. The steps and the driveway were completely covered. Visibility was poor. She yanked on her gloves and grabbed her purse and briefcase.

Daniel rested a hand on her shoulder. "I don't think you should try it."

"I have to get home," she exclaimed.

"That might not be possible."

"What are you saying?" What other choice did she have?

His gaze was steady. "I think you'd better stay here."

"Nonsense." Karen's voice was brisk as she shrugged off his touch. She couldn't stay *here*. Not with him. If she didn't leave now, she would be trapped until morning. "I have studded tires," she told him. "I'll be fine."

"Ah, hell," he said finally. "If you're that determined to go, let me get my coat and I'll help you clean off your car."

By the time he came outside, wearing his sheepskin-lined denim jacket and scarred leather work gloves, his Stetson on his head, Karen had the engine running and she was brushing snow from the back window. Even walking was treacherous; she had slipped and stumbled with every step. She wondered how Daniel could be so surefooted in his cowboy boots.

He looked down the long road and started shaking his head. "I don't think—"

"I'm going," Karen interrupted.

He shrugged and began helping her brush the snow off her car. She was eager to be on her way. After a few more moments, she opened the door and got in.

"I'd be glad to discuss Jamie with you later," she offered.

He nodded and she saw apprehension on his face. It made her feel strange, although she knew his concern was impersonal.

"I don't want you risking this," he said suddenly, jerking the car door open wider. "Come on back inside." The snow was rapidly covering his hat and his shoulders.

She tugged on the door handle. "No. I'm leaving."

His expression was grim, his jaw set stubbornly. "I'd take you home in my truck, but I can't leave Jamie and I don't want to bring him out in this when he's been sick."

She pulled on the door handle again. "I wouldn't want you to, but I have to leave. I've got school tomorrow."

"Not if this keeps up," he countered, holding the door open. He stuck out his free hand. "Come on. It's getting colder out here."

He must have assumed she would obey him. His hold on the car door slackened. With a sudden pull, she slammed it shut. Before he could react, she pushed the automatic door locks. Ignoring his thunderous frown, she eased the small red coupe into reverse and backed it around carefully.

Daniel watched with his hands on his hips as she shifted again and began to go forward. Unable to hold back a triumphant grin, Karen risked a glance at him standing in the snow. Their eyes met and she gave him a jaunty thumbs-up signal. As she did so, the car started to skid. She gripped the steering wheel with both hands but the tires spun helplessly. She saw out of the corner of her eye that Daniel, who had turned toward the house, was now watching her again. She tried everything she could think of, but the wheels wouldn't take hold. Finally, fuming, Karen shut the engine off and opened her door.

"All right," she snapped at him. "I guess I'll stay, but only as long as I have to." *If he says one word,* she thought furiously, *I won't be responsible for my actions.*

Daniel must have read something in her expression. Wisely he remained silent as he took her by the elbow and began walking toward the house.

"Just a minute," Karen cried as her feet slid on the wet snow. "Don't go so fast." Finally she yanked free of his hold. As soon as she did so, her feet flew straight out from under her and she sat down—hard—right on her rear end.

Daniel stood over her, arms folded, and Karen found out that she had been right. The man really was devastating when he smiled.

Karen sat at the table and stared out the window at the snow. "The main roads might be okay," she muttered without looking at Daniel. Her rump was still tender where she had fallen, but she refused to give him the satisfaction of knowing that she had bruised more than her pride.

"If it gets colder and the snow stops, all the roads will be solid ice," he said from the stove, where he was stirring a pot of homemade soup. The aroma made Karen's mouth water.

"I might as well do something to help," she grumbled. "Since I'm *trapped* here anyway."

Daniel sighed and put the lid back on the soup pot. "You could make some sandwiches, if you want." He had just come back in from feeding the animals and his presence made her nervous. How did he feel about having an unexpected guest?

Karen jumped to her feet. "Okay." Sitting wasn't too comfortable, anyway.

He pulled a loaf of bread from a drawer. "I think you can find the other stuff you need. There's some ham and sandwich makings in the fridge."

"I can manage," she told him, glad to be doing something.

"If you don't need anything, I'm going to see if Jamie's awake." He looked cold and tired. And relieved to be getting away from her.

"Go ahead." She felt bad that she had been inside sulking while he was out in the weather doing chores. She had offered to help, but he had turned her down. Now she heard his boots thudding on the stairs as she began looking through the refrigerator.

What she needed the most was to get away from him. She had terrible taste in men; she had learned that the hard, painful way. The summer before, her fiancé had left her at the altar. Now he was married to someone else and Karen wasn't ready to get involved again. Even if Daniel *had* been attracted to her, which, clearly, he was not.

She was almost done with the tray of thick sandwiches when Daniel reappeared. She had thought she heard a shower running and now she saw that she had been right. He cleaned up rather nicely, she noticed before she turned hastily back to the leftover ham she had been wrapping in plastic. His face was free of its dirty smudges and his damp hair was once again pulled neatly away from his face. His exquisite cheekbones stood out in chiseled relief. His faded plaid shirt was clean as were his worn jeans.

"I hope I didn't take too long," he said.

"Not at all." She kept her back turned. "I made fresh coffee if you want some."

"Great."

While he refilled his cup, Karen wondered whether the housekeeper who had made the delicious-looking chicken soup was young or old, and if she was attractive. "Shall I take a tray to Mary?" she asked innocently.

He shook his head. "I'll see if she wants anything later."

"How's Jamie?" she asked, fiddling with the sandwiches.

"Last time I checked, he was awake. He should be down in a moment."

Daniel lifted the lid on the soup pot and took an appreciative sniff. Only moments before, he would have said he wasn't hungry, but suddenly he was ravenous. "This looks about ready," he said in a remarkably steady voice. Karen set the plate of sandwiches on the table while he pulled open drawers and cupboards, looking for dishes and utensils. Mary usually prepared the meals and the kitchen was her domain. When he finally found what he needed, he set the round kitchen table for three.

"Coffee?" he asked Karen, holding up a mug. "Or would you rather have tea?"

"Coffee's fine." She still looked annoyed at having to stay here. Well, he wasn't crazy about it, either.

Daniel filled two cups and almost collided with her when he took them to the table. She jumped back as if she feared that he would bite her, or worse. He wondered just what kind of man she thought he was. Or what kind she was used to.

Maybe he should just grab her and kiss her, get it out of the way so he could stop thinking about it. No, not when they were stuck here together at least until tomorrow. He could keep his uncivilized nature under control for that long, couldn't he?

"You okay?" he asked, reaching out to steady her. She backed away and their gazes clashed for a moment. Perhaps he should tell her he hadn't taken a scalp or a female hostage in a long time, he thought resentfully. Did all men make her nervous or was it just him?

"I'm fine." Her voice sounded slightly breathless. Surely she couldn't really be nervous about staying here?

Karen saw Daniel's mouth tighten into a grim line as he turned away. Was he that resentful of her presence? The freak snowstorm wasn't his fault, she reminded herself. Nor was her misplaced attraction toward him. He probably didn't want her around any more than she wanted to be marooned here. Biting her lip, she watched him stir the soup again and then lift the big pot effortlessly. He set it on an enameled trivet that was shaped like a sheep.

"I guess we're ready to eat," he said.

Karen needed a respite from the close confines of the kitchen. "Shall I check on Jamie?" she asked.

Daniel glanced around as his nephew appeared in the doorway. "No need. Here he is."

"Why are you still here?" Jamie asked Karen. He was wearing his robe again, and blue corduroy slippers.

"Look outside," Daniel told him. "It isn't safe for her to drive home in this." His gaze dared Karen to contradict him.

"Snow!" Jamie exclaimed. "Cool. Maybe there won't be any school tomorrow."

"I doubt there will be," Daniel said.

Karen reached for one of the oak kitchen chairs and was caught by surprise when Daniel reached around her to pull it out.

"Thank you," she mumbled, flustered as he seated her. She was vaguely aware of Jamie at the place next to hers. Daniel sat across the table. He didn't meet her gaze. Had his gesture been an automatic one that now embarrassed him?

"How do the sheep like this weather?" she asked as he stirred sugar into his coffee.

He glanced at her and then his dark-eyed gaze slid away. "They'll be okay. Cully and I took care of them earlier."

Karen wondered who and where Cully was.

"It's too late in the year for this much snow," Daniel continued. "The shearing crew is coming week after next and then the ewes will be dropping their lambs. It had better warm up by then or we could have trouble."

Before Karen could think of an intelligent response, Jamie reached for the ladle. Then he hesitated and offered it to her.

"Why, thank you," she murmured, impressed. She took some soup and handed the ladle back to Jamie as Daniel passed her the plate of sandwiches. They ate without talking.

"Do you feel better now?" Daniel asked Jamie, breaking the silence.

"Yeah, I guess," Jamie replied. He turned to Karen. "Are you going to sleep over?"

Karen hadn't thought that far ahead. She looked at Daniel, feeling her cheeks flush at the speculative expression on his face. It wasn't as if she wouldn't be well chaperoned, with both Jamie and the housekeeper here. She wondered if the ranch had a guest room. If not, she could sleep in her clothes on the couch. That might be better anyway.

"I don't know how long I'll have to stay." Why hadn't she called the ranch before driving out? Why hadn't she realized the snow would get so bad? She could be home now, wrapped in her afghan and reading a good book.

"You'll be here until the roads are drivable," Daniel said. "Sometime tomorrow if the snow stops in time."

She hadn't thought that she might be stuck out here longer than one day. Surely not! The plows would undoubtedly be out in the morning. If she had to walk to the main road, she was leaving tomorrow, she decided. And Daniel Sixkiller would have nothing to say about it. Hoping that her own expression was as impassive as his, she slid back her chair and excused herself.

"I'll clean up here and keep an eye on Jamie," she told him. "I'm sure you must have more chores to do."

Daniel had been contemplating having another cup of coffee before he went out into the cold again, but he knew a dismissal when he heard one. He drained his cup and scraped back his chair. "I'm sure you'll be able to leave tomorrow," he said as he carried his dishes to the counter.

His gaze clashed with hers. "I'm counting on it." She began putting dishes in the dishwasher.

Resisting the urge to tell her he was counting on it at least as much as she was, Daniel grabbed his hat and jacket and went outside. He *knew* why she made him jumpy; what he wondered was why he apparently had the same adverse effect on her.

Chapter Three

"The kittens' eyes aren't open yet," Jamie commented softly as he and Karen watched them nurse. "I guess that's so they won't go anywhere and get lost."

"You're probably right." Karen stroked a tiny head with the tip of her finger while the mother cat watched her. It was early evening and the snow was still coming down hard. "They're cute, aren't they?" Two of the kittens were black with white feet like their mother. The third was white with black spots.

"Uncle Dani'l said that I can name them," Jamie told her, "but he doesn't know yet if they're boys or girls."

Karen was relieved that Jamie apparently hadn't given any thought to how "Uncle Dani'l" was going to figure that out. She rocked back on her heels and then got to her feet.

"Let's leave them to finish their meal while we get you ready for bed," she said.

"I don't want to go to bed. I'm not tired."

"Then why don't we find another book to read first?" she suggested, leading the way upstairs. "Or we could do some of the work sheets I brought with me from school."

Jamie wrinkled his nose. Just as she had thought, he elected to read a book. As he picked one, Karen wondered when Daniel was coming back inside. Even though she found his brooding silences intimidating, he still fascinated her.

Fervently she hoped the unexpected blizzard would spend itself by morning. Regardless, she would have to call Mr. Appleby this evening and tell him she was stranded. She only hoped he didn't ask her where she was!

Karen and Jamie were on their second book, about bats that could talk, when she heard the back door closing. Moments later, footsteps sounded on the stairs. Jamie sat up straighter and Karen dragged in a deep breath as Daniel appeared in the doorway with a long-haired dog at his heels.

"Jericho!" Jamie cried, holding out his arms. Brushing past Daniel, the shaggy black-and-white dog darted forward. His tail wagged furiously in greeting. As Jamie enfolded him into a hug, Jericho's pink tongue slurped out to lick the boy's face.

"Careful," Daniel cautioned. "He's wet and he's pretty dirty." He glanced at Karen, eyes hooded. "The other dogs stay in the run or with the sheep and Cully takes care of them, but Jericho's old and has arthritis, so he sleeps in the mudroom off the kitchen when it's cold out."

She patted the dog's wide head as he sniffed at her. "He won't bother the kittens, will he?" Even though she had been listening for Daniel, his unexpected appearance made her pulse thump like bongo drums. He looked tired and cold, and she would have liked to get him some fresh coffee, since he seemed to drink numerous cups all day long.

"Jericho likes cats," he replied. "He won't hurt the kittens."

At the sound of his name, the dog perked up his ears and glanced back at Daniel as Jamie pulled him closer and spoke into his ear in a crooning voice.

"Time for lights out," Daniel said.

Jamie made a face. "Can Jericho sleep with me tonight?"

Daniel shook his head. "Sorry, buddy. It's too warm up here for him in his heavy coat. He'd be miserable." He snapped his fingers for the dog, who immediately went over to sit obediently by his side.

"The mother cat usually sleeps at the foot of Jamie's bed," he explained to Karen before he bent and gave the boy an unselfconscious kiss on the cheek. Jamie didn't pull away but he didn't return Daniel's hug, either. "Mr. Panda will keep you company while Muffy's with her kittens." Daniel moved the stuffed animal closer to Jamie's small body and pulled the covers up over both of them. "I'll see you in the morning."

"When will the kittens be big enough for us to find homes for them?" Jamie asked him.

"Not for about six weeks, when they don't need their mother's milk anymore." Daniel glanced at Karen. "Know anyone who'd want a kitten?" His expression was innocent, but she wasn't fooled.

"I'm not sure."

Jamie lifted his head. "Where are you going to sleep?" he asked her.

Daniel's face revealed nothing. Well, it was his own fault that he had to put her up tonight. She refused to feel guilty about it, even if he found her presence inconvenient.

"I guess she'll sleep in the spare room," he told Jamie. "Now get some rest."

Cheeks burning, Karen patted Jamie's shoulder and whispered a quick good-night. Daniel turned out the light and shut the door softly after them. Without Jamie's presence to serve as a buffer, Karen was even more aware of his uncle. It was going to be a long evening.

Daniel watched her walk ahead of him down the stairs. Her waist was small beneath the red sweater and her bottom rounded out her plaid slacks. He watched the feminine sway of her hips and thought about bracketing them with his hands. Holding them still and pulling her tight against him.

Damn! How he was going to get any sleep with her in the house? A couple of times he had caught her looking at him with a speculative expression in her green-gray eyes. He had learned all about white women who were curious about how an Indian buck performed in bed. Satisfying that curiosity was something Daniel was reluctant to repeat, but it didn't stop him from thinking about Karen. From wondering if her lips would taste as luscious as the strawberries they reminded him of, and whether her hair would be as warm and soft as the sunlight that appeared to be trapped within its golden strands.

At the bottom of the staircase, she turned hesitantly and stared up at him as he quickly wiped all traces of what he had been thinking from his face. Her perfume swirled around him, clouding his senses. Its aroma was feminine and sweet, with an underlying kick that made his nostrils flair. His body reacted to her closeness and he shifted uncomfortably.

"I have to go back outside," he said in a harsh tone. "I forgot to take care of something. The TV might be out, but there are books if you get bored."

"Could I go with you?"

"Not this time. Stay here where it's warm." He hurried past her to the mudroom, where he grabbed his hat and jacket. He had to get out of here before he gave in to temptation and made trouble for both of them. Impatiently he called to the dog, who followed him outside.

From the kitchen window, Karen watched him cross the white expanse behind the house, Jericho at his heels. Daniel's expression, when he left, had been closed, almost hostile. She wondered what she could have said or done to upset him. If he didn't want her here, why hadn't he helped her to leave earlier?

Opening her purse, Karen pulled out her small address book and looked up the principal's home phone number. Mr. Appleby answered on the third ring and she told him that she was visiting a friend and had become stranded.

"Don't worry about school," he said. "No doubt we'll be closed tomorrow. The weatherman's predicting a blizzard."

A blizzard could last for days! Karen gave him the phone number at the ranch and hoped he wouldn't call.

Her duty done, she wandered into the living room. The furniture was oversized and casual, the walls were paneled and an oval rag rug covered most of the wood floor. She glanced at the blank television screen. It didn't appeal to her; she seldom watched. Instead she studied the contents of a tall bookshelf. Spotting an ancient-looking collection of short stories by O. Henry, she sat down and began to reacquaint herself with one of her favorites.

The next thing she knew, someone was shaking her gently.

"Wake up. Karen, wake up," urged a deep voice.

She blinked her eyes open to see Daniel leaning over her. In the glow from one lamp, his long hair swirled like midnight-hued silk around his face. His eyes were heavy lidded, mesmerizing. For a long moment, she stared in helpless fascination.

Then, muttering something indecipherable under his breath, he straightened.

"You might as well turn in." His voice had an edge to it.

Smothering a yawn, she swung her feet to the floor and saw that the view beyond the window was completely dark.

"Has the snow stopped?"

"No."

"What time is it?" She got up from the couch, resisting the compelling urge to stretch.

"After nine."

"Shall I fix breakfast in the morning?" she asked. "Since I'm here, I may as well be useful."

"The housekeeper makes breakfast at five-thirty."

"Oh." Clearly Daniel didn't want or need her help.

"I'll show you to your room," he said. "I put towels and a toothbrush in the upstairs bathroom for you." Before she could thank him, he added, "I found some clean clothes and left them on your bed."

Surprised by his consideration, Karen murmured her thanks as she followed him to the stairs. She had planned on rinsing out her underwear but it would be nice to have something fresh to put on, even if it was only a borrowed shirt or jeans.

As she climbed the stairs behind him, guiltily admiring the view of his taut behind and muscular legs, the house went abruptly dark. In the sudden silence, she heard the condenser on the refrigerator in the kitchen groan to a stop.

Ahead of her, Daniel muttered a curse. "The power's gone out," he said. "I expected that it might."

She sensed him moving closer, felt his body heat with a sharp awareness that stunned her. She had to press her lips together to smother the tiny sound of reaction that rose in her throat as his hands curled unerringly on her shoulders. Karen felt herself sway toward him in the blackness. His fingers tightened. Then he put her aside and brushed past her on the staircase that had suddenly become too narrow.

"Are you okay?" His voice was different in the dark, more sensual. It was filled with subtle shadings she tried, without success, to interpret.

"I'm fine," she croaked.

"Good. There are flashlights in the kitchen. I'm going to get us a couple. You stay here, okay?"

"Okay." She had no intention of stumbling around in the dark and perhaps colliding with him, but neither did she like being left alone. Intellectually she knew that the unfamiliar house was perfectly safe; on a deeper, gut level she couldn't control, she felt the icy touch of uncertainty shiver down her spine. When the house creaked in the silence, she changed her mind about waiting and decided to follow him after all.

At the foot of the stairs, her toe caught on the edge of a small rug she had noticed earlier. She stuck her hands out to break her fall, grabbed at nothingness and landed painfully on one knee and the heel of her hand.

"Damn!" she exclaimed.

Turning back in the darkness, Daniel almost fell over her. She heard his sharp intake of breath.

"What happened?" he demanded.

"I'm okay." She felt exceedingly graceless.

His seeking hand touched her head and it felt as if his fingertips caressed her hair for just a moment before he let her go.

"Stay put this time," he commanded imperiously, "while I get the flashlights."

Karen never had taken orders well. Shakily, she got to her feet. The knee she had landed on throbbed, but the pain was already lessening.

"Sorry," she called out quietly, massaging her stinging palm.

He returned with the torch, its beam pointed at the floor. "Does the dark bother you?" he asked as he switched on the other light and handed it to her. Their fingers touched and a jolt went through her, but she couldn't tell if he reacted, too.

"The dark doesn't usually bother me," she replied. "How about you?"

"I beg your pardon?"

"How about you?" she repeated. "Are you afraid of the dark?"

"Of course not." He cleared his throat. "It's going to get cold in here tonight, even with the wood stove going. If the power isn't on by morning, I'll start up the generator." He fell silent and she wondered what he was thinking.

"I'm sure I'll manage," Karen said, tempted to shine her light in his face so she could see his expression. He probably had night vision; she was surprised he bothered with a light.

"Come on," he said. "I'll show you to your room."

Daniel gripped his flashlight harder and fought to keep his breathing shallow so her scent wouldn't leak into his brain and fill it with awareness. Lord, but she was insidious, swamping his senses, stirring his hunger and setting his teeth on edge. Even in the darkness, he could picture her clearly— as if her image was already burned into his consciousness.

He wanted to throw his head back and howl at the moon, except the moon wasn't visible tonight. What would she do if he grabbed her, tangled his hands in those golden strands of sunlight and buried his mouth in hers, tasting, stroking until they were both—

The darkness must be affecting him strangely. With an effort that brought beads of sweat to his brow, he willed the direction of his thoughts to change, raising his hands to his head as if he could somehow ward off the stream of images.

"What's wrong?" she asked as the beam from his flashlight danced across the wall.

Immediately, he steadied it. He knew that sleep would elude him with her down the hall, but the last thing he wanted to do was to make her nervous. She was Jamie's teacher, nothing more, and he would do well to remember that when his blood began to heat.

She wouldn't appreciate his undisciplined imagination. Undoubtedly his hair was too long, his hands too callused and his complexion way too dark for a woman like her. And she was too pale for him. He needed to remember that.

He led her to the door of the fourth bedroom and pushed it open. It was colder inside than in the hallway.

"Be careful," he said over his shoulder. "There are some odds and ends in here that I didn't have time to clean out, but the bed's comfortable. I'll get you an extra blanket."

He played his torch across the room and stopped at the narrow bed with its red plaid spread and the pile of clothes he had taken from the master bedroom. Twyla wouldn't have minded. She probably would have liked Karen. His sister had been open and friendly, not closed up and distrustful as he was.

Daniel decided not to mention that this was the room he had always slept in whenever he came to visit. Now he used a different room with a bigger bed. Someday he supposed he would have to do something about the master bedroom, still full of John and Twyla's things, but he wasn't ready yet. It had been difficult enough to look through the drawers in search of what he thought Karen might need. The only thing he had forgotten was a nightgown, but he didn't want to go back in there and disturb Twyla's belongings again.

He sighed as Karen sat down gingerly on the edge of the bed. "I'll get you something to sleep in." Now he *knew* he would be awake all night.

"Thank you."

When he brought her back the blanket, one of his T-shirts and an old pair of sweatpants with a drawstring waist, he said, "You'll be sharing the hall bathroom with Jamie. I'll use the one off the master bedroom. That way..." His voice trailed off and he swallowed. Was her body slim and boyish or rounded and soft? Was the rest of her skin creamy, like her throat? What was it about her that had him so enthralled? He closed his eyes and willed her out of his thoughts. "That way you can shower whenever you want." Abruptly he headed for the door.

"Good night," she called quietly.

Daniel didn't bother to respond before he shut the door behind him.

Something woke Karen. The room was still shrouded in darkness and muffled in silence. She hadn't thought she would be able to sleep, but apparently she'd been more tired than she knew. Now she sat up in bed, surprised at how icy cold the room had grown, and listened to the quiet.

Maybe Jamie was awake. If he tried to turn on his light and it didn't work, he might be frightened. Karen had no idea whether Daniel would hear him if he called out, but she would bet the rancher was a light sleeper. She couldn't imagine anyone sneaking up on him.

She lifted the covers and immediately began shivering in the night air. Groping for her flashlight, she flicked it on and looked at her watch: 4:00 a.m. She straightened the T-shirt Daniel had loaned her. The sweatpants were tight across the hips. Lucky they were stretchy. She bent over and pulled down the legs which had ridden up while she slept.

As quietly as possible, she opened her door and slipped into the hall, still shivering. Her bare toes curled into the carpeting. Listening outside Jamie's room, she didn't hear a thing, so she eased the door open and shined her light around. He was sound asleep. Shutting his door again, she aimed the beam up and down the hall. The other doors, except the one to the bathroom, were shut.

Karen heard a faint noise. It sounded like a cat's cry and it came from downstairs. Maybe the dog was bothering the kittens or maybe one of them had gotten out of their box. If Muffy didn't notice right away, the cold would severely chill a tiny body. She debated waking Daniel, then discarded the idea. She would check the kittens herself. Quietly she tiptoed down the stairs.

There was a glow from the kitchen. Had Daniel left a light by the wood stove? She was about to slip into the dining room when he stepped out of the shadows. Her heart almost stopped.

"Why are you prowling around?" he asked.

She swallowed the lump that had risen in her throat. "I thought I heard a cat cry and I was just coming down to check on them," she babbled. "Jamie's still asleep and your door was shut. Why are you down here, jumping out at people?"

Daniel was a dark outline against the glow in the kitchen, his expression shrouded in darkness. Behind him, Karen saw Jericho.

"The kittens are fine. I just looked," Daniel replied. "I saw coyote tracks the other day, and I wanted to check things out."

"Would a coyote attack the sheep?" Karen asked.

He shrugged. "They usually only take lambs, but I want to see if I can find anything. I'm making coffee, if you want some."

She shuddered at the thought of a coyote killing lambs. It might be nature's way, but she still hated the idea. "I think I'd rather have a glass of milk," she said.

"There's some in the refrigerator. It should still be cold. Help yourself."

She thanked him and headed toward the kitchen, glad to put some space between them.

Daniel had noticed how carefully she moved around him. What if he told her that he had looked in on her before he came downstairs? She might not appreciate knowing that he had been watching her sleep, and she sure as hell wouldn't like hearing what he had been thinking about while he looked. It might even have been him shutting her door that woke her.

"How are you making the coffee with no electricity?"

He gestured toward the battered pot on the wood stove. "Old cowboy secret," he drawled.

Karen smiled. Then she yawned widely and clapped a hand over her mouth. "Excuse me."

He nodded toward the fridge. "Don't leave the door open too long."

She poured a glass of milk and then stood in front of the wood stove's warmth while she drank it. Neither of them spoke.

"Well, I'm going back to bed," she said when the glass was empty. "I hope the sheep are okay."

"Me, too." Daniel tried not to stare openly at her unbound breasts. She must not realize that the dark circles of her nipples showed through the thin cotton of the old T-shirt. He'd have thought they would be small and pink, like the inside of a seashell, but perhaps they were coral or tan. He wondered if they were sensitive, if they would draw up as hard as berries if he touched them. The thought made his blood surge and his body tighten.

He was sorry he had loaned her the sweatpants. He would have liked to see her legs. He bet they were long and slim. With skin like satin, especially on the insides of her thighs. Damn. He was almost as bad off as he'd been when he first woke up, hard and aching.

What would she do if he kissed her? Or put his mouth over the fabric covering one of those hard little nipples and sucked until it was wet? His body responded to the idea with a rush that had him gritting his teeth.

"I'd better go." He needed to get away from her before he did something that would drive a stake through his chances of keeping Jamie. He still had trouble believing he could lose the boy.

"What about the coffee?" Karen asked.

Daniel glanced at the pot, then at the empty cup he was holding. He couldn't even think straight around her.

"It's almost ready," he amended lamely.

She looked out the window. "Well, be careful." Her eyes had a sleepy softness to them that drove him wild. "Will you be able to get any more sleep, or are you up for the day now?"

He almost choked at her choice of words, but her concern surprised him. It had been a long time since anyone had thought to wonder if he got enough rest. "I'll be okay," he said with a slight smile. "I might go back to bed and sleep for a little while when I get done. Not much else to do at this time of the morning." As soon as he had uttered the words, he wished he could take them back. Karen must have been thinking along the same lines. First her eyes widened and then she looked away. Her cheeks turned pink.

"I guess not," she agreed faintly. "I'm going back upstairs." Before Daniel could wedge his foot any deeper into his mouth, she fled.

He watched her go, cursing his loose tongue. What some people would find to do if they woke in the night was obvious, and they had both realized it at the same time. The only difference was that he found the image tempting as hell while he obviously scared her more than a whole half-naked Comanche raiding party. She hadn't been able to get away from him fast enough.

Pouring himself a cup of coffee, Daniel took a sip and grimaced at the hot, bitter brew. So far, when it came to winning Jamie's teacher over to his side, he'd been doing one hell of a lousy job.

The next time Karen woke up, the sky was paler. The snow was coming down hard, but the light switch worked. When she peeked into the hallway, Daniel's door was open. He was probably outside somewhere.

In the bathroom, she showered quickly, enjoying the feel of the warm water and the shampoo someone had put out. After she wrapped her long hair in a towel, turban style, she realized that she had forgotten the panties and bra, with sales tags intact, in the bedroom. They must have been Twyla's. Apparently she'd never had the chance to wear them. Instead of putting on the shirt and jeans anyway, Karen wrapped another towel around her body, opened the bathroom door—and almost collided with Daniel.

"You're back," she said inanely.

He kept his gaze riveted on her face, and she decided the rest of her must hold no interest for him. She should be glad he wasn't ogling her, she chided herself silently.

"Damned stupid ewe," he grumbled, frowning, "butted me right in the back of the knees and dropped me like a bad habit." He turned around and she saw the smear of mud all down his jeans. "I had to come in to change clothes."

It occurred to Karen that this was the longest explanation she had ever heard from him about anything. Maybe he wasn't as unaffected by her as he pretended to be.

"I'm sure it's too cold out for wet pants." She gave him an innocent smile.

"Old Cully's still laughing." His voice was disgruntled. He towered over her, smelling of outdoors and hard work, and he made her achingly aware of her own femininity.

"Thanks for leaving the shampoo," she said breathlessly, as he turned to go.

He glanced at her again. Something in his gaze made her hand tighten on the terry cloth wrapped around her. She wondered what he was thinking.

"Would you take off the towel?" he asked softly.

Karen's fingers froze over her breast and her heart climbed into her throat. "What?"

He was looking at her turbaned head. "Take off the towel," he repeated. "I want to see what your hair looks like loose."

Oh, *that* towel.

Karen stared, not sure what to say. Her hair was still damp and full of tangles. She needed to comb it out and dry it somehow. "You want to see my hair?" she echoed.

One corner of his mouth pulled up in a barely recognizable grin. "Do you mind?" he asked. "You have such beautiful hair."

Karen could think of no real reason to refuse his rather odd request. She tucked her clothes under her arm. Then she unwrapped the towel, feeling a little like a stripper, and shook out her hair. It fell around her shoulders in wet ropes.

"It's pretty messy," she murmured apologetically.

Something flickered in Daniel's eyes. He lifted a soggy strand and stared at it intently. "If I had more time, I'd brush it out for you," he said hoarsely. "I used to brush Twyla's hair when we were kids. She always wore it long and it fell to her hips."

Suddenly Karen understood. Even though Twyla's hair had been black and hers was blond, it reminded Daniel somehow of his sister.

"Twyla was a lovely woman," Karen said. "You must miss her terribly."

He let go of the strand he had been rubbing between his thumb and fingers. "Yeah, I miss her."

Karen wanted to ask him more about his family, but her hair started dripping on her bare skin and she suddenly remembered that she was wearing a towel. "I'd better get dressed."

He frowned. "Good idea," he said as if she had been the one to delay him.

Karen rushed into the spare room. Annoyed by the ease with which he flustered her, she yanked on her clothes. The bra was a little snug, but it was better than nothing. She had rinsed out her own underwear the night before but it was still damp. Over matching lace-trimmed panties that made her blush to think of Daniel's hands on them, she pulled on jeans and a blue pullover sweater. The jeans were tight in the hips and a little too short. It was a struggle to zip them. The whole time she was dressing and brushing out her hair, she remembered the way Daniel had caressed it. As if he found it fascinating.

Jamie's room was empty when she checked it, so she went downstairs.

"Good morning." She assumed that the short, rotund woman with graying black hair who greeted her when she got to the kitchen must be Mary, the housekeeper. Jamie was seated at the round table, devouring a plate of pancakes. He must be feeling better.

"Would you like some breakfast?" Mary asked.

"No, thanks," Karen replied. "Coffee and toast would be fine, but I can fix it. I don't expect you to wait on me."

Mary's smile was relaxed and friendly. "It's part of my job," she said. "Besides, Jamie told me that you helped with supper last night and cleaned up afterward. I'm sorry you got stuck here, though."

Gratefully Karen accepted the coffee that Mary poured and sat down at the table. "So am I, but it hasn't been so bad." She hoped that Daniel didn't overhear her. She wanted him to feel guilty; he was playing hell with her peace of mind.

"How are you today?" she asked Jamie.

"I'm great," he said, beaming. "There isn't any school on account of the snow."

"I know," she replied.

"You do?" He looked surprised.

"I talked to Mr. Appleby last night."

Jamie looked suitably impressed. To a kindergarten student, the principal was on about the same level as the president of the United States. "Uncle Dani'l says that I can't go out today," he grumbled. "My fever's all gone and I want to play in the snow."

"Your uncle doesn't want you getting sick again," Karen told him. "The snow will still be around tomorrow."

"He doesn't want me to have any fun."

"You know that's not true," Mary chided him. "He offered to play a game with you later."

Karen smothered a grin at the picture of Daniel playing *Chutes and Ladders* or *Go Fish* with his nephew. She thanked Mary for the plate of toast the woman set in front of her. "How are the kittens?" she asked Jamie.

"They're boring. All they do is sleep and eat." He sounded disgusted. "Will you help me build a snowman tomorrow?" he asked. Milk formed a mustache on his upper lip.

"If I'm still here." Surely the roads would be drivable before then. "And if you'll spend some time today working on letter sounds with me."

His expression was so negative that she expected him to refuse.

"Okay," he agreed around a bite of pancakes, surprising her. She hid her elation behind her hand and got up to pour herself more coffee. As she did, Daniel came into the room.

"I see the clothes fit." He looked at her hair and she wondered if he still thought it was attractive, now that he had seen it wet and stringy. She had taken extra pains when she dried it, telling herself she didn't want to get a chill from leaving it damp.

"Yes, thanks again," she said self-consciously. What would he say if she told him the bra was too small? She wondered if it bothered him to see her wearing Twyla's clothes.

While Karen tried to concentrate on her toast, he carried his empty mug over to the counter. Before he could reach for the coffee, Mary took his mug and filled it.

He stood with one hip braced against the counter and drank the coffee silently. As soon as Karen was done eating, she excused herself and left the room.

Daniel watched her go, wondering if she was trying to avoid him. He knew he shouldn't have asked her to bare her wet hair the way he had. She probably thought he was crazy, but he hadn't been able to resist. He wished she would wear it loose all the time, but perhaps he should be glad she didn't. Just now, when he came into the kitchen, it was spilling over her shoulders like a river of gold. He had wanted to bury his face in its softness and breathe in its perfume. What would she have done if he had?

What was it about her that made him want to open up, to share his secrets and listen to hers? To hear all about her childhood and why she had become a teacher? And how she felt about ranching and if there was someone special in her life? And all the other things he had no right to ask?

Daniel came into the house again later to ask Karen if she wanted to go see the sheep and his horses.

"She and Jamie are upstairs," Mary told him. "She said something about doing schoolwork."

Daniel's brows rose but he didn't say anything. He wondered how Karen had gotten Jamie to cooperate. At least the two of them seemed to be getting along better. Daniel wished he could say the same. When he had told Jamie it was too cold for him to go outside in the snow, the boy had started to cry.

Still feeling like an ogre, Daniel climbed the stairs. He could hear their voices. Curious, he stopped in the hall and listened.

While he eavesdropped shamelessly, Karen was trying to think of a way to bring Jamie's parents into their conversation. If she could get Jamie talking about them, he might begin to accept their deaths.

"Do you like it when I read aloud to you?" she asked him.

He nodded. "When I learn to read all by myself, I can get books at the library," he said. Then he frowned and looked away.

"What's wrong?" Karen asked.

"Mommy said she'd take me to the library to pick out books, but now she's gone and I don't know if Uncle Dani'l will have time to take me."

"I'm sure he'll find the time." Daniel would want to encourage Jamie to keep reading. "Did your parents read to you often?" she asked.

Jamie was silent and she held her breath. "Sometimes," he said finally. "Mommy read to me from books. Then Daddy would come up and kiss me good-night. Sometimes, he told me stories."

"What kinds of stories?" Karen asked, leafing through the book on her lap.

He shrugged. "Stories about when he was little. Him and Uncle Ted."

Karen remembered a comment Jamie had made at school. She took a deep breath. "Jamie, do you remember what you said one day about wishing Uncle Daniel would leave so that your parents could come back?"

He nodded slowly, his eyes wide and solemn. "I guess."

"What did you mean?" she asked carefully. "Do you think that your uncle being here is somehow keeping them away? You don't really want him to leave, do you?"

Before Jamie could say a word, Daniel burst into the bedroom, his eyes narrowed and his face a mask of cold fury.

"Just what the hell are you playing at?" he demanded, as Jamie began to cry.

Chapter Four

"Now look what you've done," Karen exclaimed without thinking. "You've scared Jamie and made him cry."

If anything, Daniel's frown became even more fierce. "My nephew isn't afraid of me!" He came into the room and stared down at Jamie as Karen slipped an arm around the little boy's thin shoulders. Tears clung to Jamie's thick lashes and his lower lip quivered.

"It's okay," she told him quietly. "Your uncle isn't really angry at you."

"We need to talk." Daniel's deep voice was underscored with fury as he grabbed her upper arm and hustled her out of the room.

"What about Jamie?" she asked, struggling against his iron grip.

Daniel swore under his breath. "Just a minute, son. Miss Whitworth and I will be right back."

"Okay." Jamie's voice was thin, his expression solemn, as Daniel pulled Karen into the hall and shut the bedroom door behind them.

"Just what the hell are you trying to do?" he demanded in a harsh whisper as he backed her against the wall and glared down at her.

Karen wrenched her arm free, barely sparing a thought to wonder why Daniel in a temper didn't send her screaming for help. Anger glittered in his eyes and tightened the muscles along his jaw. A nerve twitched in his cheek.

"I'm trying to help." She grated out the words, standing tall and lifting her chin so they were almost nose to nose. She matched his relentless stare with her own. Did he have to be so hardheaded? "Jamie needs to talk about his feelings. He needs to be able to ask questions about everything that's happened."

"He needs to forget," Daniel contradicted her angrily. "He has to put it all behind him and move on."

Karen shook her head adamantly. "No! Not until he's dealt with it."

Daniel stared into her eyes as if he were trying to see inside her. Would he trust her? Karen reached her hand out and laid it against his chest. She could feel the strong, slow beat of his heart. "Please," she begged, as something flared across his face and then was gone. "Talk to Jamie. It will help you both."

He turned away, swearing under his breath.

"Please," she said again. "Just talk to him."

He eyed her warily and she felt a sigh ripple through him before she dropped her hand. "You really think it will help?"

She sagged with relief. "Yes. Will you come back in with me and give it a try?"

The remnants of anger and distrust faded from his face. He nodded. "All right."

Back in Jamie's room, Daniel hunkered down beside the boy, who was sitting at a small table in an equally small chair. Karen stood inside the doorway, praying that her interference hadn't been misguided.

Daniel swallowed, searching for the right words to say to the little boy who meant so very much to him. "I didn't mean to scare you," he began, feeling like a brute.

A lone tear spilled over and ran down Jamie's cheek. "Why were you yelling?" he asked. "Daddy only yelled when he was mad."

Daniel shot a beseeching glance at Karen, who merely smiled encouragingly.

"I'm sorry," he told Jamie contritely. "I shouldn't have yelled." Daniel knew he had to be honest. "I guess I got a little hot when I heard Miss Whitworth mention my going away."

Jamie ducked his head. No doubt he hadn't meant for Daniel to hear that. He reached out slowly to tip up the boy's chin so they were looking at each other again.

"I'm not going anywhere," he said. "I'd travel to the ends of the earth if it would bring your mom and dad home, but it wouldn't help. They aren't coming back, and both you and I have to accept that. They wanted me to take care of you, and that's what I'm trying to do. That's what your mom asked me to do if anything ever happened to her."

Karen could hear the pain in Daniel's voice. She knew he was baring his soul to Jamie and the sound of that pain made her eyes fill with tears that she hastily blinked back. Daniel was a proud man, but he was laying down that pride for his nephew.

"Mommy asked you to take care of me?" Jamie echoed. "Like she used to ask me to take care of Muffy and feed her when she was busy?"

"Something like that," Daniel said. "Your mommy wanted to be sure your cat was getting what she needed, and she counted on you to take care of Muffy when she couldn't. She knew she didn't have to worry about you forgetting. Because you love Muffy, and because you're a responsible person.''

"What does responsible mean?" Jamie asked.

Daniel glanced at Karen, who remained silent. "It means someone who can be trusted to do what they've been asked to do." Daniel put a hand on Jamie's shoulder. "Your mommy and daddy asked me to take care of you because they knew that I love you, too, and that I would be responsible for you. See that you go to school and have everything you need. And they knew I would run the ranch until you're old enough to do it yourself."

Karen thought that Jamie looked impressed.

"Do you understand what your uncle just told you?" she asked.

"I think so. It's just that you came here when they went away," he said earnestly, as if he were concerned about his uncle's feelings. "So I thought maybe if you left again, then they would come home."

Daniel glanced at Karen, clearly puzzled by his nephew's reasoning.

"Children have unclear concepts about death," she explained softly. "And when they hear that someone is gone or has gone away, it confuses them even more. It's difficult for a child to really understand that a dead person isn't ever coming back."

Understanding dawned on Daniel's face. He ran a hand over Jamie's head in a rough caress. "You and I are family, bud. We have to stick together."

"What if you go away, too?"

Daniel's jaw hardened with determination. "I'm not going anywhere," he promised.

When Jamie gave him a wobbly grin, Daniel leaned down until their foreheads were touching. "Okay?" he whispered.

"Okay."

Karen thought her heart would burst with relief. Daniel had done better than she had dared hope.

She thought of her own parents. They were hardworking, successful, respected. Her mother was a lawyer with a leading Denver firm, her father a judge. Karen was their only child, but she didn't feel close to them. She never had. And they had been disappointed when she decided to be a teacher. They had expected her to follow in their footsteps.

Daniel remained squatting beside Jamie's chair. "I don't know a lot about kids," he continued, his voice gruff, "but I'm trying, okay? If I make mistakes, can you be patient with me?"

With an emotional cry, Jamie launched himself into Daniel's arms, almost toppling him over.

"I love you." His voice was muffled against his uncle's chest. Over his head, Daniel looked at Karen. Through her tears, she could see that his black eyes were shining with moisture. Then he squeezed them shut.

"I love you, too," he muttered thickly, holding Jamie tight.

When Daniel opened his eyes, he saw Karen leave the room. Now he understood what she had been trying to do. He owed her some thanks or an apology—probably both, but he dreaded having to seek her out. Whenever he was around her, he was acutely aware of the magnetic pull between them. Sometimes it was all he could do to ignore it—but ignore it, he must. Indulging his interest would be a costly mistake. One with a price tag a man like him could never afford.

He let Jamie go and got to his feet. Out of habit, he fiddled with the tiny silver hoop that pierced his ear. It had been half of one of Twyla's favorite pair of earrings, one of John's first gifts to her, and Daniel wore it in her memory. The other earring was put away for the time when her son might want to do the same.

As Jamie wiped his tears on his sleeve and smiled up at him, he wondered if Karen had any good ideas on how to explain the coming custody battle to a five-year-old.

The next morning, the sky was blue and the reflection of the sunlight on the snow was almost blinding. Looking out the window, Karen could hear it melting and dripping from the eaves. The lights worked, but she didn't hear the loud drone of the generator.

Making sure that she took everything she needed into the bathroom with her, she showered quickly and donned her own dry underwear, the borrowed jeans and her red sweater.

In the kitchen, Mary told her the radio had announced that the plows were out and headed their way.

"The main road should be cleared by this afternoon," she said as she brought Karen's toast and coffee to the table. "Daniel has already plowed our driveway with the tractor."

Karen frowned thoughtfully. Now that he and his nephew were working things out between them, Daniel probably wanted her out of there as soon as possible. He hadn't wanted her help in the first place.

The evening before, Cully had come to the back door during dinner to tell Daniel that one of the horses had been kicked and was bleeding. When Karen went to bed, he still wasn't back. It was probably just as well, she thought as she buttered her toast. She was getting too involved with him and with Jamie. What she needed was to get out of there and go back to reality. And the sooner, the better.

"The radio said school is reopening tomorrow," Mary added as she set a jar of homemade jam on the table.

Jamie, who was seated next to Karen, wrinkled his nose.

"Coming back to school and seeing your friends again will be fun," she told him.

"Uncle Dani'l said I can go outside today." He ignored her comment. "Will you help me build a snowman before you go? You promised you would."

Karen drained her coffee mug. "Good idea," she said, eager to get some fresh air. "We need to wear our coats and gloves."

"Cool!" Jamie got up from the table and pushed his chair in.

"What do you say?" Mary reminded him as he carried his dishes to the dishwasher.

He glanced back at Karen. " 'Scuse me."

"You put on your warm jacket, your boots and your mittens, if you're going outside," Mary told him.

Karen promised to meet him back in the kitchen shortly. He raced up the stairs as Mary wiped off the table. "Don't forget your hat," she called after him. "It's still pretty cold out there."

The bright sun was deceiving. Karen could feel the sting of the chilly air on her cheeks as she and Jamie walked down a long, sloping hill to an empty pasture. She didn't see Daniel, but the snow was crisscrossed with tracks, both human and animal.

By the time she and Jamie had managed to form a fat body for their snowman, she was no longer cold. Instead she felt alive and happy. She envied Jamie and Daniel, living on this ranch and being able to walk out of the house and absorb the raw beauty of the surrounding country and the majestic, towering mountains whenever they wanted. She had grown up in Denver, but she thought this part of the state was by far the most appealing.

"How's it going?" Daniel called from the fence as Karen stopped to catch her breath. He looked rugged and attractive in faded black jeans and a heavy parka, together with his usual black Stetson. In one hand he carried an old brown hat with a floppy brim.

"Come and help," Jamie cried. "We're building a snowman. He's going to be very big."

Karen wished, too, that he would stay, despite the common sense that told her the less time she spent around him, the better. Along with the proud nobility Daniel carried like a warrior's shield, there was an aloofness, an air of solitude about him she doubted she would ever be able to breach.

He came through the gate and walked over to where she was packing more snow together. She glanced up as he inspected their handiwork.

"Hi." She hadn't seen him since the day before and she still felt a little awkward around him.

Politely he touched two fingers to his hat brim. "Mornin'." He seemed to hesitate. "About yesterday, I guess I overreacted—"

"Don't worry about it," Karen interrupted, straightening. "I thought your talk with Jamie went well."

He glanced at his nephew and his gaze softened. "I think we made a start."

Wondering what it would be like to have him look at her with that much tenderness, Karen managed a shaky smile. "I'm glad."

"Yeah, me, too." Daniel went over to where Jamie was piling snow around the base of the snowman. "You're doing a good job," he told the boy. "I wish I had time to help, but I need to haul hay out to the sheep."

"Where are they?" Karen asked. She hadn't seen a sign of them, but she could hear their bleating.

He pointed. "Down there, on the other side of the sheds. Why don't the two of you walk down later and take a look?"

She wondered how long he was going to be out there, and then reminded herself that he had only made the offer out of politeness. "Perhaps we will."

He held the old brown hat out to Jamie. "I thought you could use this for your snowman."

He was obviously disappointed by Daniel's refusal to stay, but now his expression brightened slightly. "Cool," he said, accepting the hat. "We can make him a cowboy, like you."

Daniel rubbed his chin thoughtfully. "Guess I'm not really a cowboy anymore. A sheepman's more like it." He shook his head as Jamie ran back to put the hat on the snowman.

"How do you like it?" Karen asked without thinking. "I mean, raising sheep instead of cattle."

He shrugged. "There are a lot of things to learn, but Cully's been teaching me. As long as I can work outside and be around animals, I guess it doesn't really matter."

"It was thoughtful of you to bring the hat. It would mean a lot to Jamie if you could stay for a few more minutes and help with the snowman."

Daniel's brow arched and his hard features thawed slightly, but all he said was, "Sorry, I just can't. This weather just makes everything more difficult, and it all takes longer."

When he called to Jamie that he'd see him later, the boy ducked his head and kicked at the snow with his boot. He looked so forlorn that Karen's heart went out to him. Was Daniel really so busy, or did she have anything to do with his refusal to stay? Without giving herself time to reconsider, she scooped some snow into a ball and threw it at Daniel's retreating figure.

While she watched, slightly horrified by her own impulsive action, the snowball hit him square in the back of the head. He stopped in his tracks, shoulders hunched against the icy onslaught. It knocked his hat askew and slithered down his neck inside his jacket collar. Slowly he turned.

Daniel was surprised that Jamie had managed to hit him. As he swung around, he reached back to brush the snow off his neck before it melted. He looked at Jamie, who was laughing, and then at Karen. Her cheeks were flushed and she looked ready to bolt.

She looked guilty.

She had thrown the snowball, not Jamie. Intrigued by her temerity, he approached her with caution. She was studying the toes of her boots as if they fascinated her, and her hands were empty.

"Did you do that?" he demanded.

"I—" She looked at him and shrugged. "Yep."

"I see." Grinning, Daniel bent to pack some cold retribution into a ball, as his pent-up frustration burst its boundaries. If she wanted to tweak the tiger's tail, she would have to deal with the consequences.

As soon as Karen realized what he was doing, she started to run. The snow was deep and she floundered, almost falling.

"You're going to be real sorry you did that," Daniel promised as he advanced on her.

She watched him, wide-eyed. "Did what?" she squeaked with an air of reckless bravado he found amusing, but her breathless laughter gave her away.

Daniel hurled the snowball at her but she ducked and it sailed harmlessly by. While Jamie shouted encouragement, she packed another of her own and chucked it back. The shot went wide and she turned to run again.

"Jamie, help me!" she cried.

"Look out!" he shrieked, tossing a lump of snow in Daniel's direction. Jamie squealed with glee when it fell only inches short of the target. Daniel realized how much he had missed this playful side of his nephew.

"You're next," he threatened with an exaggerated glare. "As soon as I deal with Annie Oakley here."

"Who's Annie Oakley?" Jamie demanded as Daniel formed another missile with slow deliberation.

"Another woman with good aim," Daniel replied without taking his eyes off Karen. While he stalked her, she bent to scoop up more snow. He couldn't decide if he would rather spank her for getting his hair and the collar of his shirt wet, or kiss her cold lips and feel them heat beneath his own. Something of his intent must have shown on his face. She looked wildly around as he moved in.

"Give up," he suggested. "I'll be merciful."

"How dumb do I look?" she demanded. "You'll probably roll me in the snow."

"That's a thought." An image of the two of them tangled together distracted him. Then Jamie ran forward, growling and waving his arms. When Daniel's attention shifted, another one of Karen's snowballs caught him on the cheek.

"Now you've done it!"

She was doubled over with helpless laughter, but she managed to take several backward steps as Daniel advanced. When he raised his arm to throw another snowball, she darted to the side.

Karen realized he had her trapped. She had retreated into a corner of the pasture and he had her boxed in.

The snowball he tossed bounced harmlessly off her shoulder. With a shriek, she spun the other way. Daniel was watching her with an evil grin on his dark face.

"You'll be sorry," she cried out, doing her best to bluff as she scooped up more snow.

He couldn't hold back a snort of laughter. Who had started the fight, anyway?

Taking his eyes reluctantly off Karen, he tossed a snowball at Jamie that knocked the boy's hat off. Karen bolted, slipped and lost her footing. Daniel tackled her and they both went down. She landed face first in the cold, wet snow with him on top of her.

Jamie ran around them, shrieking with excitement. "Wash her face with snow!" he cried.

"Whose side are you on?" Karen demanded, raising her head to glare at him. She was out of breath and Daniel's solid weight threatened to flatten her.

"Get off me," she demanded, struggling. "You'll squash me flat."

Immediately Daniel rolled to the side and got to his knees.

"Are you okay?" He turned her over and began brushing the snow from her clothes. His nearness was doing strange things to her nerves and her breathing.

"I think I'm all right," she murmured, trying to sit up.

He studied her with a concerned expression. "Are you sure?"

She grabbed a fresh handful of snow and tossed it in his face, then attempted to push him away. It was like trying to shift solid rock. She knew she had made a grave tactical error.

"So you want to play rough!" Daniel growled as she thrashed around. She twisted away from him, hands protecting her face. He went still and she risked a peek between her fingers. When she did, he grabbed hold of her wrists and pushed her down.

Lying in the cold snow, Karen stared up at him. His narrowed eyes were crinkled at the corners and his mouth had softened into a grin that made her breathless. Her body was achingly aware of every place his pressed against her. Her back was chilled by the snow, but the front of her was on fire. The new awareness must have shown in her eyes, because his grin faded and he leaned forward.

"Let me go!" she cried, afraid he could read her feelings on her face. "I didn't mean anything. Honest." Silently she prayed that he wouldn't guess at the real reason for her desperation to get away. "I'll be good, I promise. How about showing some mercy?"

Daniel laughed softly. "Where was all that mercy when you put snow down my neck?" he growled. Despite his relaxed expression, to Karen he looked more dangerous than ever.

Her struggles were futile. "Help," she called to Jamie, nervous laughter bubbling from her lips.

"No one can help you now," Daniel told her in a soft, menacing voice. "Jamie's on my side." He shifted his grip on her wrists, holding them both in one big hand. He scooped up more snow with the other and held it threateningly above her head.

"No fair." She laughed. "You're bigger than I am."

He flexed his hips, making her achingly aware of the intimacy of their positions. "So I am."

Karen tried again to dislodge him, without any success.

Daniel studied her crimson cheeks and her sparkling eyes. Her hair was spread across the snow the same way it would be spread across a white, fluffy pillow. Her lips were red from the cold. Each time she tried to buck him off, her legs chafed against the insides of his thighs.

While he struggled with his body's reaction to her, she managed to free one hand, grabbing more snow and stuffing it into the open neck of his jacket.

He roared in surprise. "That does it! Now you'll have to pay a forfeit," he exclaimed as Jamie jumped up and down, clapping his hands together.

"Kiss her, Uncle Dan'il!" he shouted.

Karen could have throttled him for his suggestion. Daniel stared down at her, one brow raised in silent query. "Now there's an idea," he mused aloud, grinning like a pirate. "I always knew my nephew was a bright kid.

"Jamie," he hollered, "run up to the house and see if Mary has a carrot you can use for the snowman's nose."

As he hurried to comply, Karen gazed up at Daniel warily, hot with embarrassment. It was intimate enough with him straddling her hips, but the fun had been fairly innocent with Jamie there. Now she wasn't so sure. Before she could utter a word, Daniel rolled onto his back, pulling her over him so her hips and legs lay flush against his own hard contours.

She burned with awareness. Her hair fell down around her face like a golden curtain. Before she could guess at his intentions, he caught the back of her head in his hand, urging her closer. Then he raised up and kissed her.

Ice and fire shot through Karen at the touch of his mouth on hers. At first, she resisted. Then something melted inside her and she began to yield. Just as she was about to kiss him back, he jerked his head away and stared at her intently. For a moment, she thought she saw a flash of surprise in his dark eyes and then his expression closed up.

"Let me go," she demanded, humiliated. While she was being seduced by his kiss, he had obviously found her wanting.

Angry, she shoved at his chest.

"Wait a minute," he protested. "I didn't mean—"

She struggled against his embrace. "I don't care what you meant. Let me go."

Instead of freeing her, he rolled again so that she was under him, his weight pinning her down, his face close to hers. "Listen to me," he said.

Far angrier with herself than at him, Karen tried to buck him off. When that didn't work, she closed her eyes against his invading stare and did her best to ignore her body's response to his.

"Have it your way," he muttered as she kept struggling. A handful of icy, wet snow made abrupt contact with her overheated face.

"*Ooooh!*" she cried in shock and angry protest. As she did, Daniel levered himself off her prone body. She scrambled to a sitting position, wiping the snow from her face and blinking it from her eyes.

When she could see again, she noticed that he was standing over her, hand outstretched, as he watched her with a hawklike stare.

"Let me help you."

Jamie ran up, brandishing a long carrot. "I got one!" he shouted triumphantly.

While Daniel was momentarily distracted, Karen grasped his outstretched hand and allowed him to pull her to her feet. As he did, she managed to spin around and grab his arm with her other hand. Shifting her weight, she flipped him neatly over her shoulder into the waiting snow.

"Wow!" Jamie exclaimed. "Where did you learn to do that?"

"In my high school gym class," she replied. "My teacher thought it might come in handy someday. I guess she was right."

"Will you teach me how to do it?"

Daniel lay on his back in the snow. His face was blank with astonishment.

"I don't think so," Karen answered Jamie as his uncle got slowly to his feet. He regarded her with a wary expression.

"Are you okay?" she asked.

"Everything but my pride." His tone was dry, his expression of blank surprise not quite gone. "I guess I had that coming." He stuck out his hand again and gave her an innocent smile. "Truce?"

Karen backed away from his outstretched hand. "Oh, no," she exclaimed. "I'm not falling for that."

Daniel winced at her refusal as he glanced down at his hand. "Don't you trust me?"

Karen couldn't suppress a grin. "Not for a minute!"

An answering smile flickered across his face and then disappeared. "I've gotta go," he said abruptly. "I've got stock to feed."

Karen and Jamie were playing a quiet game at the kitchen table after lunch when Daniel came in to tell her that the main road was clear.

"It's time I went home, then," she said, rising without meeting his gaze. She felt as if she still had the imprint of his mouth on hers and she couldn't forget how she had been ready to kiss him back when he pushed her away. "I've certainly been here a lot longer than I planned." When she and Jamie had come into the house after the snowball fight, she changed into her own plaid pants, leaving the borrowed clothes in the laundry room as Mary had requested.

"I had fun," Jamie said. "Can you come over again?"

"We'll see," Karen replied before turning to thank Mary for lunch. Then she slipped on her coat and gloves, which she had brought down with her, and bent to give Jamie a hug.

"I'll see you at school tomorrow."

He flung his arms around her neck. "Bye."

When she straightened, Daniel was watching her. "I'll walk you out," he said brusquely, indicating that she precede him.

Karen picked up her purse and briefcase and headed for the entryway, keenly aware of him behind her. Had he given any thought to their kiss, or was it already forgotten?

When he opened the door, she saw that her car had been swept free of snow. She hurried down the steps, which had also been cleared.

"Thanks for everything," she told Daniel when she was a safe distance away.

"Are you sure you can manage?" His voice was gruff with unwilling concern. "I could follow you into town if you want."

"I'll be fine." He opened the car door for her and she slid inside.

"Will you come back and work with Jamie?" he asked.

"I'd like that," she admitted. "It shouldn't take him very long to catch up."

There was nothing left to say. Daniel nodded and shut the car door. Without looking back, Karen drove carefully down the road to the highway.

"Don't fool yourself. In a case like this, appearances can be crucially important," Nick Keller said. The attorney to whom Mr. Lu had referred Daniel was sitting in a wheel-chair behind a massive old desk littered with papers. His fingers were steepled in front of his face.

Watching Daniel intently, he had asked a series of questions and taken detailed notes. Daniel wanted an idea of his chances and Keller had refused to predict the outcome of the case.

"Frankly it could go either way," he said.

Daniel sat back and slapped his Stetson against his knee. He couldn't lose Jamie! "I'll do anything to win," he told the attorney. "Anything."

"You married?" Keller asked, studying Daniel through horn-rimmed glasses with thick lenses.

Daniel shook his head.

"Any prospects?"

"No. Why?" What did it matter if he were married or not?

"Pity." Keller made another note on his yellow legal pad.

"Why?" Daniel repeated impatiently.

Keller glanced up. "Why what?"

"Why does it matter if I'm married or not?"

Keller folded his hands in front of him. "Like I said, appearances can count for a lot. A traditional family, man and wife, a home and perhaps a dog, looks like a good setup for a child. Could influence the judge." He spread his hands. "No matter," he added. "We have other things on our side."

Daniel gripped the arms of the chair hard, his gut knotted with tension. "Be honest," he said. "What chance do I have to keep Jamie?" He had already shown Keller the will appointing him as Jamie's guardian and manager of the sheep ranch.

Keller studied him thoughtfully. He was wearing his usual clothes, clean jeans, western shirt and his Stetson, with his hair pulled back into a neat ponytail. Under Keller's perusal, he resisted the urge to fidget like a nervous schoolboy.

"We've got two things in our favor," Keller said. "The will and the both of you having Native American blood."

"Is that enough?"

Keller scratched his chin thoughtfully. "I don't know."

"What else can I do?" Daniel asked. "There must be something."

"Get a haircut," Keller said abruptly.

Daniel bristled at the order. "How short?"

Keller grinned. "How short can you stand it?"

"I'll shave my head if it will help."

"No, don't do that!" The man laughed, and then his expression became serious again. "It doesn't have to be that extreme, just something a little more moderate than it is now, okay?''

Daniel nodded. "Okay. What else?"

Keller made another note on the legal pad. "Why do you think Ted Powell is suing for custody?" he asked. "Do he and his wife have a close relationship with Jamie?"

Daniel shrugged. "I don't think so. They haven't seen him since the funeral."

"Interesting." Keller glanced at his legal pad. "Is there money involved in the estate?"

Daniel shook his head, confused. "No. There wasn't that much cash. Some life insurance that Mr. Lu put into a fund for Jamie's college tuition."

Keller jotted something down and nodded absently. "I'm fishing for motive," he explained.

Daniel remembered the late-model black sedan Ted had driven to the funeral. Something long, foreign and luxurious, with tinted windows. In contrast, Daniel's own red-and-white pickup truck looked decrepit.

And Ted's wife had been wearing a full-length fur the color of her blond hair. He remembered because it stood out so amid the somber blacks and grays of the other mourners. "If there's any money to speak of, I'd say Ted's already got it." He went on to explain that his brother-in-law was some kind of real estate developer, with a plush office in Steamboat Springs.

"All I want is to raise Jamie and run the ranch until he grows up and can take it over himself," Daniel concluded. "Like my sister and her husband wished me to do."

Keller sat up straighter. "The sheep ranch, right?"

"Right." Daniel wondered at the sudden show of interest.

"How many acres?" His pencil was poised.

Daniel described White Ridge, its size and location. And the number of sheep he was running.

Nicholas Keller pointed his finger at him and mimed the pulling of a trigger. "Bingo," he said with a satisfied grin.

"What do you mean?" Daniel wasn't sure what he was getting at.

"I'd bet my wheels that Uncle Ted wants the land," he mused. "That's pretty country up there and you've got a big enough parcel to make a real estate developer drool."

Daniel shook his head in disbelief. "Jamie is Ted's nephew, his flesh and blood, just as he is mine. You must be mistaken."

Keller pushed his chair back from the desk, signaling the end of the appointment. "Perhaps I am, but somehow, I don't think so. I'll contact your brother-in-law's attorney," he said, waving the letter that Daniel had brought with him. "Maybe we can find out for sure what he's up to." He wheeled over to where Daniel had gotten to his feet. "Meanwhile, take good care of the boy," Keller continued. "Stay out of trouble and get that haircut. I'll be talking to you."

Daniel shook his hand and thanked him, then left his office. Keller's secretary, a brunette with startling blue eyes and long red nails, gave him a lingering smile as he walked past her desk.

School was through for the day and Karen had gone down the hall to visit with Terry Polaski, the first-grade teacher, when she glanced up to catch a glimpse of Daniel passing the open door and heading in the direction of her room. At least, she thought it was Daniel.

"Excuse me," she told the other teacher, who had been speculating about the rumors that Mr. Appleby, the principal, was going to retire early because of ill health. "I think the guardian of one of my kids just went by."

"Lucky you," Terry murmured as Karen hurried back to her own room.

She wasn't sure it was Daniel because the man had short hair, but something about the way he moved was familiar. She hurried through the open doorway of her classroom and almost collided with him.

"Oh!" she exclaimed, her upraised palms warding him off as one of his hands grasped her shoulder to steady her. "You got your hair cut."

He was holding his hat in his other hand, and he looked embarrassed by her comment. Instantly she regretted the thoughtless way she had blurted it out. "It looks nice," she added lamely. Actually the new style, short and combed off his face, longer and touching his collar in back, was wildly attractive. It emphasized his high cheekbones and straight nose, making him appear more sophisticated and yet not the least bit tame.

Obviously self-conscious, he ran a hand through his hair. "I'm still trying to get used to it," he confessed.

She found his vulnerability endearing. Dangerously so. "Why did you decide to get it cut?" she asked to hide her own reaction.

He looked surprised.

"I'm sorry," she amended quickly. "I didn't mean to be so personal. You certainly don't owe me any explanation."

He glanced around the empty room. "Do you have a few minutes or am I keeping you from something?"

His question surprised her. "No, you aren't," she admitted, intrigued. Later, she would deal with the pleasure she felt at his unexpected visit. A visit that was, no doubt, purely professional. "Come on back and have a seat."

He waited until she was settled behind her desk and then he walked restlessly to the window, jamming his hands into his pockets and staring out. He had wanted to tell her while she was at the ranch. He needed someone to talk to, and something about her invited him to take a chance.

"I need your help," he blurted, turning to look her full in the face. "Without it, I might lose Jamie."

Chapter Five

Karen stared at Daniel, stunned by his announcement. "What do you mean, you might lose Jamie?"

"His father's brother is suing for custody." Daniel's expression was bleak and Karen saw something in his eyes that hadn't been there before. Fear.

Without thinking, she threw her arms around him. "I'm so sorry," she said into his shoulder. His arms remained at his sides. Embarrassed, she let him go. "It will work out, you'll see. Didn't Jamie's parents appoint you guardian in their will?"

He smiled reluctantly. "I see that Mary has been talking to her cousin Rose again."

Karen could have bitten her tongue. She didn't want to get anyone in trouble, least of all Daniel's housekeeper or the school secretary. Mary had been very nice to Karen when she stayed with them. And Rose was always doing little things to make the teachers' jobs easier.

"Don't worry about it," he said abruptly when he saw her discomfiture. He hadn't come to berate her about the gossip. What had he come for? To find solace in her arms? He had been shocked when she hugged him, but it felt good. If he hadn't been caught off guard, he might have wrapped his arms around her and held her close, absorbing her warmth and the sweet scent of her. Perhaps it was just as well she had released him when she did; he wouldn't have stopped without tasting her lips again. Hardly appropriate behavior in a classroom.

"Is there really a chance you could lose custody?" she asked.

Daniel nodded, the now-familiar chill of fear washing over him. "I could."

"How can I help?"

He reached a hand up to caress her hair. Part of it was pulled back into a ponytail, but the rest hung loose around her shoulders in shining waves. Lacy silver hearts dangled from her ears. He touched one with his finger and it swayed.

"You could testify for me at the custody hearing," he said softly, wondering what she would do if he indulged his galloping hormones and dipped his tongue into her mouth. If he stroked the sides of her breasts. If, just for one wild, sweet moment, he rested the ache that tormented him against the feminine cradle of her thighs.

His body was heavy with arousal, his mind clouded with desire. The last thing he wanted to do was to talk about lawsuits and hearings. Then he thought of Jamie—about losing him. Immediately passion was doused with a cold shower of icy control. Anxiously he awaited her response.

"Of course," she said, touching his arm. "I'd be glad to. Just let me know in time to arrange for a sub here at school."

The tension that had been building inside him dissolved so suddenly that it left him shaken. "I can't thank you enough," he said.

Her smile was gentle. "What does this other uncle hope to gain?" she asked. "Why is he doing this against the wishes of Jamie's own mother?"

Daniel's jaw clenched with anger. "Apparently Ted doesn't approve of a savage like myself raising Jamie."

"Savage?" Karen echoed, and then felt herself blushing as his meaning dawned. She hadn't thought about Daniel's Indian blood, other than to be aware that his bronzed complexion, black hair and dark eyes made him compellingly attractive. "That's ridiculous," she snapped. "I have no patience with that kind of narrow-minded attitude."

Daniel's brows rose at her outburst. "Thanks for the vote of confidence, if that's what it was."

"I know you're good for Jamie," Karen went on. "I've seen how you are with him. The judge will see it, too, believe me. He'll have no choice but to let you keep Jamie."

Daniel's smile was faint. "I hope you're right." It was obvious that her praise made him uncomfortable. His eyes were narrowed, unreadable, as he watched her. "Thank you."

Karen would have liked to ask how he was really handling all this. She wondered if he would open up if she did ask.

Daniel sighed wearily. His guard slipped for a moment, allowing her to see the exhaustion and strain he was under.

"I've been to see a lawyer," he said, studying the gray afternoon through the window. His fingers flicked at the ends of his hair. In back, it barely brushed the collar of his heavy denim jacket. Karen's gaze drifted downward, to the trim male buttocks and long, muscular legs encased in matching denim. Then, realizing that her perusal bordered on lascivious, she turned her attention sharply away, to the children's drawings displayed on the bulletin board.

"My haircut was his idea," Daniel added. "As if anything this simple can help."

Karen walked around to where she could see his face. "I imagine that appearances carry a certain amount of weight," she said carefully, "but you have a lot more on your side."

His lips twisted into a bitter smile. "Ted's in real estate," he muttered. "Big house, nice car, pretty wife."

"You can run the ranch," Karen argued, trying to reassure him. "That's Jamie's inheritance. He loves you, and your sister wanted you to raise him. That's a pretty powerful endorsement. What kind of relationship does Jamie have with this Ted?"

Daniel's grin widened and lost its bitter curl. Apparently, he approved of the disdainful tone to her voice when she spoke the other man's name, as if he were of little consequence.

"I wish I had your confidence," Daniel admitted. "I don't think Jamie knows Ted very well at all. He told me they wanted him to keep his hands in his pockets when he visited their house. Why would people like that want custody of a small, active boy?"

"I don't know." Karen wondered, too. "Did you get a good lawyer? One with lots of experience handling custody cases?" She thought of her mother's successful corporate practice. To Karen, it sounded so dry and dull.

"I got Nick Keller," Daniel replied. "Have you heard of him?"

She nodded. "He has the reputation of being a real bulldog in court. Tough and aggressive."

"The lawyer who handled the will recommended him," Daniel continued. "I like him."

"I meant what I said," Karen repeated after a moment. "Anything I can do..."

"Thanks."

"If you ever want to talk, let me know."

Daniel's gaze met hers. His expression softened. "I appreciate the offer."

Somehow, she was pretty sure he had no intentions of taking her up on it.

"How's Jamie's behavior been here at school?" he asked, deliberately changing the subject.

"Better," she was pleased to be able to tell him. "He's not getting into as many arguments and he's been paying more attention. He's got some catching up to do, but he's a bright boy. If I come out to the ranch a few more times, I'm sure he will get caught up."

At her words, some of Daniel's tension seemed to fade. Karen was surprised at how good that made her feel. He was only here because of Jamie, she reminded herself. Getting stranded at his ranch didn't mean the two of them were even friends, never mind anything more. Now it sounded as if Daniel's spare time, if he had any, and his attention would be wholly taken up by the custody case ahead.

"Good luck with everything." She extended her hand.

Daniel gripped it firmly and thanked her again. She thought his gaze lingered for a moment longer than was strictly necessary, but as he turned to leave she decided it must be her own wishful thinking.

"Feel free to come by anytime," she called after him as he went down the hallway.

He turned and touched the brim of his hat with his fingers. "Thanks again."

Feeling slightly foolish, she ducked back into her classroom to grab her purse and lunch sack. Before she could leave, Terry Polaski poked her head in the doorway.

"Was that him?" she asked in a stage whisper.

"Who?" Karen asked as Terry came into the room. A long, bright orange shirt and navy leggings outlined her curvy figure.

"The guy you thought he was, you know, when he walked past my room."

Karen felt her cheeks grow warm and knew they had turned the particular shade of pink that was a dead give-away to her feelings. "Yes, that was Jamie Powell's guardian," she replied coolly.

"What a hunk!" Terry's dimples flashed, her wide mouth curved into an appreciative smile. "I can't wait until next year," she trilled. "I certainly hope the boy's in my room. I can see *lots* of parent-teacher conferences in that kid's future."

Karen couldn't help but laugh at her friend's avid tone. "He's not married," she volunteered, wondering what Terry's reaction would be if Karen admitted to being snowed-in with him. Terry was a good friend and they often shared confidences, but Karen hadn't told her about being stranded during the storm.

Terry's eyes gleamed. "Not married, huh?" she echoed. "Are you interested in him?" Terry was divorced. She made no secret of the fact that she would rather be married again. More than once, she had invited Karen to go out with her, but Karen had turned her down.

"Am I?" she echoed. "Not really." Even as she voiced the denial, she knew she wasn't being truthful. After Mark Gresham, she just had no faith in her own judgment.

Terry looked slightly embarrassed. "I'm sorry, honey. I just assumed you'd be over that other bum by now."

"I am," Karen said honestly. "I'm just not in any hurry to make that same mistake again." She had transferred to Mountain View Elementary after Mark ended their engagement in a humiliatingly public way that had made teaching at the school where he was vice principal an impossibility.

Gossip had followed her here, but Terry, a college friend, was one of the few people to whom she had told the whole story.

"You know, all men aren't jerks," Terry insisted. "Just because the ones you and I chose to get involved with happened to be."

Karen could see that Terry wasn't really convinced she was over Mark. Well, there were lengths she refused to go to in order to prove it. Making a fool of herself again was one of them. "As far as I'm concerned, Mark is history. Besides, he's married now, with a new baby, you know."

Terry frowned. "Oh, I know. The man is slime, and you're well rid of him."

Karen smiled at her friend's assessment. She tended to agree. "That doesn't mean that I have to take an interest in Daniel Sixkiller," she protested.

"Is that his name? Is he Indian? I thought so, with that black hair and those awesome cheekbones. Is that why you aren't interested?"

"No!" Karen's denial was firm. That had never entered into it. She might deny her interest to Terry, but she couldn't deny it to herself. The truth was that she did find him attractive, devastatingly so, from the top of his black head to the heels of his cowboy boots. And every compelling masculine inch in between. She remembered the way his mouth had brushed hers during the snowball fight with Jamie, and she went hot all over.

"I'm sure he's not looking for a girlfriend," she told Terry, "and I'm definitely not looking for a man."

Terry held up her hands in protest. "Okay, you've convinced me." Her eyes twinkled when she grinned. "I just think you're crazy," she added over her shoulder as the two of them left Karen's classroom.

Karen's smile faded before she got to the front door of the school a few minutes later. Undoubtedly, she and Daniel had

come from vastly different backgrounds. She wasn't familiar with his, but she didn't imagine there were many paral-
lels between it and her privileged childhood in Denver.
Probably the only common ground that she and Daniel
shared was their interest in Jamie. Lord knew that wasn't
enough for a relationship, no matter how one looked at it.

While Karen was assuring herself that she and Daniel were
an unlikely pair, he was on the phone with his attorney.
They were discussing the hearing in family court to begin the
process of investigating Ted's petition.

"Don't worry about it," Nick Keller told Daniel. "It's
routine. I'll go with you. The judge will assign a social
worker to investigate you and Powell. He'll most likely leave
Jamie in your custody while that's being done."

Daniel gripped the receiver tighter. "Are you telling me
that the judge could decide to take Jamie away right then?"
he demanded. "That he could be put in a foster home or
something during the investigation?" An icy sweat chilled
Daniel and his stomach writhed with tension. It had never
occurred to him that he could lose the boy so soon. And on
someone else's whim.

"Now, hold on." Keller's voice was rock-solid calm, as if
he'd had plenty of experience soothing clients' worries. No
doubt he had.

"How can I hold on?" Aware that his voice had risen,
Daniel lowered it deliberately. He was in John's office, with
the door shut, but he didn't want Jamie to overhear him.

"Take it easy," Keller cautioned. "The court just isn't
going to jerk him out of there when he's in the family home
with a relative. There's been no accusation of abuse or anything, so don't go borrowing trouble."

Daniel was silent for a moment, trying to absorb the lawyer's words of assurance. The man was right; he had enough
to worry about without that. Damn Ted Powell, anyway!

"Okay," he said on a long sigh. "Where shall I meet you?"

After several more directives from Keller that he remain calm and confident, Daniel ended the conversation. He had barely hung up from talking to his attorney when the phone rang again. It was the leader of the shearing crew reminding Daniel that he and his men would be at the ranch first thing the next morning. Thank God the snow and cold weather from the week before had melted away as if it had never been.

As soon as he replaced the receiver for the second time, Daniel went out to find Cully and make preparations for the next day's shearing.

"I told you the judge would leave the boy with you during the investigation," Nick Keller said as he and Daniel left the courtroom.

Daniel's insides were still shaking from the strain of the last few stressed-filled moments. The preliminary hearing in family court had gone just the way the attorney had predicted that it would—routinely. A social worker named Mrs. Duggan had been assigned to investigate Jamie's present home situation and to interview Ted and his wife before filing a report with the judge, a balding man with glasses and a double chin. Keller had told Daniel that Judge Hagen had a reputation for being conservative but fair.

Court would reconvene in a few weeks, after the judge had read Mrs. Duggan's report. At that time, he would hear the testimony of witnesses for both sides and would also talk to Jamie.

"I'm not looking forward to explaining all this to my nephew," Daniel admitted as he followed Keller's wheelchair down the ramp at the front of the courthouse. "He's only five and he's just lost his parents. How do I tell him he may be moving to Steamboat Springs to live with people who expect him to keep his hands in his pockets when he's in their house?'' He could hear the bitterness in his voice, but damned if he could cover it up.

Nick stopped at the bottom of the ramp and swiveled his chair around to face Daniel. "Don't get discouraged," he said. "I expect the judge to rule in your favor. You have a lot going for you. There's the will, your capability to manage the ranch, plus its being the home where Jamie has lived until now." He ticked each point off on his fingers and then let his hands fall into his lap. "And there's your shared heritage. Under the Indian Child Welfare Act, some courts are routinely placing Native American children with tribal members." Keller's normally tenacious expression radiated confidence. "Go home and get some rest," he advised Daniel. "And strengthen those ties with Jamie. We don't know how much weight the judge will put on his testimony, but it won't hurt for the boy to tell him that he wants to stay with you."

Daniel's grin was wry. He couldn't even count on that, although Jamie and he had been getting along much better since Karen had forced them to talk. He shifted his shoulders, confined in the unfamiliar dark suit he had bought for the hearing. The discreetly striped tie Keller told him to wear with it threatened to choke him.

"I'll talk to Jamie before we go back to court," Keller continued. "I can be good with kids when I need to be, so quit worrying."

Daniel had spent the last hectic couple of days before the hearing getting his sheep sheared. He was tired to the bone and he still had chores waiting for him. The sheep didn't care about the custody hearing, and neither did his horses.

Perhaps he'd go for a ride when he was done with the work. Being on horseback always relaxed him. He wondered if Karen rode, then hastily dismissed the thought. He needed to concentrate on Jamie.

"I'm not worried," he told Keller, sure his expression must belie his words.

Keller emitted a short bark of laughter. "That's the spirit. Go on," he repeated. "There isn't anything else you can do today. Call me when you hear from that social services woman and we'll talk, okay?"

"Okay." Daniel stuck out his hand. "Thanks," he said. "I appreciate your help."

Keller pumped Daniel's hand. "You can thank me when we win," he said with another grin.

Exhausted, Daniel walked across the street to where his pickup was parked. The shearing crew had been the ones to do the real work, sitting each sheep up onto its rear end and stripping away the fleece with long, sure strokes of their electric clippers in less time than it would have taken Daniel to get an animal into position. Still, he felt as if he had personally dealt with each ram and ewe himself.

As Daniel climbed into his truck and started the engine, he remembered Cully's cheerful warning. "Mate, if you think this was tough, just wait for them ewes to start dropping their lambs all over the place."

Daniel ripped off the hated tie, freed the top button of his dress shirt and gratefully slapped the Stetson Keller had made him leave in the cab back onto his head. Sighing with relief, he turned his truck toward home.

When he passed the road to Jamie's school, he had a moment's tempting thought that he would have liked to stop by and see Karen Whitworth. He could have taken her out for coffee and told her about the hearing. She would have listened to him, really listened. He wondered if she wore her hair loose today or pinned up on her head.

He could have described the shearing to her—how fast the members of the crew worked to separate the sheep from their wool, how pure and creamy white the underside of each fleece was compared to the dirty, matted outer layers. How slippery the floor got from the lanolin in the wool.

Even if she wasn't really interested, she would have let him talk. She had offered to listen when he needed an ear, but he could barely understand this new urge of his to share so much, he who usually had little to say and never minded being alone.

Daniel was well past the turnoff to the school before he relaxed his rigid hold on the steering wheel. He needed a strong cup of coffee, a hot meal and a good night's sleep, in that order. What he didn't need was to torment himself yet again by thinking about a woman he had no time to spend on and no right to covet. A woman as unsuited to him as he would be to her.

He had seen her sidelong glances. She might be curious about him, but she would bolt if he lifted a finger. He was still surprised that she hadn't freaked when he kissed her during the snowball fight. She had said she hated narrow-minded thinking; perhaps she was telling the truth.

No, he reminded himself. It was one thing to mouth platitudes about all men being equal; it was another thing to crawl into bed with a redskin.

He slapped the steering wheel hard enough to make the palm of his hand sting. Hadn't he learned anything from the white witch who had allowed his baby to be taken from her body and disposed of like garbage?

"Naturally a two-parent household is the preferable environment for a child," Mrs. Duggan said, glancing over the tops of her bifocals at Daniel. "Especially a child as young as James."

Daniel sat across from the social worker in the living room of the ranch house. He swallowed the angry retort that rose in his throat and forced his fingers to keep from wrapping themselves around her crepey neck. "Jamie and I have always been very close," he said, remembering his attorney's advice to keep a firm lid on his temper and not bad-mouth Ted and Dixie. "His mother was my only sister. We understood each other. I know the values she wanted Jamie to learn. I know what was important to her, and to John. Jamie and I share the same heritage and the same blood."

The social worker flipped the page on her notebook. Was she writing down what he said or commenting on his dirty fingernails? He had spent the morning with Cully, inspecting sheeps' feet for hoof rot and replacing broken boards in the lambing shed. He'd barely stepped out of the shower when Mrs. Duggan had showed up—early. He had no doubt that her timing had been deliberate. To catch him before he had a chance to hide the scalps and the bloody tomahawk?

"Would you like more coffee?" he asked her. He was the one who needed the caffeine, to keep him alert.

She glanced at her half-empty cup. "No, thank you."

Mary had taken Jamie to the library and then for ice cream, to get him out of the house. Daniel had yet to explain this mess to him. How would Jamie take the news? he wondered distractedly.

"I'm sure you were close to your sister," Mrs. Duggan said, making another note on her pad. "But I have to determine the best situation for the boy."

Daniel wanted to tell her that Jamie's life was more than a situation, but he held his tongue. "He loves it here," he said instead. "It's a good place for any child to grow up and learn responsibility."

"Does he have a lot of chores to do?" she asked smoothly.

Daniel saw the trap. Was he overworking Jamie? Expecting too much? "Jamie's only five," he said. "Sometimes he helps me after school. Later on, when he's older, he'll have more responsibilities, but I'll never forget that he's a child. And his schooling will always come first."

Mrs. Duggan made another note. Then she smiled for the first time since she had introduced herself. He was amazed at the change it made in her plain face. "I quite agree." She closed the notepad and put it and her pen into a black vinyl briefcase. When she rose from the couch, Daniel sucked in a deep, steadying breath. For better or worse, the interview was over. Too bad he couldn't ask how he had scored.

"I still have to visit Mr. and Mrs. Powell. Then I'll be turning my report over to Judge Hagen."

Not for the first time since she had arrived, Daniel found himself wondering what to say. He settled for silence.

Mrs. Duggan shook his hand with a firm grip. "I've been doing this for a long time," she said. "I can tell that you care about your nephew. Unfortunately that isn't always enough." She crossed to the entryway and Daniel reached around her to pluck her coat from the coat tree. He was surprised to see her cheeks flush slightly when he held it for her.

For one wild moment, he wondered if she would be susceptible to bribery. He had money put aside. Or what about a threat to some member of her family? Or blackmail? Although he doubted she had anything to hide. Then there was always seduction.

He studied her close-cropped gray hair and sturdy figure. Realizing he must be dangerously close to cracking from the strain he had been under, Daniel ignored the wild ideas sprouting in his brain like so much loco weed.

"If there's anything else I can do," he heard himself offering instead. "Any other questions I can answer..."

Before he could finish, she was shaking her head. "Thank you, but I've heard quite enough."

He had no idea how to take that last remark. Her expression revealed nothing as she allowed Daniel to open her car door for her.

After he had watched her drive away, Daniel once again had the urge to contact Karen. Perhaps she might have some idea what chance he had.

His shoulders slumped wearily as he realized that even his attorney, who was experienced at this kind of thing, could offer no real guarantees. What good would Karen's reassurances do him? *A lot of good,* a tiny voice inside his head whispered. Daniel ignored it, wondering instead if he had just furthered his case to keep Jamie, or demolished it? Unfortunately he had no clue.

Maybe he had no business burdening Karen with his problems, but there was one person to whom he could appeal. Jaw set with grim purpose, Daniel went into the office and flipped open John's phone book.

He dialed Ted's number at the office, only to be told he had left for the day. Some long hours the man was putting in, Daniel thought sarcastically as he glanced at the desk clock. Consulting the book again, he dialed his brother-in-law's home number.

When Ted answered on the fourth ring, Daniel swallowed the lump of pride blocking his throat and got to the point.

"I want you to drop the custody suit," he said. "I haven't told Jamie about it yet and I don't want to. He's lost enough already." He paused for breath and realized he was shaking all over. Gripping the receiver tighter, he waited for Ted to say something.

"I can't do that." The other man's voice was expressionless. "I have to follow my conscience."

Daniel would have liked to dive right through the phone line and shake John's brother for what he was doing to Jamie. How could two men be so different? "You know that he's happy here. This is his home. How can your conscience let you disrupt his life so completely?" He was genuinely puzzled. According to John, neither Ted nor Dixie had ever wanted a family of their own. Why the sudden interest in Jamie?

"My conscience will permit me no other course of action," Ted replied in answer to Daniel's spoken query. "I'm determined to see young James's inheritance developed to its utmost potential." His oily voice droned on, but Daniel barely heard him. "I'm in a position to maximize the value of his holdings, that land you're desecrating by running sheep across it."

"But it's a sheep ranch," Daniel protested. "Your brother's sheep ranch." His gut threatened to twist itself inside out as he realized what Ted was admitting. It wasn't Jamie he really wanted but control of Jamie's legacy! White Ridge sprawled across a beautiful valley, almost untouched by signs of man's greed and shortsighted destruction. Now he could see that someone like Ted would view the land as a prime parcel for development into something that would completely violate its pristine beauty.

"You're making a big mistake," Daniel growled into the receiver. "And I'm going to fight you with everything I have."

"Somehow, 'everything you have' doesn't concern me overly much," Ted replied coolly.

Before Daniel could slam down his own receiver, he heard a click at the other end. With fingers that shook with frustration and fury, Daniel dialed Nick Keller's number. At least now they had a motive for Ted's sudden interest in his nephew. Perhaps the attorney could use the information to someway further Daniel's own case.

When he was done talking to Nick, Daniel sat back in his chair and blew out a long breath. He contemplated saddling Ringo and going for a ride, but then he had a better idea. Grabbing his hat, he hurried from the room. Moments later, he was headed for town.

Chapter Six

Karen was walking to the parking lot beside Mountain View Elementary when she saw a familiar red-and-white pickup truck parked on the street. While she was staring, Daniel Sixkiller straightened from the nearby tree he had been leaning against and began walking toward her.

Karen stopped and waited for him to approach. She could admit to herself, at least, how much she had missed him. That knowledge, much more than his presence in the deserted parking lot, was something she found truly scary.

With a pounding heart, she watched Daniel walk toward her. As usual, the brim of his Stetson hid most of his face, so she couldn't read his mood. Had something happened with Jamie? With the custody suit? Anxiously she nibbled at her lip and wished she had taken the time to freshen her makeup and run a brush through her hair before leaving school. She had worn her hair loose today. No doubt it was tangled and flyaway.

Daniel's hands were jammed into the pockets of his denim jacket. The collar was turned up to ward off the late-afternoon chill.

"I'm glad I caught you," he said, looking down at Karen. Now she could see that his expression was solemn, his shadowed gaze intense.

"I was just leaving." Breathlessly, she asked, "Is something wrong?"

His grin was crooked as he took her elbow. "Not really. Do you have time to get some coffee?"

She was surprised at his request, pleased that he was here. She was sure she could feel the heat from his hand through the sleeve of her heavy coat. His gaze was intent, as if he were totally focused on her.

Daniel would have liked to take her into his arms. His hand on her elbow wasn't nearly enough contact to satisfy him. He wanted to touch her skin and feel its warmth. For now, though, he had to settle for what he could get.

"Where do you want to go for coffee?" she asked.

A grin touched the corner of his attractive mouth as he glanced around. "I'm not sure."

"Have you been to My Mother's House?" she asked. "They have great pie, if you're hungry."

He looked confused. "Your mother's house?"

Karen smiled. "No, that's the name of the café—My Mother's House. It's a couple of blocks over." She pointed. "You could follow me, if you'd like."

"Lead the way." When he walked back to his truck, she watched him. Then, with a little shake, she dug her keys out of her purse and got into her car. He probably only wanted to talk about Jamie, she reminded herself. After all, she had offered to lend an ear if he needed her.

"I like your hair that way," Daniel said when he joined her in front of the small café.

"Messy?" she asked, pulling it out of her collar in back.

He leaned close. "Sexy," he whispered. His breath touched her cheek. For a moment, their eyes locked. Then he broke the spell, leaving her shaken as he opened the door of the café. Emotionally Karen was treading on dangerous ground and she didn't even care.

Daniel helped her off with her coat before he slipped out of his own jacket and put them both over the back of a chair by an empty table. Karen was glad she had worn a new mauve sweater and a long, flowered skirt to school that day. Daniel, as usual, was dressed in jeans and a Western shirt, this one a blue plaid that hugged his broad shoulders. The tiny silver hoop, more noticeable since he had gotten his hair cut, only added to his masculinity.

As soon as the two of them were seated, a waitress brought menus.

"Just coffee for me," Daniel told her. He looked at Karen. "Would you like anything else?"

She shook her head. "Coffee's fine."

Daniel removed his hat and put it on an empty chair. Then he raked a hand through his hair. The shorter style emphasized the slash of his distinctive cheekbones and the nobility of his profile. He could have been posing for a commemorative plate.

While Karen studied him, he shifted and his gaze met hers. "Did I cut myself shaving?" he asked, touching his jaw.

Her cheeks flushed and his mouth relaxed into a smile as he leaned closer. "You must have a devil of a time hiding your feelings," he said in a low voice.

Shivers of reaction made her tremble. She felt her blush deepen. "Most people are too polite to comment," she retorted.

"I'm not most people." He leaned back in his chair as the waitress poured their coffee.

"I know," Karen muttered.

It was obvious that he heard her, but he didn't say anything. Instead he took a sip of his coffee as he watched her.

"What about you?" he asked suddenly.

"What do you mean?"

His gaze searched her face. "Tell me about yourself. I don't know much except that you're a teacher, a dedicated one." He took another drink of his coffee. "Fill me in. Where are you from? How did you get into teaching? The usual."

She wondered if he was really interested or just making conversation. He was waiting expectantly, so she told him about growing up in Denver, but not about her privileged background. She had an idea that knowing she came from a wealthy family would put him off.

"It sounds as if your childhood was lonely," he said. "With your parents both working and no brothers and sisters."

She shrugged. "I guess it was. I read a lot, and I didn't mind my own company."

"Is that why you became a teacher, because you liked to read?"

She thought a moment, remembering her parents' disappointment when she chose education over law school. Her mother had suggested she at least teach at the college level.

"Sometimes it's hard to remember just why I wanted to teach," she admitted with painful honesty. "I thought I could make a difference, but now I'm not so sure."

When her voice softened and her gaze became unfocused, as if she were talking only to herself, Daniel reached across the table and took her hand in his. He caressed her knuckles with his thumb as he waited for her to continue.

"There's so little I can do to combat the poverty and abuse," she muttered. "There are children whose only decent meal is the hot lunch at school, and little ones who already trust no one because the people they should be able to trust the most have let them down." She shook her head and he saw that her eyes were moist.

"You expect too much of yourself," he told her, tightening his grip on her hand. She squeezed back and a tremor went through him. He wished they were alone, so he could sweep her into his arms and comfort her. He'd use any excuse available to hold her.

"What about you?" she asked, breaking into his thoughts. "You gave up everything to take care of Jamie."

He shrugged and released her hand to drain his coffee cup. "That's different."

She cocked her head. "Oh? How so?"

"He's family. All I have left." The way her eyes tilted up at the corners fascinated him. While he stared, they fluttered shut.

"How's the custody suit going?" Karen asked, intent on distracting him from his contemplation of her face.

Immediately his speculative grin faded, making her sorry she had reminded him. "The social worker came out the other day. She asked a hundred questions, but I don't know if I gave the right answers." He sounded weary.

Karen ached to reassure him. It wasn't fair that he had to go through this when all he wanted was to raise his nephew with love. "You're too hard on yourself," she said. "I'll bet you did just fine. I'm sure she can tell when someone genuinely cares."

"And you know that I do?"

Her opinion seemed important to him. "Absolutely."

He wrapped his hands around his empty cup as if he were trying to warm them, but his steady gaze never left her face. "Tell me something," he said, leaning closer. The noise around them seemed to recede until there was only the two of them.

Karen fidgeted with her napkin. "I will if I can." What was he after?

When he hunched forward, she caught the aroma of coffee mingled with the fainter scents of soap and the outdoors. Tiny lines radiated outward from the corners of his eyes. The grooves that ran from the sides of his nose to the edges of his mouth were deeper. Karen didn't think it was because he had been smiling a lot. The startling blackness of his eyes was as utterly unreadable as usual.

Impatiently she waited for him to continue as she moistened her dry lips with her tongue. A strand of her hair fell forward and she tucked it back.

Daniel watched her like a hawk ready to pounce on an unwary target. "What chance do you really think I have to win?"

"I think you have every chance," she declared stoutly.

"Even though I'm unmarried?"

She started to answer but he kept talking.

"Even though I got my high school equivalency in the army? I was a sniper, trained to kill people." His eyes seemed to go darker. "And I was good at it."

"If that was your job—" she began.

"I'm a full-blooded, uncivilized savage with a police record." His voice droned on.

She wondered what he had done to get a police record.

"I've got a misdemeanor for starting a fight in a bar," he continued, answering her unspoken question. "I was drunk at the time and I spent the night in jail."

She was still looking at him. At least she hadn't gotten up and run away.

"So what do you think of me now?" he asked, wondering why he was so determined to shock her, to drive her away. "Would you award me sole custody of a small child?"

"I don't think you can say that you're uncivilized," she replied.

Startled, Daniel burst into laughter. Then he looked down at his hands, studying the scars and calluses. "Ted has money," he continued after a moment. "He has a successful business and a big house in Steamboat Springs." He turned one hand over and looked at the short nails. They were reasonably clean for a rancher's.

Karen wanted to reach over and touch him. While she watched, he curled his fingers into a loose fist.

"I drove by his house yesterday. It's pretty fancy, set back from the road down a long concrete driveway, behind a wrought-iron fence. Intercom in the gate. Nice yard, lawn like artificial turf."

"That shouldn't matter," she insisted. "Jamie's home is at the ranch, with you and Mary and the animals."

His gaze was steady. "Maybe it shouldn't matter, but it does. And it matters a hell of a lot to some people. Ted's married, financially stable. My lawyer says that looks good to a judge. I'm a cowhand." He shut his eyes and shook his head. "Sheepman," he corrected. "I'm a sheepman now. If you don't know it, in some circles that's considered even worse." His face was bitter.

"So, tell me," he prompted when Karen remained silent. "What do you really think?"

"I think that any judge with a heart will leave Jamie with you." She looked him straight in the eye, but she didn't add that, after her own affluent but very lonely childhood, the ranch seemed like a dream world.

Daniel covered her hand with his, and Karen looked at the contrast. Dark to light, strong to delicate. Hard to soft. Their differences made her tremble.

She could feel the strength of his grip, and the warmth. It occurred to her that she would have liked to be the one to comfort him, to bring that rare smile back to his face. To see laughter in his eyes. She was in big trouble here.

"You know the right thing to say." His voice was deep, slightly rough, as if he were keeping something under tight control.

She turned her hand over and tangled her fingers with his. "That's not why I said it. I was telling the truth."

Daniel grabbed his hat with his free hand and put it on. He tossed some coins on the table and got to his feet. "Let's go."

When they were outside, Karen stopped on the sidewalk by her car. "Thanks for the coffee. Keep me posted on what's going on, won't you?"

He glanced up at the sky in the growing darkness. There were clouds over the moon. He seemed tense. "I'll follow you home."

Karen felt warm despite the chill of late afternoon. "That's not necessary."

His eyes narrowed. "Don't you want me knowing where you live?"

She rolled her eyes in disgust. "What kind of women have you been hanging out with?" she demanded, circling her car and opening the door. "Come on." When she glanced up, Daniel was headed for his truck, a grin on his face. He stayed on her bumper until she turned in at her building. When she stopped at her assigned spot, she waved, expecting him to keep on going.

Instead he parked his truck beside her car and climbed out.

Would he get the wrong idea if she asked him in? Had she picked up the place that morning? Or was the door to her bedroom open and her bed unmade? She couldn't remember.

"I could make some coffee if you'd like another cup," she offered as he followed her to the front door. It was almost dark now and the outside lights were on.

He glanced at his watch. "I'd better go. I have to relieve Cully. I left him with the lambs, and I want to see Jamie before he goes to bed."

Karen subdued a shiver from the cool air. Knowing the way his mind worked, he might think it was nervousness that made her tremble. "I could come out tomorrow and help him with his schoolwork," she said. "As long as it doesn't snow."

Daniel stepped closer, watching her carefully for any signs of skittishness. He gripped her elbows lightly. "I'd appreciate that."

She was looking at him, eyes wide and appealing. He wished he had taken her up on that offer of coffee, even though common sense told him he'd been smarter to refuse. Just as he'd be smarter now to turn around and walk away.

Damn, but he was fed up with doing the smart thing. Usually he had no problem resisting a woman's interest. Right now, it was suddenly more than he could manage.

"Why are you always so nice?" he asked quietly as he slid his hands up to grasp the lapels of her quilted coat.

She didn't back away, just looked perplexed. "I haven't done anything especially nice."

"That's a matter of opinion," he muttered. "And I sure hope that what I'm going to do right now doesn't blow your willingness to be so helpful." He saw the light dawn in her eyes the instant she realized what he was about to do. He waited for her hasty retreat. When she didn't pull away, he dipped his head. Anticipation roared through him as he hovered with no more than a breath between them. His heart thundered, the sound of it like a kettledrum in his ears.

Karen wasn't backing away as he had feared she might— she was actually lifting her face to meet his hungry, descending mouth.

He let go of her coat and slid his arms around her trim body. Despite the bulky garment, she felt fragile in his embrace, even delicate. He tried to hold her gently. Then his head filled with her scent. His lips touched hers and he registered how soft and sweet her mouth was. He forgot about being careful, forgot about not scaring her, almost forgot where they were.

He was barely aware of her gloved fingers coming up to rest against his cheek as he opened his mouth and deepened the kiss. She followed his lead, fingers tightening as she allowed him entrance. Her taste was sweet and dark, incredibly intoxicating. He shuddered as his tongue touched hers and she shyly stroked him back. His head was spinning, his breathing tortured. Drawing her flush against his aroused body, he kissed her as thoroughly as he knew how.

Finally, slowly, he felt her begin to pull away. No wonder, he was holding her as tightly as a life vest in a flash flood. Forcing his arms to release her, he allowed her to break off the kiss.

Her lips looked swollen, bruised. Shame washed over him like hot tar. "I'm sorry," he croaked, mortified by his loss of control.

To his bewilderment, she shook her head. "No," she whispered softly, confusing him even more. Then she touched his soul by pulling his head back down and kissing him again.

"Don't you dare be sorry. I'm not."

Her whispered words were like a benediction. He swallowed and sought a worthy response. Before he could come up with one, she pulled her keys out of her coat pocket and unlocked her front door. "Thanks again for the coffee," she said with a funny little smile he had no time to interpret. Then she slipped inside.

"I'll see you later," he managed to rasp before the door closed.

Daniel hadn't expected her to repeat her invitation that he come in. Not after the way he had fallen on her like a starving mongrel on a bone. Hell, the most he had hoped for was that she didn't slap him senseless.

The lady was full of surprises. The question that hammered at him as he drove away was whether he was jeopardizing her offer to testify for him or strengthening it. He was still so rattled by her response that he couldn't begin to sort out the possible answers.

Inside her apartment, Karen leaned against the closed door and listened to the sound of Daniel's departing truck. She was breathing as if she had just run a three-minute mile and her pulse rate was undoubtedly in the critical zone. She looked down at her hands, which were shaking, and pressed one over her pounding heart. She could hardly believe that she had acted as she had, not only returning the kiss that had scorched her to her toes but also initiating a second kiss when Daniel would have let her go.

She touched a trembling finger to her lips. They still tingled. Echoes of her response to him rippled through her like aftershocks. She had been wrong in thinking she was attracted to him; her feelings toward Daniel were more complex than that. And ten times stronger than anything as lukewarm as attraction. She was coming to care for him and for Jamie entirely too much for her own peace of mind.

Daniel might desire her, might even have some feelings for her, but it would never go further than that, she was sure. He was a man who kept his emotions fiercely in check while hers were getting perilously close to the surface.

Karen moved away from the door on legs that were still unsteady and picked up the morning newspaper she had left on the couch. She carried it out to the kitchen and dumped it into the recycling bin under the sink. Then she looked in the refrigerator for something to fix for supper, although she had no appetite. Perhaps going through the familiar routine would somehow bring her back to earth.

Several times, while she was fixing a salad and scrambled eggs, Karen found herself reliving the scene on her porch.

Each time she thought about the way Daniel had kissed her, she felt a surging response. She had been right, she realized as she sliced a tomato and barely missed her finger; she had it bad. Would she never learn to guard her heart more carefully?

"We may have trouble," Nick Keller told Daniel as the two of them sat on opposite sides of the lawyer's big desk. "Judge Hagen has taken a medical leave and Judge Greenburg has been assigned to some of his cases."

Daniel shrugged. "So, why is that trouble?" When the secretary had summoned him to the attorney's office, Daniel hadn't figured it was because Ted had dropped the suit.

"Greenburg's so conservative that he makes Hagen look like a flaming liberal." Keller waved his hands, clearly agitated by the switch. "He's on record for disregarding the Indian Child Welfare Act and he almost always rules in favor of the traditional family unit in custody cases."

Daniel felt his body go taut with tension. "By traditional family unit, you mean a married couple, right?"

Keller nodded. "Bingo. You sure you don't have a wife or a fiancée stashed away somewhere? Don't misunderstand," he cautioned. "I'm not suggesting that you get married to win this case, but Ted has a wife." He pushed his thick glasses back up on his nose and his voice became edged with sarcasm. "I talked to his attorney. According to him, Powell's got some influential friends, and they're lined up to testify that he and his wife would make wonderful parents."

Daniel set down his coffee cup and rested one booted foot on his other knee as he struggled with the sudden, chilling fear that sliced through him like the blade of a knife. He could *lose* this case.

His social life had been limited since his discharge from the army. He always steered clear of women looking for anything more than satisfying but uncomplicated sex, and he couldn't imagine proposing to any one of his faceless partners, no matter what the stakes.

He thought of Karen and dismissed the idea before it was fully formed. He had already learned that lesson. Perhaps a cat could look at a king, but the cowboy didn't marry the queen. Not in real life.

Keller was a good lawyer; Daniel had to believe they would win. Anything else was unthinkable.

"I talked to Jamie's teacher," he told the attorney. "She said she'd be glad to testify for me."

"Good!" the other man exclaimed. "Is she single?"

"Why don't you have any kids of your own?" Jamie asked as Karen drove the two of them out of the school parking lot. Since she was going to the ranch to help him with his schoolwork, it seemed only practical to drive him home. Now he looked at her expectantly. From experience, she knew if she didn't answer his question, he would only ask it again.

"I don't have any children because I'm not married." She stopped at the first intersection, glanced around and then turned right onto the road that led out of town.

"Why aren't you married?" Jamie waved out the window at another boy from his class, who was walking home from school. The other boy waved back.

Karen made a face at the back of Jamie's head. How many more questions could he think up? "I guess I haven't met anyone I liked enough to marry," she said. She thought of Mark, her former fiancé. It was hard to remember why she had believed she loved him at all. Originally she had thought him an attractive, intelligent man who cared deeply for her. One who respected her and put her happiness ahead of his own. Now he seemed like a stranger. She could recall only his selfishness and the humiliation he had put her through, but none of the reasons for her earlier devotion.

With a jolt, Karen realized that she must be well and truly over him. Maybe she had been ever since he jilted her; she just hadn't realized it. A feeling of freedom lifted her spirits. She flashed a grin at Jamie, but he was too busy looking out the window to notice.

After discarding several outfits that morning, she had finally settled on slim black jeans and a print top made out of sweatshirt material. Her old boots and a parka that had seen better days were in the back of the car in case she had a chance to go outside with Daniel. He had been so busy with lambing that she hadn't seen him since they had gone out for coffee.

Since that kiss.

For a moment, Jamie's attention was captured by three dogs trotting along the shoulder of the road. The respite from his constant stream of questions was a welcome one—until the memory of Daniel's kiss invaded Karen's thoughts. Now she wished that Jamie would start grilling her again. Anything to keep her from trying to analyze what was happening between Daniel and herself.

"Do you like my uncle enough to marry him?" Jamie asked, resuming his former line of questioning as he swiveled his head around to stare at Karen expectantly. The gleam in his dark eyes reminded her of his uncle's glittering gaze. Someday Jamie would be breaking hearts—the same way Daniel threatened to break hers.

"Tell you what," she said to Jamie, slowing down as the car in front of her made a left turn, "let's see how high you can count, okay?"

Karen was sitting on the couch in the ranch house living room, listening to Jamie recite the alphabet and cuddling the kittens, when she heard the back door shut. As usual, when she and Jamie got here, Daniel hadn't been around. Mary told her that, between lambing and the regular chores, he barely slept at all. No wonder Karen hadn't seen or heard from him.

Since he had kissed her and she had kissed him back. And probably scared him away.

"Miss Whitworth, what comes after *R-S-T?*" Jamie asked. "Miss Whitworth!" He tugged insistently on her arm.

"I'm sorry." Part of her listened to see if it was Daniel who had come in the back door. "What did you say?" she asked Jamie as the spotted kitten, Moo, climbed up her arm.

Gently she pried loose the tiny claws, almost smiling at the look of exasperation on Jamie's face. Before he could repeat his question, Daniel walked into the room.

He looked wonderful; a strong, elemental male doing what he was born to do on land that was meant to remain scenic and unspoiled. He had taken off his hat; his hair was in disarray and his cheeks were red from by the wind. When he saw Karen, his eyes narrowed but she thought his hard face relaxed just a little.

"I'm glad you're still here," he said without preamble. "Stay to dinner and then I'll show you some of the newborn lambs."

"I want to go, too," Jamie said.

"I'd love to see the lambs." Pleasure flowed through Karen. Had he missed her, as she had him?

Something flared in his eyes. "Good." He lingered only long enough to ask Jamie how the work was going, then left without a backward glance. Clearing her throat, Karen did her best to subdue her foolish grin and turn her attention back to the book on her lap and the playful kittens.

It was a good thing that Jamie couldn't tell she had no idea what the words in front of her said.

Chapter Seven

Daniel steered the Jeep through the herd of sheep with care, marveling at their oblivion to its presence, while Cully kept a sharp eye out for ewes with new lambs, ones having trouble delivering or any that might have rejected their newborns. Sometimes a ewe was unable to nurse or delivered triplets and a baby needed to be transferred to a substitute mother whose offspring hadn't survived or who had only a single lamb. To fool the ewe into accepting a bummer lamb, they had to permeate it with the ewe's own scent. One method, often used when a lamb died, was to tie the dead lamb's hide over the replacement. After a few days, when the new bond had been forged, the hide would be removed.

Occasionally an orphan lamb had to be bottle-fed several times a day until it was about a month old and could eat hay and grain. Cully and Daniel took turns with the feedings. All the extra responsibilities of lambing, in addition to the regular chores, left both men exhausted. Daniel was glad that Rudy, one of the Mexican shepherds who took the sheep to their mountain pasture for the summer, was arriving early the next week. With the sheep population more than doubled by new lambs, there would be plenty for Rudy to do. The other shepherd, Marco, wasn't coming until later.

"Everything looks okay to me," Cully said as he and Daniel made a slow sweep through the last pasture. "Wait a minute." He pointed at the far corner. "Stop over there. I want to look at that ewe close up."

Daniel drove the Jeep to where Cully had indicated and watched while he climbed stiffly down and walked over to examine the ewe standing alone by the fence.

After several moments, Cully got back into the Jeep. "She looks okay for now. I'll check her again later."

Heading back toward the lambing shed, Daniel wondered if Cully was as old as he looked. Maybe not; Daniel suspected they both had aged during the lambing. Even Cully's weathered skin, scraggly gray beard and thinning hair didn't make him look as tired as Daniel felt. He was ready to fall asleep over the wheel.

The night before, five ewes had delivered, including two sets of twins, a lamb that was stillborn and one whose mother couldn't nurse him. While Cully grabbed some sleep, Daniel had dealt with them all.

Now he sneaked a peek at his watch. He had hoped to get done in time to take a shower before dinner, but it didn't look as if he was going to make it.

"Why don't you drop me at the barn and head up to the house," Cully suggested after spitting a stream of tobacco over the side of the Jeep. Daniel had mentioned that Karen was staying for dinner. "You need to get washed or that uppity housekeeper won't let you in her kitchen."

"Don't worry about it," Daniel replied. "They know I might be too busy to eat with them."

"Well, you ain't," Cully said. "Go make yourself pretty." He gave Daniel a sideways grin as he tucked the wad of tobacco into his cheek. "That is, if you can manage it," he added with a cackle.

Daniel didn't need any further persuading. After making sure Cully would be okay by himself for a couple of hours and promising to relieve him so he could eat, too, Daniel went up to the house. Already, his exhaustion was fading.

When he walked into the kitchen, Mary turned away from the stove and gave him a disapproving look. "Least you could have allowed the time to clean up before dinner."

Daniel raked a hand through his hair. "I'm headed for the shower right now."

"Then I guess I can hold the food for twenty minutes more," she said begrudgingly. "But it's your fault if everything's dried out."

Daniel spread his hands helplessly. "I'll take full responsibility," he offered, although Mary's dinners were never dry, no matter how long she kept them warm for him.

He ducked through the dining room and sprinted up the stairs without seeing Jamie or his teacher.

In the living room, Karen heard his footsteps and a kernel of expectation began glowing deep within her. She wondered whether he would engineer a moment of privacy for them later, or if her lack of constraint before had put him off. His ancestors had been hunters; he might not appreciate her lack of reserve.

Anticipation warred with apprehension. If he retreated behind his mask of indifference, it would be all she could do to keep her disappointment from showing.

Giving her attention to Jamie sitting beside her, Karen said, "I think we've done enough for today. You're making amazing progress. Let's see if Mary needs any help in the kitchen."

"Okay." He hurried from the room with the black-and-white kitten on his heels. Taking a deep breath and smoothing her hair back, Karen followed.

During dinner, most of the conversation flowed unnoticed around Daniel. He tried to follow its meandering course, but he was so preoccupied with the idea of getting Karen alone later that Jamie had to repeat every question twice.

When the meal was finally over, Daniel gained an unexpected ally in his housekeeper. When Jamie wanted to go to the barn with him and Karen, Mary asked him to stay and help her clean up the kitchen instead.

"I have a bit of a headache," she said, without meeting Daniel's gaze.

He almost groaned with frustration when Karen offered to lend her a hand.

For a moment, Mary's expression was one of almost comical dismay. Then she said, "Thank you, but Jamie's used to my routine. Between the two of us, we'll be done in no time and I can lie down." She smiled at Daniel's nephew. "You don't mind, do you? There's an extra brownie in it for you."

Daniel wasn't sure he approved of Mary bribing the boy with sweets, but he sure as hell wasn't going to object if it got him alone with Karen. Since the last time they were together, she had taken over his thoughts. If he didn't get her into his arms soon, he would be going up in flames.

Jamie looked at Karen and then at Daniel. "Do you mind if I stay here instead?"

"No!" Daniel said.

"Not at all," Karen replied at the same time, coloring when Daniel caught her eye.

Smothering his pleasure at her quick denial, Daniel offered her a jacket.

"Actually I have an old coat and some boots in the back of my car," she admitted. "I put them in there one morning when it was icy and I thought I might get stuck. I just haven't bothered to take them out." She spoke quickly while he watched the color in her cheeks change like a barometer. Had she anticipated his offer to show her the lambs? Did she think he would mind if she wanted to be alone with him, too?

While he toyed with the idea of her wanting to kiss him again, she paused in the doorway. "I'll go get them."

He offered to go, instead, but she refused. "I'll just be a moment."

While he stared after her consideringly, she fled.

He was vaguely aware of Mary's speculative expression. At least with Jamie in the room, she wouldn't dare comment. For that, Daniel was grateful.

Making sure Karen was bundled up, Daniel took the foil-wrapped plate with Cully's supper on it and assisted her into the Jeep. He let her go reluctantly and circled to the driver's side. When he climbed in beside her and set the plate behind him, he didn't start the engine immediately. Instead he looked at her for a moment in the glow from the utility light.

"Have you ever been around a sheep operation before?" he asked.

"Not for a long time," she replied. "Actually one of my cousins used to spend her summers with her grandfather on her other side. He had a sheep ranch. Once she invited me to go with her. I really enjoyed it, but I never had the chance to go back again."

Daniel tried to picture her as a child, with freckles across her face and her hair in pigtails. He failed utterly. She had probably been cute even then.

"Well, if I tell you anything tonight that you know isn't accurate, you can correct me, okay?"

"I only spent one summer there," she reminded him. "I'm hardly an expert on the subject."

"Neither am I, but I'm learning." Daniel started the engine and they drove down the hill. When he parked and they got out, he took Karen's hand in his and kept it there.

She told herself that he was probably only worried that she might slip in the mud and sue him, but knew she didn't buy her own explanation.

Around them, the darkness seemed peaceful, even protective. Not like Denver, where she had grown up, could often be, or even some parts of Craig.

Karen tipped her head back and looked up at the clear, dark sky strewn with a profusion of stars. As she made a small sound of delight, Daniel followed the direction of her gaze.

"Pretty, aren't they?" he asked quietly as they both studied the glittering canopy overhead.

"Gorgeous," Karen breathed. She'd kept walking while she looked. Suddenly, she stubbed her toe on an uneven clump of grass and pitched forward.

Daniel hooked an arm around her waist, steadying her. "Okay?" he asked.

His closeness raised a lump in Karen's throat that proved impossible to speak around. She bobbed her head instead, wondering why she always seemed to be losing her balance around him. His arm loosened its grip but remained anchored around her waist as they approached the lambing shed.

Jericho rushed out, tail wagging.

"Hi, boy. How are you?" As Karen stopped to scratch behind his ears, an older, grizzled man of indistinguishable years stepped into the light.

"This is Cully," Daniel said. "He's the brains behind this operation."

The other man let out a sharp crack of laughter. From the lump in his cheek, she suspected he was chewing tobacco. As Daniel made the introductions, Cully wiped one hand on his overalls and extended it to Karen.

"How do, ma'am?" he said in a voice that held a trace of an accent. He held her hand a moment longer than was strictly necessary as he looked her up and down with a friendly grin.

"You married?" he asked bluntly.

Taken aback by the directness of his question, she admitted that she was not. Beside her, Daniel shifted uncomfortably.

"Cully—" he began in a warning tone.

Cully ignored him. "If I was a mite younger, I'd be bringin' you apples and hangin' around the classroom," he told her with an impudent twinkle in his faded blue eyes.

Unable to take offense at his brazen flirtatiousness, Karen teased him back. "Then I might just have to keep you after school," she warned.

He chuckled again and slapped his thigh. "What's wrong with you, mate?" He prodded Daniel with an elbow to his ribs. "You out of practice with the ladies?"

Karen gasped.

With one finger, Daniel pushed his hat back on his head as he appeared to consider Cully's question. "I gave them up for lambing season," he drawled.

"Ain't that God's truth," Cully exclaimed. "Boy might make a decent sheepman yet," he told Karen, who could feel her cheeks glowing like twin beacons.

"Mary sent you a plate of dinner," Daniel interjected quickly. "I left it in the Jeep. Why don't you take it over to your place and stick it in the oven? It's probably cold by now."

Cully turned away and spit. "Tell the old bat I said thanks." He rubbed his stomach with his free hand. "I'm hungrier than I thought, so I guess I'll do just that." He gave Karen another friendly smile. "I 'spect I'll be seein' you again."

"Nice to meet you," she replied faintly as he turned and walked away.

"I'm sorry about that," Daniel told her in a quiet voice when Cully was out of sight. "He's usually not that rude, but he can be a regular curmudgeon."

"He's quite a character. Australian?" she asked, not wanting Daniel to dwell on Cully's teasing.

"I don't know for sure, but he calls me 'mate,'" Daniel replied. "Let's go look at lambs."

He led her around, showing her the ewes and their babies that were still inside the shed. Several of the lambs were only a day or two old, and they were all cute. Karen stroked their woolly heads and spoke to them in a crooning voice while the ewes looked on placidly.

"They're all so precious, almost like stuffed animals," she murmured while one little fellow on wobbly legs sniffed her hand and then tried to suck her fingers. "You're so lucky to be here. I really envy you." As she said the words, she realized they were true. She envied him the ranch and the quality of his life here.

"Why do you say that?" Daniel asked, his eyes shadowed from the overhead light by the brim of his hat. "You're educated and you have a profession. You must love what you do."

"Sometimes." Karen took her hand away from the lamb that was butting against it. "I know this ranch must be a tremendous amount of work," she continued thoughtfully. "Especially now. But you get to be outside in this beautiful setting and you're caring for animals that couldn't survive without you. It's an awesome responsibility, but it must be wonderfully rewarding, too."

Daniel searched her face, as if he were trying to decide if she was sincere.

"It is that," he said. "And I can't imagine doing anything else. But what if I lose Jamie? If Ted wins custody, I have a feeling he's going to turn this land into a dude ranch or pave it over and build condos around an artificial lake."

"Oh, no!" Karen exclaimed. "I thought this was in trust for Jamie. Could Ted do that?"

"He could try. I guess he could say he was increasing Jamie's inheritance by making the holding more valuable, or something like that. I don't know how far he could go if he got control." Daniel spun away from her, jamming his hands into the back pockets of his jeans. The muscles of his jaw were rigid and his eyes were narrowed to slits.

He turned back around and searched Karen's face, wondering how much he could trust her. "Sometimes I think about just taking him and..." His voice faltered and he swallowed hard. "And just running. Going somewhere no one could find us." He looked at her sharply. "Can you understand that?" He was talking about breaking the law, disregarding the courts. She must be shocked and repelled by what he had told her.

He expected to see disapproval in her eyes, but she surprised him. Instead of frowning and backing away so she wouldn't be tainted by him, she moved closer.

"Of course I understand." She gripped his arm and her fingers dug into the hard muscle beneath his heavy jacket. "Jamie means everything to you and you don't want to lose him. This waiting must be hell for you."

"That's right. I'd do anything—" he began, curling the fingers of one hand into a fist. He bowed his head, fighting for control.

Karen rubbed his arm. "You can't think like that. Concentrate on winning in court."

"I don't know that I *can* win." Frustration boiled up inside him. "Even my lawyer isn't sure what kind of chance we have."

"Listen to me," she said urgently. "If you run, you'll be caught. Jamie will be taken away and you won't be allowed to raise him the way your sister wanted." She swallowed and released his arm. "Even if you weren't caught, he wouldn't grow up here, at the ranch. You'd be in hiding, maybe hungry, always on the move. He wouldn't be in school. You wouldn't be fulfilling Twyla's wishes then, either."

"How can I count on the court's respecting her wishes?" he demanded. "She was just an Indian. So am I. Ted's white, he's rich and he knows the right people. How can I fight that?" The words almost tumbled on top of each other as they spewed out of him, all the pent-up worries he hadn't even realized were festering inside him like a boil that needed to be lanced. And Karen had lanced it with her concern.

Contrite about his outburst, he gathered her close and smoothed one hand down her back, covered by the thick quilting of her old parka. "I'm sorry," he muttered. "I don't know what got into me."

She pulled loose from his embrace and gripped his chin with her fingers. "Please, promise me you won't think about running."

When she released him, he missed her touch.

"No matter what happens. Promise me," she repeated.

"I don't know if I can." He put his hands on her shoulders and drew her close again. "Why do you care so much?" he asked softly as he rested his cheek against hers and savored her warmth and the heady scent of her.

"I—care about what happens to Jamie," she whispered haltingly. "I like him a lot."

Daniel felt as if a light had gone out inside him. What had he expected, anyway? A declaration of undying devotion? He already knew the two of them were an impossible mix. Like cowboys and queens.

So why did he keep torturing himself? What did he want? If she didn't run away screaming when he kissed her, wasn't that enough?

No, he realized as he studied her beautiful face, it wasn't. He wanted to claim her in the most basic way a man could claim a woman. He wanted to be inside her so badly, he was all but shaking with the need. And he wanted her to tell him she cared about him, too.

Some of his hunger must have showed on his face; Karen's eyes widened and the tip of her tongue darted out to moisten her lips.

"Do I make you nervous?" he demanded, suddenly angry though he didn't know why.

"No." Her voice was even. "I'm not afraid of you."

"Perhaps you should be." He let his hands slide across her shoulders, down her arms. He gripped her waist and felt her tremble. When she didn't resist, he urged her forward until her hips were pressed against his and he knew she could feel his arousal through their clothing.

He meant to caution her, to warn her that he felt unusually vulnerable and she might be smart to leave him—to go back to the house. Instead he widened his stance and wrapped his arms around her. Pulling her with him, he braced his spine against the wall.

She lifted her hands to his chest and he waited, breathless, to see if she meant to push him away or keep him close. She flattened her palms against his chest beneath his open jacket and slid them up to his neck. He felt her fingers tangle in his hair. A savage tide of response ripped through him, threatening to tumble him end over end.

"Honey," he said hoarsely, "if you have any second thoughts about kissing me, you'd better stop this now. Once I start, I'm liable to keep going until I've sucked the breath right out of you."

Karen just looked at him. "Are you always this talkative?" she asked lightly.

Daniel felt his control, usually unshakable, falter. He only hoped he could stop at kissing and keep himself from doing all the other things he had dreamed about doing to her.

Deliberately, giving her time to change her mind, he began unbuttoning her parka. He spread the edges wide and ran his hands down her hips in the black jeans. Before him, she stood unmoving. Waiting, while he tortured them both, drawing out the anticipation until he was weak from it. Then he slid his hands back upward, over her hipbones and her waist, slowing their movement as they glided up and over her breasts. She moaned. He froze when he heard it. He caressed her throat, resting his fingers lightly against her pulse, baring his teeth in a satisfied smile when he felt the rapid flutter. Finally he cradled her jaw and tipped her head back.

While he watched her, Karen's eyelids drifted shut and her lips parted slightly. His control disintegrated. With a rough groan, he kissed her.

He kissed her again and again, breaking away to draw in a tortured breath and then returning to rub her lips, to plunge his tongue deep into the dark recesses of her mouth and claim it as he wanted to claim her body. All of him and all of her. Only when he felt the last of his good sense swirling away, leaving nothing but his fierce hunger to guide him, did he finally lift his head.

She leaned her cheek against his chest and he felt her shaking. She wanted him, too. The realization almost brought him to his knees.

"Do you have any idea what you do to me?" he demanded.

Karen's breath froze in her throat. She could feel the latent power in him, felt the heat and the raw sensual promise. Instinctively she crowded closer, craving more of what only he could give her.

Daniel stiffened. "Be careful," he warned. "I haven't had a woman in a long time, and you're so damn tempting." He scraped his knuckles along her jaw in a rough caress.

Karen searched his face. "You do the same to me," she confessed.

His black eyes glittered with heat and fire. Then he grasped her hand in his and pulled it down over the fly of his jeans. He rubbed it up and down his hard length before he released her.

"If you want me, don't admit it." He grated out the words. "If you're so hot and wet that I could slide into you right now—" She saw the muscles working in his throat. "Don't tell me," he finished. "I swear, I'll lay you down in the straw and crawl on top of you. I'll stay inside you till we're both too sore and tired to move."

The raw emotion in his words was so erotic that she wanted to sink to the floor and take him down with her. She wanted to touch him, but something stopped her. Perhaps it was the stark hunger she saw on his harsh face; perhaps it was knowing that, deep down, she wasn't ready to give herself so totally.

Maybe she'd never be ready.

He must have seen her retreat.

"Always remember," he said softly, "that I'm a savage, after all."

"You aren't a savage!" Karen's voice shook. "Don't talk like that!" She knew that someone, in Daniel's past, had hurt him badly. She could hear it in his voice and wished there was something she could do to ease his pain.

Instead, heeding his warning, she kept her distance.

"Come on," he said after a moment of nearly unbearable tension, "I'd better get you back up to the house. I have to put Jamie to bed and then come down and check the sheep again."

His recitation of mundane considerations was like a splash of cold water. It was clear that he, at least, had recovered from their encounter. Touching her swollen lips with her tongue, Karen watched him walk away. After a moment, she realized he wasn't coming back or waiting for her. Slowly, on shaky legs, she began following him to the Jeep.

The next afternoon, Daniel delivered hay to the sheep, medicated lambs and took his turn at bottle-feeding a couple of orphans. The whole time, his thoughts zigzagged between Jamie's custody battle and what had happened in the lambing shed with Karen the night before.

The two of them had been leaving the shed when they met Cully coming back to relieve Daniel. From the look on Karen's face, it was clear she realized how close they had come to being interrupted.

By the time they got back to the house, her retreat behind a protective wall of cool civility had been complete. Daniel was tempted to kiss her again just to bring that wall crashing down around them both.

After thanking Mary for dinner and saying goodbye to Jamie, Karen had raced away in her car with unflattering haste—leaving Daniel to wonder momentarily if he had imagined the scene in the shed.

Now, alone with his thoughts, he finished mucking out stalls and was pushing the last wheelbarrow load of dirty straw outside when he glanced up the hill. Ted's black sedan was coming down the road from the house.

Daniel set down the wheelbarrow and waited, unsmiling, for Ted to stop the car. What the hell did he want? The last time Daniel had spoken to Nick Keller on the phone, there had been no new developments in the case. As Ted and his wife got out, Daniel felt a surge of hope inside him. Had Ted finally found a drop of compassion and canceled the suit?

One look at his expression was answer enough. Daniel shoved his hands into his pockets so that Ted wouldn't make the mistake of extending one of his.

"Where's the boy?" he demanded without bothering to greet Daniel first.

"At school, where he belongs. What do you want?"

Ted flushed at the hostile tone. "We came to visit him." Dixie was carrying a box wrapped in gift paper and tied with a big red bow.

"We brought him a present," she said.

"Next time, call first." Daniel turned his back and began pushing the wheelbarrow around to the side of the stable. Fury roiled inside him, but he refused to give Powell the satisfaction of seeing his anger.

"You can't deny us access," Ted said in a loud voice. "If I have to, I'll have my attorney petition the court."

Daniel considered his options. Hearing that he had refused to let them see Jamie wouldn't sit well with ultraconservative, family-oriented Judge Greenburg.

"Why the sudden interest?" he asked insolently as he once again set down the wheelbarrow full of manure.

Ted looked as if he had bitten into a wormy apple.

"He's our flesh and blood," Dixie said.

Cynically Daniel wondered if their lawyer had advised them to pay a visit to the nephew whose custody they were trying so hard to attain. They were screwing up Daniel's life, and Jamie's, for, he suspected, a reason no more altruistic than plain, old-fashioned greed.

Before he could suggest again that they come back some other time—preferably when hell froze over—Jamie burst out the back door of the house. Spotting the big, black car, he immediately slowed his steps. Daniel would have liked to holler at him to go back inside. Instead he watched, jaw clenched, as the little boy drew closer.

To Daniel's private satisfaction, Jamie made a wide circle around the other two adults and came to Daniel.

"You remember Uncle Ted and Aunt Dixie, don't you?"

Jamie nodded, crowding closer. He eyed the brightly wrapped package under Dixie's arm.

"Why are you here?" he asked with the bluntness of youth.

"This is for you, sweetie," Dixie told him, holding the present out temptingly.

Jamie looked to Daniel for permission before taking it. Then he unwrapped it and lifted the lid. Inside was a teddy bear with a blue bow.

"Thank you," Jamie said politely.

Daniel suspected that he might consider a stuffed animal too babyish for a boy who was five, even if he did still sometimes sleep with a ragged panda, but that was the Powells' problem.

"We'd like to look around," Ted said. "As John's surviving brother, I feel a responsibility to make sure you're maintaining Jamie's estate."

Ignoring the implied insult to his integrity, Daniel took his nephew's hand.

"Shall we give them a tour in the Jeep?" he asked.

Jamie was holding the teddy bear as if he had no idea what to do with it. Stuffing it under his arm, he said, "Sure." He liked riding around and checking on the livestock with Daniel and Cully.

On the way to the Jeep, Daniel glanced behind him and saw Dixie almost lose one of her high-heeled shoes in the soft ground. Too bad there wasn't any quicksand on the property.

As he took them to the winter pasture to see the herd, he made little effort to avoid the bumps and dips in the land they covered. He might have to be polite, especially in front of Jamie, but he sure as hell didn't have to like it.

The Jeep bounced over another rut, and he heard Dixie's exclamation of discomfort.

"I think we've seen enough," Ted said as Daniel slowed to point out a group of breeding rams. "Let's head back."

"Sure thing."

Ted gave orders as if he had already taken over. Daniel refused to let his irritation show.

"This land is almost priceless," he heard Ted mutter to Dixie. "Think how much people would pay to stay here. People from all over the country, all over the world."

Daniel was curious, but Ted didn't say any more until they were again parked beside the barn.

"I want to have my accountant go over the books," Ted announced. He hadn't bothered to thank Daniel for the tour and his contempt was plain to see. Daniel wondered how Ted would treat Jamie's Native American heritage if he did win custody.

"I have nothing to hide," Daniel replied. "Your accountant can check the books anytime he wants."

"He'll be calling you. Perhaps we should take an inventory, too." Did Ted expect to find hordes of thieving renegades making off with whatever wasn't nailed down? While he craned his neck, Dixie spoke to Jamie in a voice as phony as artificial sweetener.

"How would you like to come over and visit sometime?" she asked. "We'll redecorate one of the guest rooms in your favorite colors and fill it with toys."

Daniel winced at the shabby attempt at manipulation.

"Would I have to keep my hands in my pockets?" Jamie asked her.

Daniel quickly covered his grin. Perhaps he hadn't given his nephew enough credit.

Dixie blinked, her false eyelashes fluttering in confusion. "Well, I—I guess not," she stammered.

Jamie mulled over the offer. "No, thank you," he said. "I have my own room here. I don't need one at your house, too."

Ted glared at Daniel. "Haven't you talked to him?"

Daniel pushed the wheelbarrow around to the driver's side of Ted's expensive sedan and opened the door. Lifting the wheelbarrow so the odorous contents began to slide forward, he said, "I'll talk about things when I decide the time is right, and not before. Now I think you'd better leave."

Ted's expression radiated fury at being thwarted, but he swallowed whatever he had been about to say. "All right," he growled, hurrying over to the car. "We're going."

Daniel moved the load of manure out of the way as Jamie grinned and clapped his hands. "Was that a joke?" he asked. "Were you kidding Uncle Ted?"

"Something like that."

"Come on," Ted told Dixie. "Let's go."

Ignoring his order, she swooped down to give Jamie a hug. Before she succeeded, he scrambled behind Daniel.

"Thank you for the bear," he said, holding tight to Daniel's leg.

Dixie shrugged, waved a last goodbye and climbed into the passenger seat.

"I can see that the boy needs a firm hand," Ted said. "It's obvious that you've been cutting him too much slack."

Telling Jamie to stay put, Daniel strolled over to Ted. Inches away from the man's smoothly handsome face, he muttered, "Get out of here. Don't come back without either an invitation or a court order."

Ted glanced down at Daniel's hands, which were bunched into fists, and ducked into the car. He locked the door and rolled the window down about an inch. "That can probably be arranged. I don't want my nephew unduly influenced by a savage like you."

As Daniel took a threatening step closer, Ted started the car and shifted into reverse. Spinning around, he drove away without a backward glance.

Daniel felt like throwing up. He had to maintain custody of Jamie and control of White Ridge. He had to!

Chapter Eight

As he punched in Joe Sutter's phone number, Daniel asked himself what he expected his former boss to do. Daniel was standing in the room he still thought of as John's office, looking at the stack of paperwork that had gotten away from him since lambing began. He had deliberately waited until evening to call Joe, figuring to catch him in his office, too.

When Joe answered on the third ring, Daniel asked after Emma, answered Joe's questions about Jamie and the sheep and then got down to the reason he was calling.

He told Joe about the custody suit and explained his suspicions as to why Ted Powell was so determined to gain control over the estate.

"I can't believe the judge would take Jamie away from you," Joe insisted. "You're the appointed guardian and I'm sure you're the best thing for Jamie and the ranch."

"Thanks for the vote of confidence," Daniel said, shifting the receiver from one ear to the other. "Care to repeat that under oath?"

"You know I will."

Joe's positive outlook made Daniel feel better. "Thanks," he told the man who had been his friend as well as his employer for the past nine years.

"I've got one more suggestion." Joe's voice had lost its serious tone.

"What's that?" Daniel asked eagerly.

"Have you given any thought to getting married?"

After she read the memo in her teacher's box, Karen joined the rest of the staff after school in the lounge for a meeting with the principal. Rumors had been flying and she was reasonably sure she knew why the meeting had been called. Terry had just slid into the chair next to Karen's in the back of the room, when the door opened and Mr. Appleby walked in. He was followed by an attractive man with blond hair who was wearing a well-cut gray suit.

Terry leaned over to Karen. "Oh, my God! Isn't that—?"

Karen nodded, frozen with shock. "My ex-fiancé," she finished. "Mark Gresham, in living Technicolor. I wonder what the heck he's doing here."

Terry's expression was sympathetic. "Mr. Appleby's replacement?" she suggested gently.

Karen felt an icy chill steal over her. No! She couldn't work for Mark. Not after what he had done to her.

A smattering of polite applause interrupted her tortured thoughts, making her realize she had missed most of what the principal said.

Now Mark stepped forward. "I know how difficult these transitions can be," he said in the voice that once had held the power to raise or plunge Karen's spirits with a single word. Now she thought his voice contained a nasal quality she had never noticed before. His waist had begun to thicken beneath that elegant suit, and his hairline was receding.

Terry nudged her, making Karen realize once again that she had missed what was being said.

"As your new principal, I'll do everything I can to carry on the tradition of successfully meeting challenges that Mr. Appleby has so aptly encouraged," Mark concluded.

Had he always been this pompous?

This time, the applause was livelier. Karen was well aware of how personable and charming Mark could be. After all, she had been a victim of that charm, and now she considered herself a survivor. But that didn't mean she wanted to work for him.

Nor was she ready to shake his hand and welcome him to Mountain View as if there had never been anything between them. As soon as the meeting broke up and Mark was surrounded by the rest of the staff, she and Terry made their escape.

"What are you going to do?" Terry asked as the two of them headed back to their classrooms.

Karen was still trembling from the shock of seeing Mark again. She hoped he hadn't seen her slip from the room and assumed she couldn't face him, even if it was the truth. She was sorry that chronic hepatitis was forcing Mr. Appleby to retire early, but she was sorrier that Mark was going to replace him.

"I'll put in for a transfer," she said in response to Terry's question. "There's no way I can report to that man. No way."

Terry gave her a supportive hug before going into her own classroom. "I don't blame you," she said. "Or you could run off with that handsome visitor you had last week," she added in a teasing tone. "You said he's not married."

"Who?" Karen asked, puzzled.

"You know." Terry stuck her head back out the open doorway. "The cowboy with the black hair. The one I said I was going to call in for lots of parent-teacher conferences if his nephew's in my class next year."

Daniel! Karen blushed. "Oh, him." She hoped her voice didn't reveal any of the turmoil she felt at the mention of his name.

"Just a thought." Terry's grin was unrepentant as she ducked back into her classroom.

Karen's smile faded as she went into her own room, collected her briefcase and looked down the hallway to make sure the coast was clear before effecting her escape. She didn't want to run into Mark any sooner than was absolutely necessary.

As she walked past the principal's office, she could hear the two men's voices through the partly open door. Nausea rose in her throat at the thought of the gossip that would fly when the other teachers found out she had once been engaged to the new principal. The whole ugly story would come out again, and she would relive every humiliating detail. Again.

There were only a few weeks of school left. She had to survive them. Next year, she could teach somewhere else. For now, though, she had no other options.

Daniel was saddling up his pinto gelding when he heard a car door slam outside the stable. Leaving the horse cross-tied in the aisle, he went outside to see Cully slapping the back of a dark-skinned man with long, gray-streaked black hair.

"The reinforcements have arrived!" Cully cried when he saw Daniel. "This is Rudy, one of our summer herders."

Daniel shook the other man's hand while Cully introduced him. "We're glad you're here," he said truthfully. Although lambing was officially over, neither Daniel nor

Cully had gotten much sleep during these past weeks. Another pair of hands and eyes was very welcome.

"I'm glad to be here," Rudy replied in heavily accented English.

While Cully asked him about the drive north, Daniel glanced at the battered pickup truck and weathered camper Rudy had driven up from Mexico. He would live in it all summer while he herded sheep on the mountainous summer range, not returning to the ranch until September. Daniel wondered if Rudy minded the solitude and the months separated from his family back in Chihuahua. Cully had told Daniel before that the majority of summer herders came from Mexico, South America and even Spain. They came to America on special visas, since the job was too isolated and the pay too low to attract local workers.

Rudy and one of the sheepdogs would live out of his camper while they moved the herd over the summer range. Every week, Daniel or Cully would take them fresh supplies while the lambs grew fat in the highland meadows.

"Now that Rudy's here, you could take an evening off if you wanted," Cully told Daniel in an undertone.

Daniel glanced around at Rudy, who had climbed into the camper to get something.

"Why would I want an evening off?" Daniel asked as Cully transferred his wad of tobacco from one cheek to the other.

His thick brows rose in disbelief. "If that's the case, mate, you stay here an' I'll have the time off. I think I'll take a certain schoolteacher to dinner. Okay by you?"

Confounded by the jealous rage that gripped him at the idea of Karen seeing anyone else, even Cully, Daniel managed a weak smile.

"Tell you what," Daniel said, clapping a hand on the old herder's shoulder, "I'll ask her first. If she turns me down, then you can take her."

"And I will, too," Cully said, spitting. "You better believe it."

When Karen opened her door and saw Daniel standing there in new, neatly creased jeans and a white shirt under a black suede jacket, she was glad she had decided to wear the simple royal blue sweater dress, a gold locket and tiny matching earrings. She had curled her hair and it rippled past her shoulders.

With his shorter hair, Daniel could go almost anywhere and not look out of place, she thought as she invited him in.

"Hi," he said, as he took his hand from behind his back. In it, he held a bunch of yellow flowers shaped like stars. "These grow wild out at the ranch, but I thought they were pretty."

The unexpected gesture surprised Karen and charmed her more than long-stemmed roses ever could. "Thank you," she said softly as she took the flowers. "I'll put them in water."

Looking around, Daniel followed her into the tiny kitchen. "This is a nice place." Privately he thought the apartment was too small and impersonal, one cubicle in a row of identical cubicles, but she had made it cozy.

A colorful afghan covered the back of the couch. A bunch of dried flowers, secured with a blue bow, hung on one wall. A faded quilt was tossed over a rocking chair. In the kitchen, children's paintings covered the door of the refrigerator and, on the counter, a wire stand held an assortment of mugs with cats on them. A row of painted tiles hung above the stove.

Karen put the flowers into a pottery vase and set them in the center of the kitchen table.

"Don't they look nice?" she asked.

"Mmm-hmm." Daniel put an arm around her waist and rested his cheek against her hair. "You need a cat," he said, as pleasure at her closeness flowed through him. "And I know where you can get one."

Laughing, she pulled away and looked up at him through her lashes. "I don't think I'm ready for that kind of commitment. Would you like a beer or some coffee?"

He glanced at his watch. "Perhaps we'd better go." If they didn't leave right away, he would be tempted to stay here. He wanted to take her to bed, but he sensed she wasn't ready for that yet, either.

They went to a popular bar and grill in downtown Craig. While they ate, they talked about the case, movies, books and Karen's class. Daniel didn't talk as much as she did, but he listened attentively and he answered her questions, as well as asking a few of his own.

When Karen was done with her chicken, she sipped the last of her wine. Daniel had ordered a steak, rare, and a beer. Even watching him eat fascinated her. His white teeth contrasted brightly with his bronze complexion.

"How about dessert?" he asked when Karen set her wineglass down. "They make pretty good pie here."

She leaned forward conspiratorially. "Don't let Mary hear you say that. Her pie is in a class by itself."

Daniel returned her smile with a slight grin of his own. "I only said it was pretty good," he reminded her. "I'd be the first one to admit that Mary's cooking has pretty much ruined me for ordinary food."

Karen was about to make a teasing comment about him cleaning his plate when he stretched out his hand and covered hers.

"Dessert?" he asked again, one brow raised in query.

She felt her cheeks begin to heat as his fingers stroked the sensitive back of her hand. Well, if he wasn't used to watching her blush, he hadn't been paying attention, she thought. Since she had met him, her cheeks took on color with annoying regularity. God only knew how Daniel interpreted her tendency to turn red in his presence. She didn't think she wanted to know what he thought.

"No dessert for me, thanks, but you go ahead, if you want." His touch was sending erotic shivers throughout her system, making it hard to concentrate. Would he misinterpret her intentions if she once again invited him in for coffee back at her apartment? And what exactly were her intentions, anyway?

His expression was, as usual, difficult to read, but his hand tightened on hers while she studied him. The waitress came by to see if they needed anything else. When Daniel replied negatively, she handed him the bill.

"Are you ready?" he asked.

Karen nodded so he rose and pulled out her chair. Glancing at the dinner tab, he left some money on the table.

"How do you feel about country music?" he asked as they walked back to his truck.

"I like it. Do you?"

He slipped an arm around her shoulders. Two women passed them on the sidewalk and Karen saw the approving glances they gave Daniel. He didn't appear to notice as his fingers caressed her curly hair.

When they got to the truck, he rested his hand on the door, effectively trapping Karen between the vehicle and his own body. When he leaned close, she could only stare, mesmerized, into his black eyes.

"I'd like any kind of music that gave me an excuse to hold you in my arms," he said. "Let's go down to Red's and dance."

Overwhelmed by his admission, Karen managed to bob her head. For a moment, she thought he was going to kiss her right there, but another couple walked past. Daniel merely touched her cheek before he stepped back to open her door.

The relationship between the two of them was shifting. At some point, they had crossed an invisible line. Karen might come to regret it, but for now, she couldn't seem to think of a single reason to resist his magnetic pull.

Daniel's hand cupped her elbow and he helped her into the high truck seat. As she scrambled inside, Karen followed the direction of his interested gaze and saw that her skirt had ridden up her thighs. Quickly she tugged it back down. Daniel didn't comment but his expression was intense as he shut the door.

She was fumbling with the seat belt on the passenger side when he got behind the wheel. Sighing, he drew her over to the middle of the seat next to him and fastened her in.

"Okay?" he asked gruffly.

"Okay," she echoed.

The bar he took her to was crowded, the music loud but good. A man in a bow tie showed them to a small, round table and a waitress in Western attire took their drink order. After she left, the band switched abruptly to a ballad about lost love and heartache.

"I was in the army with the man who made that song a hit," Daniel whispered into Karen's ear.

"You knew Chase Cantrell?"

He grinned at her expression. "We keep in touch." Getting to his feet, he held out his hand. "Dance with me."

Remembering what he had said earlier about getting her into his arms, Karen stood, weak-kneed, and followed him onto the large dance floor.

Daniel was a good dancer, moving to the beat of the music with an inborn sense of rhythm. Instead of merely following the music, he seemed to absorb it and make it his own. Karen was cradled tight in his arms and they danced more as one entity than two separate beings.

When she tipped her head back to look at him, the expression in his eyes was veiled by his short, thick lashes. A crooked smile softened his mouth. A moment passed in silent communication and then he tucked her close again. She could feel his head resting against her hair, feel his breath on her cheek. She pressed one hand to the front of his shirt. Beneath her palm, his heart pumped, strong and steady.

Too quickly, the song ended and the lead vocalist announced that the band was taking a break. Daniel's hands dropped to bracket Karen's waist. Then he took a deep breath and let her go.

She was preceding him off the dance floor when someone bumped into her, making her stumble. Daniel steadied her before she could fall. When she looked up, a stocky man in a tan cowboy hat was glaring at them.

"Tell your squaw to watch where she's going, Indian," he growled at Daniel. His voice was loud and he slurred his words.

Karen was shocked at the hostility on his homely face. She stiffened as Daniel's arm came around her shoulders and he stepped protectively between her and the drunk.

"Are you okay?" Daniel asked her, his expression like stone.

"I'm fine." She would have liked to scratch the other man's eyes out for insulting Daniel, but she knew that would only make the situation worse. And more painful for the proud man at her side.

The woman who was with the jerk who had shoved Karen tugged at his arm. "Come on, Earl. Come and sit down." She glanced at Karen and then her gaze slid away. Other people were trying to see what had happened.

Karen touched Daniel's forearm, feeling his tension in the rigid muscle there. "Let's go back to our table."

For a moment, she thought he intended to pursue the argument, but then the anger seemed to drain out of him. The other man glared at them again and then turned to the woman pulling on his arm.

"Yeah, yeah," he told her. "I hear ya." The crowd parted and they walked toward the other side of the dance floor.

The man in the bow tie bustled up and demanded, "What's going on here?"

"Just a shoving match," someone told him.

He turned to Daniel. "You two okay?"

To Karen's relief, Daniel merely nodded before he led the way back to their table. Karen held on to his arm.

When they sat down, his face was blank, his dark eyes opaque. "I'm sorry that happened," he told her.

She could hear the mortification in his voice and her heart ached for him. She linked her fingers with the hand resting on his thigh. "So am I," she said. "But it's over now."

"I bet you've never been called a squaw before." His voice was edged with bitter anger.

Karen wondered how many other times things like this had happened to him. She leaned closer and looked into his eyes. "I consider being called *your* squaw a compliment."

Disbelief flickered across Daniel's face and then was gone. He lifted her hand and kissed it.

"You're crazy," he muttered, but she could see that he was pleased. He glanced around. "Let's get out of here."

"We don't have to go," she said, refusing to be driven away.

"I know that," he whispered into her ear, "but I want to get you alone as quickly as possible."

They didn't talk much on the way back to her apartment. Country music played on the radio and he kept her hand captured in one of his. When they got inside, Daniel kicked the door shut and pulled her into his embrace.

"You're unreal," he muttered into her hair. "I would have liked to kill that guy for insulting you."

"I already told you, I wasn't insulted."

He groaned and bent his head to hers. The kiss started slowly, a sweet joining. Then Karen buried her fingers into the hair at his nape and pressed closer. Immediately Daniel changed the angle of the kiss, turning it to a sensual assault that rocked her to her foundation. The kiss he took was raw; it was carnal and it was emotionally devastating.

When Daniel let her go, she knew she'd had no idea what passion was before meeting him. When she would have kissed him again, he set her roughly aside and walked over to sit down on the couch. He was breathing deeply. His nostrils flared and the muscles in his jaw were tight.

"How about some coffee?" he asked, resting his head against the back of the couch and closing his eyes.

As Karen went into the kitchen to fix it, she noticed that the message light on her answering machine was flashing. Without thinking, she went over and pushed the button.

Vaguely she was aware of Daniel's footsteps coming up behind her as Mark Gresham's voice filled the kitchen.

"Sorry I missed you," the machine recited. "Since we're going to be working together, I just wanted you to know that I don't hold any grudges."

Karen wanted to scream. As her body went rigid with fury, she felt Daniel's hand close reassuringly over her shoulder.

"I don't want any trouble with my staff at school," Mark's voice continued. "Just thought I'd clear the air."

Karen doubled her hands into fists and let out the breath she'd been holding. "Ooh, that creep!" she exclaimed, so angry that tears formed in her eyes.

"Who was that?" Daniel asked, gently turning her around. He looked into her eyes and then caught one of her tears of frustration with his thumb before it could spill down her cheek.

"That was Mark Gresham, the new principal at Mountain View," she said through clenched teeth. "He just happens to be my former fiancé."

Daniel bent his head to peer into her averted face. "Want me to kill him for you?"

His question had the desired effect. It made her laugh. "Could I let you know?" she asked. "He isn't taking over until a week from Monday."

"Why don't you come and sit down?" Daniel suggested. "You can tell me all about him."

She hesitated. "What about the coffee?"

"Forget the coffee. I want to hear about this creep who makes you cry."

When they were seated on the couch with Daniel's arm wrapped protectively around Karen's shoulders and her head resting against his chest, she began to talk. Dredging it all up was painful, but perhaps by getting it out she could truly purge herself of the memory.

"Mark was the vice principal at the last school where I taught," she said as Daniel absently stroked her hair. "We dated for a while and then we got engaged. I didn't know he was seeing another woman on the side until he stood me up on our wedding day last year. Naturally a lot of people from the school district were there to witness my humiliation."

Her smile wobbled and she rolled her eyes. "The gossip mill buzzed for weeks afterward. It was, to say the least, extremely embarrassing and painful for me. Not only had I lost the man I loved, but everyone I knew kept asking questions until I thought I'd go crazy."

Daniel made a rough sound in his throat. "I was right. I think I'll kill him for you." One of his big hands began to knead her shoulder. "What happened to the other woman?" he asked.

"That's the best part," Karen said, allowing some of her bitterness to seep into her voice. "He married her, instead, and now they have a baby." There was more to the humiliating story, but no way could she bring herself to tell Daniel about it. Instead she turned to him and smiled brightly. "So, do you want that coffee now?"

His eyes narrowed as he stroked one hand along her chin and circled her throat with his fingers.

"What I want can't be brewed in a pot."

Karen's eyes widened as she stared at his intense expression. She knew that he was waiting for some sign from her. A sign that she was ready to make love with him. She would have in a heartbeat if she thought his feelings for her ran deeper than mere attraction or sexual desire. What stopped her was knowing how serious her own feelings were getting. She had thought she loved Mark—and he had hurt her. But if she gave her heart to a man like Daniel and he refused it, he could very well destroy her.

Before she could say anything, he rose to his feet and grasped both her hands. "I'm rushing you," he said, bringing them to his mouth and kissing them. "I'm sorry, I don't want to pressure you."

Karen leapt to her feet. "You aren't," she cried. "It's just—" She stopped, unable to explain. How could she tell him that she already loved him so much that she was afraid to take that last step? That if she did, she might lose herself and never recover?

On the drive back to the ranch, Daniel began to wonder what Karen thought about his fast exit. He'd had to get out of there before his shaky control gave way and he did something she didn't want. When a woman said no, that was it. He'd never forced an unwilling female in his life and he wasn't about to start with Karen. Even though he was still half-aroused.

His hands tightened on the steering wheel as he drove through the darkness. It was just that he was so damn hungry for her, especially after what she'd told him at the bar.

Braking at the turn into the ranch road, he remembered the feelings that had exploded inside him at her healing words.

I consider being called your squaw a compliment.

Had she any idea how what she said had redeemed him? Probably not. He had wanted to fall to his knees before her. At the same time, he had wanted to make her his squaw for real, to lift her into his arms and shout to the whole word that she was his. Only his!

And that was what had him running scared. The feelings she drew out of him. The feelings that could hurt him more than any drunken slur.

The next day, Saturday, Karen was in the midst of her weekend housecleaning when the phone rang. She had called Terry earlier to tell her about Mark's call and his arrogant, self-centered message, but Terry hadn't been home. That was probably her returning Karen's call now.

"Hi," she greeted in a deliberately cheery tone. She had already decided not to let either Mark's call or Daniel's sudden departure the night before ruin her weekend.

There was a moment of silence on the other end of the line.

"Hello?" she repeated.

"You sound like you're in a good mood." Daniel's voice sent a shiver of reaction through her.

She had dreamed about him the night before—heated, erotic dreams—and when she woke, blushing from head to toe, the bedclothes were hopelessly tangled.

"Of course I'm in a good mood," she replied briskly. "It's the weekend and I have two whole days away from the classroom. Believe me, at this time of year, that's a definite plus."

"Do you ride?" he asked.

Confused by the rapid shift in gears, she blurted, "Ride what?"

There was another long silence, but she thought she heard him chuckle. "Ride horses."

Idiot, she told herself silently. What else could he have meant? Llamas? Camels? "Oh, sure. I mean, it's been a while, but I used to ride a lot in Denver." Horseback riding had been one of the things her parents thought a well-rounded child should master. It was one of the few lessons she had truly enjoyed.

"Good. We're driving the sheep to their winter pasture tomorrow and I wondered if you'd like to come along."

His invitation surprised her. After the way he had left the night before, she hadn't expected to hear from him again so soon.

"Is Jamie going?" she asked, wondering suddenly if that was why Daniel was asking her, to keep an eye on his nephew.

"Jamie? No, why?" He sounded surprised.

"I just wondered," she said lamely. "I'd love to go. What time should I be there and what should I bring?"

"Be here at five," Daniel told her. "Wear riding gear and don't forget your gloves and a hat. It will be chilly in the morning, and we'll be gone most of the day."

After they had talked for a few more minutes, Daniel excused himself, saying that the other shepherd had just arrived. As she replaced the receiver, Karen thought about spending the whole day with him. Refusing to analyze her feelings too closely, she danced happily down the hall to clean the bathroom.

Chapter Nine

When Karen got to the ranch the next morning, she drove down to the barn the way Daniel had told her, and parked next to two dusty pickup and camper rigs. She had barely gotten out of her car when he appeared in the stable doorway, leading a mare as dark as his hair. She was already saddled. From nearby, Karen heard Cully's voice, followed by a burst of masculine laughter.

"This is Midnight," Daniel told her as he caressed the mare's flank.

"She's beautiful." Karen held out her hand. Midnight sniffed her fingers and snorted loudly.

"You're the beautiful one." Daniel's voice had deepened as his gaze traveled the length of Karen's tight jeans to her riding boots and back up to linger on the swell of her breasts in her embroidered chambray shirt and open parka. A tingling response made her aware of him on the most basic level.

Karen's gloves were in her back pocket and she had on a Stetson she'd bought the day before. It was a deep rose color.

Daniel was wearing his usual Western attire. Around his neck was a blue bandanna. He pulled a matching kerchief from his pocket.

"Wear this for the dust." He held it up. "Let me tie it for you."

Karen turned around and lifted her braid out of the way. She could feel his breath on her nape. It made her shiver with longing as she faced him again. "I hope I'm dressed all right."

"You're fine. New hat?"

She nodded. "I needed to get one."

"May I see it?"

Karen took it off and handed it to him. As soon as she was bareheaded, he leaned over and gave her a brief, hard kiss.

"I'm glad you're here." He glanced at the hat and then gave it back to her with a cocky grin. "Nice."

Before she could reply, three more men dressed like cowboys came around the corner of the barn, followed by Jericho, the herd dog.

Karen said hello to Cully and Daniel introduced her to Rudy and Marco. Both men doffed their hats and greeted her shyly. As soon as the rest of the horses were saddled and they got to the pasture, the drive began.

As the riders and the sheepdogs herded the sea of sheep and their lambs up the road toward the summer range, Karen began to relax in the saddle. After the first few moments, it felt perfectly natural to be back on a horse and Midnight was a sweetheart to ride. Overhead, the sun was shining and the sky grew more intensely blue as the morning progressed. It was good to be outdoors. The sheep bleated and the dogs barked as they meandered down the road.

Daniel hadn't given Karen a very difficult job; the sheep-dogs seemed to do most of the work. All she had to do was keep the sheep moving and stop them from wandering off if a dog didn't notice.

Cully and Marco rode up ahead; Daniel and Rudy, the other Mexican herder, rode at the back. As the day grew warmer, the sheep kicked up quite a cloud of dust. The sun climbed higher, but there was a breeze. Karen took off her jacket and stuffed it into her empty saddlebag. She took a sip from her canteen, savoring the beauty and peace around her. *This is the life!* she thought as she rolled up her shirt-sleeves. Once again, she envied Daniel and hoped he would be able to keep the ranch and Jamie.

Then she had a new thought. If he lost the custody case, might he go back to the other side of the state where he had worked before? There was no way he would stay on at White Ridge if his brother-in-law took charge.

The idea was a sobering one. All the more reason for her to pray that Daniel won. She was thinking about the very real possibility that he might leave the area, when he rode up beside her and reined in his paint gelding.

"That's a beautiful animal," she said, eyeing his mount.

Daniel leaned forward to pat his horse's neck below his cropped mane. "Joe gave him to me when I left the Blue Moon. His name's Ringo."

"Was Joe your boss?" she asked.

"Yep. He understood just how I felt about this horse."

"Joe sounds nice." She watched while one of the dogs nipped at the heels of a ewe that had stopped to graze on the wildflowers.

"You'd like him and his wife, Emma," Daniel said as he rode along beside her. "She used to be a teacher, too."

"Near their ranch?" Karen asked.

Daniel shook his head. "No, she's from Seattle. Joe's mother invited her to stay at the ranch for the summer. Marian lives with them, and she and Emma's mother had been good friends." Daniel chuckled at some memory that apparently amused him.

"What's so funny?" Karen demanded.

"I knew the first time I laid eyes on Emma that old Joe didn't stand a chance." Daniel was still grinning.

"What do you mean?" Karen prodded. "Didn't have a chance for what?"

Daniel looked at her and his eyes were twinkling. "Between Emma and his mom, Joe was throwed, hog-tied and branded before he knew what hit him."

Karen couldn't hide her smile. "It sounds as if his mother was matchmaking."

"She invited Emma to stay with them for three months," Daniel continued. "I'd say it took Joe about two weeks to fall for her and the next two months to face up to it. Then Emma almost went back to Seattle before they finally worked things out."

"You make it sound like something terrible he had to get used to, like an incurable disease," she exclaimed.

"I think Joe looked at it that way at first."

"Do they have children?" Karen asked wistfully, wishing she had a matchmaker to help her with Daniel.

He shook his head. "None of their own, but they take in foster kids and they've adopted one of them, named Kenny. They've got a big old house and there are always kids running around." He looked thoughtful for a moment. "Joe was married before, and they didn't have any kids of their own, either." He shrugged. "Maybe there's a problem, I don't know, but it hasn't stopped him and Emma from being about the happiest couple I know."

"That's nice," Karen said as her spirits rose. Didn't the experts say that a man with married friends was more likely to think about marriage himself than one whose friends were all carefree bachelors?

The thought stopped her cold. Marriage? Was that what she wanted? With Daniel?

She watched him as he touched his heels to his mount and cut out after a trio of strays, sitting the horse as if he had been born to it as he headed the sheep off and turned them back to the herd.

Daniel had told her once that he was Comanche. If she remembered her American history correctly, they had been a Great Plains tribe, raising horses and hunting buffalo. Riding was bred into his blood and bone.

He turned back to her. He was magnificent, head high, shoulders wide and powerful, muscular legs gripping the horse. He looked as if he had just stepped out of a Western movie.

Leaning over, he touched her gloved hand. "You doing okay?"

"Sure."

"Not sore?" he asked.

She shook her head. "That will come tomorrow," she predicted.

Daniel glanced down at her leg. "I'd be glad to rub some liniment wherever you might need it," he offered shamelessly. "A good massage could make all the difference in how you feel tomorrow." His grin flashed devilishly. "I wouldn't even charge you for the rubdown."

"I'll keep that in mind," she replied dryly. They exchanged knowing glances as he tipped his hat.

"You do that, ma'am. Meanwhile, I'd better get back to my post. Mary will be up in a while in the station wagon with lunch. I'll see you then."

Karen turned in the saddle and watched him ride back past the endless flow of sheep. He had told her they would divide the herd when they reached the high range. Marco would take half and Rudy the rest. For now, she was content to ride along on Midnight and watch the sheep as they moseyed up the road beside her.

While they ate the lunch that Mary had brought, fried chicken and potato salad, baked beans and biscuits, with gallons of ice tea and fresh-baked chocolate cookies for dessert, the conversation was sporadic. Afterward, Karen found a private spot to take care of nature's call, the only drawback she had experienced so far on the drive.

When they mounted up after lunch, Daniel again rode along with her. Once in a while, a car would come down the road, but no one spooked the sheep.

"You know all about my family," he said as they rode, "but you never talk about your own."

Karen thought for a minute. "Actually I know something about Jamie's family but nothing of yours," she corrected him.

He whistled sharply at one of the dogs. It immediately went after a straggler.

"What do you want to know?"

"Are your parents alive?" she asked gently.

He frowned and continued looking straight ahead. "Mom's dead. I don't know about the old man. He cut out when Twyla and I were little. A couple of stepfathers came and went, but they weren't so bad."

The subject was obviously an uncomfortable one for him. "My parents live in Denver," Karen volunteered. "My father's a judge." She didn't add that her mother was an attorney at one of the top firms there. She suspected that knowing too much of her background would put Daniel off.

"Do you see them often?" he asked. "You don't mention them."

"No." She groped for an explanation. "I was an only child. They were always busy and we just weren't close."

Daniel's expression was puzzled. "Were they mean to you?"

She remembered her lonely childhood, crammed with private school and endless lessons. With a series of baby-sitters while her parents went to parties and traveled without her. They had been wildly in love with each other, and obviously still were. Karen had made an awkward third.

"They had each other," she said bluntly. "They didn't need me."

Instead of offering platitudes, Daniel squeezed her leg. "I'm sorry."

She shrugged. "I survived it. We speak on the phone occasionally. I go home a couple of times a year." If he thought that was odd, considering the relatively short distance between Craig and Denver, he didn't say.

Daniel was relieved when they got the sheep to the high meadow without any mishaps. As soon as the shepherds were all set, he rode up to Karen, who had dismounted and was stretching her legs. Despite the heat and the dust, she still looked good enough to fire his blood and make sitting a horse damned uncomfortable.

"Ready to head back?" he asked her.

"Sure."

He held Midnight's reins while she mounted. "How do you like her?" he asked.

"Midnight? She's wonderful, sweet tempered and comfortable to ride. I bet you trained her yourself."

Midnight's ears pricked back and forth, as if she knew she was being discussed.

"Guilty," Daniel admitted. "I have several horses that I'm training to sell, but you can ride her anytime." He made the offer without thinking about it. God, but he was a glutton for punishment. "I've been considering getting Jamie a pony. It's past time he learned to ride." An image formed in his mind of the three of them riding together. Daniel blinked it away. He wanted to bed her but that didn't mean he wanted anything permanent. Nor would she. Not with him.

Slapping his hat against his thigh to knock off the dust, he set it back on his head. "Let's go," he said gruffly. "Cully and I still have to drive the campers up here." At least the ride back wouldn't take nearly as long without the sheep to slow them down.

Hollering for Cully to join them, Daniel turned Ringo's head toward home.

Karen tried to savor the last week of school before Mark took over as principal. The days went by too fast, and the only highlight came when she went out to the ranch to tutor Jamie. The kittens ran all over the house now, climbing curtains and knocking over vases as they chased one another from room to room.

As Karen was getting into her car after a lesson that had gone very well, Daniel cantered up the road from the barns and asked her to dinner the next night.

"Why don't you come over to my place instead?" she suggested, heart racing at his sudden appearance on the big pinto. "I'll cook for you." The day after that was a school holiday, but no doubt he would have to be up early.

"Well, I don't know," he drawled, eyes dancing. "Can you cook?" His hands were folded on the saddle horn and he was leaning down toward her.

Karen kept her expression serious. "I'm no Mary in the kitchen but I can read the directions on the box with the best of them."

"Sounds fine. When do you want me?"

What would he do if she answered "all the time"? They settled on six o'clock and then he straightened and touched his hand to the brim of his hat. "I'll bring the Pepto-Bismol."

Before she could think of a suitable comeback, he'd ridden away, leaving her chuckling at his unexpected streak of humor. How had she ever thought him silent and incommunicative?

"Is it pretty quiet with most of the sheep gone?" Karen asked him as the two of them sat at her kitchen table eating the salad, lasagna and garlic bread she had fixed.

Daniel took a sip of the wine he had brought with him, telling her the store was out of Pepto-Bismol. "I like having more time to work with the horses. And there's a lot of repairs that need to be done."

He had been pleasantly surprised when Karen served dinner. It was delicious, despite her earlier disparaging remarks. He wouldn't have cared if she'd fixed him frozen pizza, he realized with a sigh of contentment. Her company was at the same time undemanding and exhilarating. As relaxed as he had become around her, there was still that sizzle of awareness between them, the raw heat of sexual desire he was pretty sure she felt, too.

When they were done eating, she rose to clear off the dishes. Daniel pushed back his chair.

"Let me help."

Smiling in a way that fanned the flames of his desire, she asked him to load the dishwasher while she wiped up and put things away. When the kitchen was spotless, she poured coffee for them both and he followed her into the living room.

"You need a cat," he said as they sat on the couch. "You must get lonely here."

"I've been considering it seriously. I'd have to pay a deposit, but a cat would be company." She sipped her coffee without looking at him, and he sensed that she was nervous. Probably waiting for him to pounce. He would have liked to ask her if she had invited him tonight because she was ready for a more intimate relationship or just because she thought it was her turn to feed him.

He decided it was time to convince her of the former. Setting aside his untouched cup, he slid his arm along the back of the couch. In the light from the lamp, Karen appeared almost ethereal, her hair hanging in tangled waves like a halo of gold around her face. More often than not, she wore it loose now, and he wondered if it was because she knew he liked it that way. He wanted to tell her she looked like an angel in a church painting he remembered from childhood. Karen was the most beautiful creature he had ever seen.

She touched his cheek with her fingertips and his voice dried up in his throat. "I'm glad you're here," she whispered, her sweet breath fanning his face.

It occurred to Daniel that he might have had sex before, even made love a few times in his life—but with Karen he would truly mate. The magnitude of the step he was about to take made his hand shake as he grasped hers and brought it to his mouth.

"It's time," he murmured as he kissed her palm. Her hand smelled like herbs and spices. He licked the fragrant, sensitive skin with a rough stroke of his tongue.

Heat flooded her at his words and the erotic touch of his mouth against her hand. She had no need to ask what he meant; she knew. She had already weighed her decision, realizing it went against everything she had ever learned about emotional survival and self-preservation.

She no longer cared about either. Next to Daniel and the promises she read in his dark eyes, the future faded to a gray haze lacking significance. The only important things in her life right now were Daniel Sixkiller and the immediate present.

"Yes, it's time," she echoed.

If he was surprised by her answer, he didn't show it. Instead he rose from the couch and scooped her into his arms. "Where's your bedroom?" He cradled her protectively against his heart.

When she gave him directions, he shouldered his way down the short hallway and gently kicked the door of the bedroom shut behind him. Light from the utility pole down the street came in through the high window and illuminated the room faintly. Daniel made his way to the bed, bracing himself on one knee as he lay her on the quilted spread and followed her down.

Where Karen had expected him to overwhelm her with passion, he wooed her with tenderness. If he had ever waited impatiently for her to be ready for this, he showed no impatience now. Instead he kissed her forehead and her closed eyelids, then her earlobes and the corners of her mouth. When she parted her lips, eager to meld them with his, he soothed her with gentle touches and then began kissing her chin and her throat.

Beneath him, Karen's hands moved restlessly and then settled on his muscular shoulders. When she stroked them down his sides, she felt him tremble. Somehow, knowing his vulnerability calmed her anxiety about pleasing him. She threaded her fingers in his straight, silky hair as he undid the buttons of her blouse. He freed them so slowly and lingered over each new patch of exposed skin so patiently that Karen was beginning to wonder if a person could die of anticipation.

Finally her blouse was completely unbuttoned. Carefully he laid the edges open. Beneath it she wore only a lacy, sheer bra. Daniel's glittering gaze met hers for a heartbeat before he bent and put his mouth on her through the lace. When he drew her nipple into his mouth, Karen arched off the bed, her fingers biting into his shoulders. The warm coals smoldering deep within her burst into flame.

She moaned and he transferred his attention to the other nipple. When she thought she could stand no more, he raised his head.

"I've wanted to do that since I saw you wearing my T-shirt." His voice was hoarse with passion.

She was unable to speak, so she caressed his cheek with her hand. Then she began to unsnap his shirt.

"I don't have your patience," he declared, sitting back and peeling it off. Beneath it, his exquisitely formed torso was bare—and free of hair except for tufts beneath his arms.

Karen reached up to touch his chest. It was warm and hard. Beneath her palm, his heart ricocheted.

"You're beautiful," she murmured, running her hand over his satiny bronze skin. Her fingers brushed the small copper disks as he sucked in a breath through clenched teeth. The tensile nubs beaded as her own had done.

In the dim light, she noticed a narrow line of dark hair that started above his navel and disappeared under his belt. She traced its downy path with her finger and his muscles quivered beneath her touch.

"You're a goddess," he replied, bending over her and undoing her jeans. He placed a wet kiss on the V of bare skin above her bikini panties while her hands smoothed down his arms, savoring their sinewy strength. Then, to her surprise, he shifted so that he was on one side of her and gently rolled her onto her stomach. Her blouse was tossed aside. Brushing away her long hair, he unfastened her bra and whisked it away. He followed the curve of her spine with kisses, stopping at the waistband of her jeans. Bending down, he removed her shoes and socks. Then he pulled off her jeans.

Karen lifted her head but he covered her body with his and gently bit her neck. The heat of his hard chest scorched her back. She struggled to turn over and face him, but he lightly held her down.

"Wait." She could feel his arousal resting against the cleft of her buttocks. He bit her neck again and stroked it with his tongue as he shifted his hips off her and slid his hand past the small of her back, taking her panties down her legs. His fingers against her bare skin sent a shower of sparks through her. As he kissed his way back up her calves and knees, a fire was growing—threatening to burn out of control.

"Beautiful," he murmured as he stroked his hand up her thigh and over her hip.

At last, he raised and turned her gently over. She was dying to kiss him. Still wearing his jeans, he knelt on the bed beside her. Karen rose until they faced each other. He waited, eyes hooded. His cheeks, though, were flushed dark with passion, his features drawn tight with desire.

Karen grasped his shoulders and leaned forward to place her lips against the hollow of his throat. His pulse raced. As her hands slid to his waist, she kissed her way clear down to the Western buckle on his belt. He rolled away from her and disposed of his boots, socks and jeans. Then he hooked his thumbs into the waistband of his dark shorts and stripped them off.

Karen looked at him and felt her cheeks go warm with color. He was magnificent. She raised her gaze to his and he must have read something of what she was feeling in her eyes. With a low sound in his throat, he pulled her down beside him.

Using his hands and his lips, he showed her how lovely and precious she was to him.

"You're a witch," he murmured. "You've enchanted me."

"The spell is on me, too." It had never been this way for her. His touch was magic, his kiss a burning brand that consumed her even as it fed the fire within her.

Karen's hands were busy, too. As she touched and explored his powerful body, tremors went through him and his breath caught. Her fingers scraped over his hipbone and he groaned. When she would have caressed his length, his hand caught hers and put it gently aside. He turned away, dug into his pocket and tore a foil packet open with his teeth. When he rolled back to her, he captured both her wrists and held her arms above her on the bed. His knee nudged her legs apart. Then he released her wrists and braced himself on his arms.

Holding him tight, Karen wrapped her legs around him as he flexed his hips.

He eased into her.

She sighed.

He groaned. Holding each other tightly, they raced toward completion, fitted together like two halves of a perfect whole. Faster, deeper, harder he thrust. With a tiny cry of surprise, Karen soared.

"Yes," Daniel growled. "Yes." With one last powerful stroke, he buried himself deeper still and gave up the last shred of his control.

When Karen woke, she was alone in the bed. The sound of running water came from the bathroom; Daniel must be taking a shower. He probably had to go back to the ranch, she thought with regret. Her body tingled as she stretched; she ached pleasantly from his possession. Blushing, she remembered the things they had done and the way he had made her feel.

Feminine, beautiful and desirable. She was smiling secretively when the sound of the water stopped and she saw Daniel's outline in the doorway. As he crossed to the bed, she sat up, surprised that he was still naked.

"Good. You're awake."

Before she could speak, he lifted her effortlessly in his arms and carried her back to the bathroom.

"What are you doing?" she asked.

"Taking care of my lady."

In the bathroom, she saw that he had found the candles she kept for emergencies and lit them. Reflections of their flames danced in the mirror over the sink. As he set her on her feet, she saw that the tub was full of soapy water.

"I used your bubble bath," he said. "I hope you don't mind."

Wordlessly she shook her head. He picked up a stretchy loop she used on her hair and fastened it into a ponytail atop her head. Then he took her hand and helped her into the tub.

The water was heavenly, warm and scented. She sank into the bubbles and slid forward when he stepped in behind her.

"This is wonderful," she breathed, leaning back against his chest.

His arms came around her. "You won't tease me if I smell like flowers?" His deep voice rumbled in her ear.

"Never."

He worked up a lather between his hands and began to wash her, shoulders, arms, wrists, fingers. By the time he rubbed his soapy hands over her breasts, the flame deep inside her was burning again. When he was done, she turned around to face him, with her legs over his. She washed his body as he had hers but, before she could get past his hips, he urged her forward and arched into her.

After he had taken her to heaven and back again, he helped her up and wrapped her in a towel. Kissing her tenderly, he proceeded to dry her off and then himself as the water drained from the tub. He blew out the candles and carried her back to bed.

When Daniel woke again later, she was curled against him like a trusting kitten, her bottom pressed into his aroused flesh. After fumbling in the pocket of his jeans, he stroked her awake with his hands. When he took her, hard and fast, she was with him every step of the way, crying out his name as he joined her in a heated explosion that left them both weak.

It was only afterward that he realized he had forgotten to use a condom in the tub.

He got up and pulled on his jeans, jerking up the zipper but leaving them unsnapped. Then he sat on the edge of the bed and hung his head. How could he have been so irresponsible? So caught up in his own needs that he could forget something so crucial?

What if she got pregnant? Did he want another child of his aborted?

"What's wrong?" she asked, reaching out to smooth her hand over his rigid shoulder.

Furious with himself, he turned to tell her.

Karen's face flamed at his blunt words. She could see that his annoyance was directed toward what he perceived as his own lapse of responsibility. Still, she hadn't given the subject more than a passing thought as something to be dealt with "soon." *She* hadn't noticed his failure to use something in the tub.

"I'm sure it's okay," she told him. "This is a safe time for me."

His gaze narrowed. "You have to tell me when you're certain whether or not you're pregnant."

"Of course." She sensed his withdrawal. It left her floundering, unsure how to proceed with him. She pulled the sheet up higher, held it over her breasts. "I really doubt that I am."

"Tell me when you know," he repeated.

"Have you heard anything more from your lawyer?" she asked, hoping to draw his attention from his self-condemnation.

"Only that he'd rather I was married."

She didn't know what to say.

Daniel stared at the window. "What would I do with a wife?"

"You have a lot to offer," Karen said hesitantly. "And I'm sure many women would love the ranch."

He fixed his attention on her, scowling. "Oh, yeah? And what if I lose the case? I wouldn't have the ranch, then. I'd be down the road with nothing to call my own except a string of ponies. What woman would have me then? Who would marry a man like me?"

Karen knew he didn't expect a reply. The opportunity was too great, though, the temptation too strong for her to resist. She took a deep breath and answered with her heart.

"I would."

Chapter Ten

Daniel glanced at Karen and smiled. "Thanks," he said absently.

"I mean it."

His head whipped back around. "Karen, I'm serious."

"So am I. Dead serious. If you need a wife, I'll marry you."

His eyes narrowed, screening his thoughts as he stared at her intently. She could see the wall going up. "Why?"

"What do you mean, why?" She stalled.

He turned completely around, resting one bent leg on the mattress so he faced her. "Why would you be willing to marry me? Just because we're great in bed together?"

She flushed, a small part of her basking in the knowledge that she had pleased him. She thought fast, knowing he wouldn't accept a declaration of love. Not now.

"I told you about my fiancé," she began haltingly. "But I didn't tell you everything."

He waited silently.

She took a deep breath and moistened her lips. "We didn't sleep together after we got engaged," she continued. "Mark told me—and our friends—that he wanted to wait for me, until we were man and wife. He said it would make our wedding night more special."

She shook her head and blinked away the moisture that gathered in her eyes as she dredged up the painful memories she had finally managed to bury.

Nothing of what Daniel might be feeling showed on his face. She had no idea if she was reaching him at all.

"As I waited in the back of the church, in my long white gown, someone brought me a note from Mark. In it, he confessed his affair with a cocktail waitress from a bar with a really bad reputation for drugs and prostitution. It was only when she got pregnant that he realized he couldn't give her up for a more 'advantageous' marriage to me."

Karen dashed the tears from her eyes, wishing that Daniel would say something, anything, to let her know what he thought. Instead he sat before her, tall and still. Only his whitened knuckles revealed his inner tension.

"He and Marie got married. I transferred to Mountain View. The marriage doesn't seem to have hurt his career any, either. After all, the ultraconservative school board *did* just promote him as the new principal at Mountain View."

"And that's enough to make you want to marry me?" Daniel questioned, his tone disbelieving. "Pretty drastic."

"Look," Karen told him, afraid her impulsive offer was about to blow up in her face. "He starts on Monday. Once the word gets around that we used to be engaged, the whole sorry story is going to get dragged up all over again. Mark has his nice little family, beautiful wife, adorable baby son. I'm still single. I'd much rather marry you and have everyone at work think I've been swept off my feet by a dashing rancher than pity me for losing the only man in my life."

He smiled ruefully at her description of him. "Dashing rancher?" he echoed, rubbing one finger along the side of his cheek.

"Whatever," she snapped, getting impatient. What did he want? She had just offered to solve all his problems, for Pete's sake!

"I don't know," he muttered, obviously still unconvinced. "That's a hell of a commitment to make just to avoid a little embarrassment."

"Maybe it's more than a little embarrassment to me," she countered. "I was the one waiting at the altar. I was the one who had to face our guests—our co-workers—and tell them he wasn't going to show up." She shuddered, remembering. "On top of all that, I lost the man I loved."

"And do you still want him?"

The question astounded her. "Heck, no! I wouldn't take him if he was the last man on earth and came with a big, red bow around his—"

"I get the picture," Daniel interrupted. He took her hand. "I'm sorry," he said as he stroked the back of it with his thumb. "I'm sorry you were hurt by him. I just don't know—"

"Listen." It was her turn to cut in. "I care about Jamie and I don't think this Ted character really sounds like parent material. Even if he can double the value of Jamie's estate. I want to see Jamie stay where he belongs. In my book, that's with you. And I, we . . . we get along," she added, gesturing with her hand. "In bed and, uh, otherwise. I mean, we seem to like each other." She shrugged, unable to meet his gaze. "We've got more reasons than a lot of people," she murmured, pleating the sheet with her fingers.

Daniel let her go and rose to pace the length of the room. "I see what you're saying." He turned to face her, raking one hand through his hair. "It's just—"

"What?" she demanded, the tension threatening to unravel her composure entirely. Was he going to marry her or not?

He put his hands on his hips and bowed his head.

"We can help each other," she said quickly. "And having a teacher in the family certainly won't hurt Jamie." She wondered if Daniel would want her to keep working. *If* he ever got around to accepting her proposal.

He sat back down on the side of the bed, staring at his hands. Then he looked up. "Okay. Let's do it."

Inside her, something broke free. She wanted to throw her arms around him, but then he really would be suspicious of her motives. Besides, if she did that, the sheet she was holding up would drop to her waist.

She could hardly believe they were having this discussion while she was still naked under the covers. At least Daniel had had the chance to put on his jeans.

"But I want to warn you," he continued. "There's no way that this is going to be one of those marriages in name only. If we hadn't made love, it would be different. But I can't live with you like that now, not after I've had you. I couldn't do it."

Karen was blushing again. "I understand." He wanted her, and that was a start. In time, who knew what might happen? He could come to love her. At least she had a shot.

"I will, of course, give you a divorce if I still lose Jamie. Or, after a reasonable time has passed, if I win."

His words brought her sharply back to earth. He might find her fairly attractive, even desire her in his bed. But his emotions were clearly not involved. If she didn't remember that, she would end up with her heart in so many pieces that it could never be mended again.

Daniel watched the emotions chase one another across Karen's expressive face. Desire rose within him, drawing him up tight. He was about to force it back down when he realized that, very soon, he would be able to make love to her whenever he wanted. The thought was nearly enough to shatter his control.

Instead he leapt to his feet. "Why don't you put some clothes on?" he suggested, glancing at the clock on her nightstand. "It's almost morning. I'll make some coffee and we can figure out the details."

"Okay." She was staring down at her fingers as they played with the lace along the top of the sheet. Suddenly Daniel realized the true immensity of what she had offered to do for him. Cursing himself for being such an insensitive jerk, he leaned closer and gently lifted her chin.

"I'm sorry I gave you the third degree when I should have been thanking you," he said softly. "You might very well be giving me the one thing I want most in this world."

Hope flared within Karen, and then she realized that he was talking about Jamie and not about her.

They decided to tell no one about their agreement. As far as anyone else was concerned, except Daniel's attorney, the marriage was a real one, the result of a whirlwind courtship. They set the date for two weeks from that Saturday, after school was out for the summer.

Daniel surprised Karen by asking if she wanted an engagement ring. "It wouldn't be the Hope diamond, but I did manage to save part of my pay over the past nine years," he explained. "I thought you might like something that sparkles to wave beneath Gresham's nose."

His thoughtfulness made her love him even more. "I appreciate the offer." Her eyes were misty. "But we're getting married so soon. I'd rather have matching bands. Would you wear one?"

She thought he looked pleased. Then his expression sobered. "Sure. It wouldn't hurt my image in court, would it?"

* * *

"The first time I laid eyes on her, I knew something was going on," Mary crowed when Daniel gave her the news. "When's the wedding? Where are you having the reception?" she demanded expectantly. "Do you want me to do the food? I've got a few cousins who could help out."

Feeling like a fraud in the face of Mary's excitement, Daniel stopped her barrage of questions. "We're having a very small ceremony two weeks from Saturday. And we're not having a reception." He saw her disappointment. "But we'd like you to be there for the wedding," he added hastily. Karen would have to understand that he couldn't hurt Mary's feelings.

"No reception?" she asked. "Why not?"

He slapped on the hat he'd been holding, turning the brim around and around in his hands. Filling a mug with coffee, he made his escape. "I don't have time for all that foolishness," he growled defensively as he went out the back door. "I've got a ranch to run." Women!

Already, he hated the pretense.

Later that morning, Karen called her friend Terry and broke the news.

"You sly fox!" Terry exclaimed. "You told me you weren't even interested in the man. You let me go on about him like a star-struck teenager!"

Karen could tell from the tone of her voice that she wasn't really upset.

"It caught us both by surprise." Daniel, at least, had been stunned. Did that make it only half a lie?

"When did all this happen?" Terry prompted. "What did he say? Did he propose or did you just decide together? What did you say when he asked you?" Her questions tumbled out. "Come on, girl. I want details! When's the wedding? I'm invited, aren't I?"

"Of course you are." How could they have assumed they could tie the knot with just Jamie and two witnesses? Daniel would have to understand. She explained to Terry that they were keeping it very small and simple, but of course she wanted her friend there.

Karen had already called her cousin, Laurel, and asked her to be a witness. Laurel and her husband, both college professors, taught at UC Boulder and would drive to Craig early that Saturday morning.

"Well," Terry said, "this should kill any old gossip that crops up about you and Mark."

"Oh, I suppose you're right," Karen agreed brightly, as if the idea had never occurred to her.

Terry lowered her voice conspiratorially. "Tell me," she almost whispered. "Is your cowboy as good in bed as he looks like he would be?"

"Better."

"You lucky girl," Terry groaned.

"I'm speechless," Joe Sutter drawled when Daniel called to ask if Joe would stand up with him. "I never dreamed, the last time we talked, that you were even seeing anyone."

"It happened kinda fast," Daniel mumbled, hating the necessity of lying to his best friend. Not that Joe would ever say anything to the wrong party, but they couldn't start making exceptions to the secrecy pact or word of their arrangement was bound to leak out.

"Sometimes it happens like that. We can't wait to meet her," Joe told him after a brief consultation with his wife. "Emma says to make sure Karen knows how lucky she is."

Daniel laughed obligingly. "Maybe I'm the lucky one," he said. Or he would be, if the marriage had the right effect on the judge.

"We wouldn't miss it."

Mentally Daniel added two more guests to the growing list. They made arrangements for the Sutters to come to the ranch the day before the wedding. Joe congratulated him again before they broke the connection.

Emma's remark lingered in Daniel's head. Lucky? He and Karen were using each other. If that made them lucky, then so be it.

Daniel punched in Nick Keller's number and waited while the secretary connected them.

"Terrific," Nick said when Daniel told him the news. Then there was a pause.

"What's wrong?"

"If, by any chance, you're doing this to swing the custody suit your way, I don't want to hear about it."

Jamie was at least as enthusiastic about the news as Nick had been. "Will I call her Aunt Karen?" he asked. "Will she sleep in Mommy and Daddy's room with you? Will she still be my teacher?" He stopped long enough to take a breath.

"Whoa, there!" Daniel grinned and ruffled his short black hair. At least the boy wasn't upset about his uncle taking a wife and bringing her into his parents' home. "I'm sure she'd like it if you called her Aunt Karen." He thought for a moment. "We haven't decided yet where we'll sleep." He supposed he'd have to do something about clearing out the master bedroom before the wedding. Maybe paint the walls and invest in a new bedspread and curtains. Perhaps he could get Mary to pick them out. If he didn't have time to paint the walls, Cully could do it for him.

"What else did you want to know?" he asked Jamie, who was trying to keep his balance while he stood on one leg.

"Will she still be my teacher?" he asked again.

They hadn't discussed whether she would continue working. Daniel had assumed she would prefer it. Then he realized that he wanted her to stay home, greeting him with that special smile of hers whenever he came up to the house.

With her cheeks all rosy with that particular mixture of excitement and nervousness that made him want to either kiss her or protect her—he wasn't sure which. But then, maybe he was the one she needed protecting from.

He pictured her stretched out beneath him on the big bed, the coral tips of her breasts beckoning to him, her thatch of downy blond curls waiting for his invasion, and his whole body clenched. If she was here all day, he'd never get any work done.

"Will she?" Jamie repeated.

"Will she what?"

He rolled his eyes dramatically. "Still be my teacher?"

"I don't think so, not unless you're planning to repeat kindergarten," Daniel responded with a chuckle.

Jamie looked puzzled but didn't ask any more questions.

Daniel wondered if she had told her parents yet. She hadn't mentioned wanting them to be at the wedding. Maybe she didn't want to admit she was marrying an Indian. Especially not when the situation was temporary.

Karen waited until the week before the ceremony to call Denver. When there was no answer at the house for two days, she called her mother at her law firm.

"She and your father are in Europe," Julie, her mother's executive assistant, reminded her. "You just missed them. They'll be gone for a month. I can give you their itinerary, if it's something important."

"No, thanks." Karen was flooded with relief. "I didn't want anything special. I'll call them when they get back."

In February, the last time they had spoken, her mother had mentioned the trip, but Karen hadn't paid much attention to the dates. It was better this way. She and Daniel would already be married when he met them.

She had one more call to make. It would be easier to give him the news over the phone than to see the relief on his face.

"I'm not pregnant," she said.

On the day of the wedding, Daniel put on the same dark suit he had worn to court. Jamie was dressed in a white shirt, navy blue pants and a bow tie that Mary had bought him. He rode into town with her and Cully, since Daniel was picking up Karen. Daniel had been shocked when Cully offered to take Mary and Jamie with him, even more surprised when she agreed. Perhaps they had signed a truce while they were redoing the master bedroom.

"You look very handsome," Mary told Daniel when he came down the stairs, tugging self-consciously at his tie.

He ducked his head, feeling as if he should scuff the toe of his boot on the rug and tug at his forelock. "Thanks." He checked his pocket for the dozenth time, making sure he had the ring box and the license, then glanced at his watch.

"I gotta go." He swooped down to kiss Jamie's cheek. His skinny little arms came up to give Daniel a choking hug.

"'Gratchalashuns," he said, beaming proudly.

For a moment, Daniel's own arms tightened and his eyes grew damp. Blinking rapidly, he let Jamie go. "I'll see you there," he said hoarsely.

Mary gave him a pat on the back. "Relax. It's not gum surgery."

By the time he pulled up in front of Karen's apartment in the ranch station wagon that Cully had washed that morning, he had regained his composure.

Then she opened the door and he lost it all over again.

She looked like the angel from atop a Christmas tree.

"Come in," she said, voice taut with nerves.

Daniel stared, wordless, for so long that she looked down at herself.

"What is it?"

He swallowed. "You're beautiful. Turn around."

She wore a cream lace suit, with a short-sleeved jacket and a row of pearl buttons down the front that matched her earrings. The suit had a straight skirt that showed off her long legs. Her hair was caught up with a matching bow and a puff of veiling, with long curls falling down in back. Her skin reminded him of roses and cream. Her eyes, within the frame of her lashes, shone more green than gray.

She was a bride any man would be proud to have stand beside him. Daniel was humbled; damn, but he didn't deserve her.

Wordlessly he extended the corsage he had picked up on the way to her apartment. It was a single orchid, a creamy velvet creation so fragile it looked like porcelain, with a rich burgundy throat and green-tipped petals that almost matched her eyes.

"It's lovely." She took it from the box and held it out. "Would you?"

His hands shook when he pinned the corsage on her jacket. He wanted to kiss her, but she turned away and hurried into the kitchen. He heard the refrigerator door close and then she came back, holding a deep red carnation.

"I got you a boutonniere," she said shyly.

He thanked her and she fastened it to his lapel. When he glanced up, he saw their reflections framed together in the hall mirror. For a moment, he wished the wedding were a real one in every sense of the word. Then he reminded himself: cowboys didn't marry queens. Not marriages that lasted. He had better remember that or she would take his heart with her when she left. And leave him she was bound to do.

Everyone knew what happened to a man without a beating heart.

* * *

Karen gripped Daniel's hand as they walked down the courthouse hallway. He was stunning in the white shirt and dark suit, the silver earring adding a rakish note to his civilized veneer, and she was bursting with pride to be with him. The few people they passed stared and smiled.

"Aren't you the beautiful bride!" Terry exclaimed, dashing up to give Karen a hug. When she introduced Daniel, Terry hugged him, too, winking at Karen over his wide shoulder. The other people waiting quickly surrounded them as more introductions were made.

"The judge is ready for you," a woman in a pink dress announced.

With a solemn glance at Karen, Daniel patted his pocket, clasped her hand tightly and led her inside.

When the short ceremony was over and he kissed her, drowning in her sweetness, he had to remind himself once again that the marriage wasn't a real one. When he lifted his head, she looked as starry eyed as any "real" bride, and his heart lurched at the idea that she was his, at least for a while.

Joe had insisted on taking the whole party to dinner afterward. He had rented a private room at the nicest restaurant in town.

When they were seated and Karen was sneaking an admiring glance at her ring, a wide silver braid dotted with turquoise stones, Daniel leaned over to her.

"Are you okay?" he asked. A matching ring shimmered on his dark hand.

"I'm fine. I like your friends." She glanced shyly at Joe and Emma. As she did so, Joe happened to look up. He raised his champagne glass to her in a silent salute.

"I like your cousin," Daniel whispered back. Laurel had already teased him about his comedown from cattle to sheep, and made friends with Jamie. Daniel wasn't as sure about her husband, who appeared much older and was rather quiet.

Before Daniel could add anything, Joe stood and tapped a fork on his upraised glass.

"I'd like to propose a toast," he said as Emma smiled up at him. To Daniel, they looked even happier than they had been on *their* wedding day.

"To Karen and Daniel, who have chosen to walk life's path together. May your love grow, your happiness multiply, your problems diminish and your sorrows disappear. May your lives be forever entwined like the vines on the matching rings you wear. May your skies be as blue as the turquoise stones therein, and may neither of you walk life's path alone."

As glasses were raised around the table and Daniel bent to kiss her, Karen almost forgot the marriage wasn't a real one. Not yet, anyway.

Joe and Emma took Jamie back home with them for a visit and Mary insisted on spending the night with her cousin Rose. Daniel wished that everyone hadn't made such a point of giving them privacy on their wedding night.

When they returned to the ranch after the dinner party and the others had all gone, Karen went up to the master bedroom to change. While she did, Daniel showered in the hall bathroom and pulled on a pair of jeans.

He was sitting in the living room, doing his best to make sense of the newspaper, when Karen floated down the stairs in a sheer green nightgown that swirled around her like sea foam. Her hair fell in soft waves past her shoulders and there was a tentative smile on her face.

"I thought you'd be waiting in the bedroom," she said.

Telling himself he had made the right decision, Daniel went over to her. Her perfume, dark and sensuous, wove a spell around him that he tried hard to ignore. Steeling himself against the erotic pull between them that had never been stronger, he put a hand on her bare shoulder.

Touching her was a mistake. Warmth seeped into him, all but melting his resolve.

"You're probably worn-out," he said, forcing the words past lips that burned to kiss her. "I thought you might want to get a good night's rest."

Her eyes searched his. He could see that his words had hurt her, despite his attempt to spare her feelings.

"What's really going on?" She backed away, crossing her arms protectively over her lace-covered breasts. His hand dropped back to his side.

Unable to bear the sudden wariness in her gaze, Daniel turned away. His shoulders slumped and he shoved his hands into his pockets.

"I've changed my mind," he said, telling himself he was doing the right thing. The only sensible thing. "Waiting to hear whether you were pregnant made me realize the risk we'd be taking if we shared a bedroom."

He turned to face her. "I won't be sleeping with you after all. Not tonight, not any night of this marriage. I won't risk making you pregnant."

Chapter Eleven

Daniel's lips were pressed together, his eyes opaque. His announcement had caught Karen totally off guard. She debated salvaging what pride she had left and marching back to the lonely bedroom, her head held high. Then her love for the man standing before her won out.

"Why?" she demanded. "Why have you changed your mind?"

He looked surprised by her question. Had he expected her to slink from the room like a whipped puppy?

"I told you, I don't want to risk a pregnancy."

If he thought she would be satisfied with that pitiful explanation, he was mistaken. She sat down on the couch, crossed her legs and folded her hands over her knee.

"There are ways to prevent a pregnancy."

"I know that!" His voice thundered. "And the most effective way is abstinence."

She wondered what he was afraid of. That she would use a baby to hold him? That she might refuse him visitation? He didn't even know that she loved him—why would he think she might try to keep him? Puzzled, she studied his tension-filled face.

He shifted and glanced away, refusing to meet her eyes.

"When I was in the army, I met a college girl at a local hangout," he began. "She was beautiful. Smart, sophisticated, classy—everything I wasn't. When she agreed to go out with me, I thought I was the luckiest man alive." He studied his fingernails. "I adored her. She—" He shook his head, a bitter smile on his face. "She wanted me every way I knew to take her and a couple of ways I didn't. I thought that meant she felt the same."

A surge of jealousy rose inside Karen, as corrosive as bile. Then, hard on its heels came a wave of anger at the girl who had dared to hurt the man *she* loved. "You don't have to tell me this."

"Yeah, I do," he said, eyes hooded. "One weekend, she stood me up. None of her friends would tell me where she was. I was frantic, sick with worry. It took me days to find her."

He swallowed hard and Karen watched the muscles work in his strong brown throat.

"She had aborted my child."

"Oh, Daniel!" Karen was halfway to her feet, but she made herself sit back down. There was more; she could sense it.

For a timeless moment, she didn't think he was going to continue. Then his jaw clenched as his gaze focused, blindly, on the far wall.

"She told me that having my 'half-breed brat' didn't figure into what she called her 'Native American studies.' All along, she had been entertaining her ritzy white friends with details about our relationship."

Karen remained where she was, speechless. One look at Daniel convinced her that he wouldn't welcome her sympathy.

"People can be such jackasses."

He rose and headed for the stairs. For a moment she thought . . . "Where are you going?"

He didn't reply but she heard a door shut. With her heart aching for the betrayal he had suffered, she followed him. Then she saw that it was the door to the spare room that was closed. As she stood in the hallway, wondering what to do, he came back out, fully dressed.

"Where are you going?" she asked again as he brushed by.

When he turned to look at her, his gaze raked down her body in the sheer nightgown. A nerve in his jaw twitched as he clenched his teeth together.

"Go to bed," he said as he clumped down the stairs. Moments later she heard the back door slam.

Karen didn't think she would ever sleep that night—her wedding night. But, eventually, she got fed up with crying. That night and each one that followed, she slept alone in the king-size bed and Daniel slept down the hall.

During the daytime, he was polite, even friendly. The two of them kept up a pretense in front of Mary, whose frown of concern continued to deepen. Cully, too, watched them speculatively, but Daniel ignored him and Karen avoided him.

Instead she reminded herself that all she had hoped for was the chance to make Daniel fall in love with her. No one had told her it would be easy. Nothing was going to be accomplished by pouting because he refused to sleep with her.

Right from the morning after the wedding night that wasn't, Karen went out of her way to be attractive, agreeable and helpful. She helped Mary in the kitchen, she helped

Daniel with the horses. Whatever boring, dirty job he gave her, she did without complaining. If she noticed him watching her, she smiled innocently and went on with whatever she was doing.

The nicer she was, the more wary he became. The more he tried to avoid her, the harder she dug in her heels.

She was determined to wear him down, to broach his defenses, to send his formidable control up in flames and to seduce him into loving her. With a man like Daniel, she decided, the way to his heart was definitely *not* through his stomach.

She was driving him crazy. They had been married little more than a week now, and if constantly being in a state of semiarousal could kill a man, Daniel would already be dead.

He might have managed to keep his sanity if Karen were willing to leave him the hell alone, but she wasn't. Every time he turned around, she was there, bringing him a cold beer, asking questions about the horses, the sheep, the ranch, helping with the endless chores, smiling at him as if he were some kind of rock star.

When he took supplies to the shepherds, she went along. When he mended fences, she helped. When he drove into town, she rode with him. Try as he might, he couldn't escape her without hurting her feelings, and that he wouldn't do. He had already hurt her enough.

One afternoon, Daniel was getting ready to bathe two of his horses that a prospective buyer was coming to see the next morning. Hotshot was a bay gelding, Rowdy a flashy chestnut.

"What are you doing?" Karen asked as he led Rowdy outside and tied him to a post. Her cutoff jeans, faded and worn, were so short they should have been illegal. With them she wore a pale blue shirt with the tails knotted below her breasts, exposing her narrow waist. Her hair was pulled into a sassy ponytail and tied with the blue bandanna he had given her when they drove the sheep to higher pasture.

The day was hot; Daniel had an idea it was about to get a whole lot hotter. He told her what he was doing and she offered to help.

"It's too nice to be cooped up in the house," she added as she uncoiled the hose. A lick of fire went through him when he realized she was braless. He hurried back inside to get Hotshot and to regain his equilibrium while Karen fetched the shampoo, sponges and the other things they would need.

For a while they worked silently, side by side, wetting down the horses and working the shampoo into their hides. Every time Daniel risked a peek in Karen's direction, his whole body clenched with desire. Her cutoffs cupped her behind and bared an indecent amount of her long, lightly tanned legs. While he stared helplessly, she bent over to soap Hotshot's belly. Daniel's blood pooled in his groin so fast it left him light-headed.

Grabbing the hose to rinse off Rowdy, he told himself if she so much as tried to wear those cutoffs in front of anyone else, even Cully, he would lock her in her room. She was *his wife,* dammit, and she had better not forget it—he sure as hell wouldn't.

She managed to get the front of her shirt wet so her nipples were clearly delineated against the now semitransparent fabric. The sight made Daniel's hands itch and his mouth water.

He wanted to send her up to the house to change into something less revealing, but he wasn't about to admit how much she was getting to him. If he thought for one moment that she was doing it deliberately, he might have been able to ignore her, but he was positive she had no idea he was ready to explode.

Beads of sweat popped out on his skin, so he stripped off his own shirt and turned away, running the squeegee over Rowdy.

Icy water spattered against his back.

"Sorry," Karen called when he looked over his shoulder. Apologetically, she waved the hose from where she stood on Hotshot's far side.

Daniel managed a tight smile as he turned away again.

The full blast of the hose hit the back of his head.

"Damn!" Ducking, he whirled around.

Karen's hand was clamped over her mouth and her eyes danced with laughter. Daniel snagged the dripping sponge from the bucket of water at his feet.

"Lady, you're asking for trouble." He threw the sponge, but she darted behind the big bay and the dripping missile sailed harmlessly past her head. As Hotshot stamped his foot, she moved away from him and squirted Daniel again.

"Gotcha!" she cried triumphantly as the water hit his chest.

Itching for revenge, he glanced around for a weapon and noticed the faucet where the hose was connected. As he ran over to it, Karen followed, soaking him with water until he managed to shut the faucet off.

"No fair!" she hollered, dropping the useless hose as Daniel tackled her. She screamed as they slipped and fell into a puddle of dirty water. Shouting threats and laughing, they rolled around in the mud like puppies as the horses edged nervously away.

Finally Daniel managed to pin her down and sit on her. Karen was covered with mud, her hair was filthy and there were dirty smears on her face. Grinning at her comical appearance, he was about to let her up when she grabbed a handful of mud and hit him in the shoulder.

He narrowed his eyes and did his best to look menacing as they struggled, each trying to gain the upper hand, but he couldn't suppress a smile. Then his knee slipped on the wet ground and he fell forward. His hand shot out to save him and covered her soft breast beneath her wet shirt. Her nipple pressed into his palm and Daniel froze.

Silently Karen waited to see what he would do. He moved his hand with great care and rolled off her. She scrambled to her feet. Heat surged through her; she was starved for his touch.

Without a word, Daniel went over to the faucet and cranked the water back on. Then he took the hose and rinsed the worst of the mud from her clothes and hands. Even the cold water wasn't enough to drown Karen's longing for him.

"Daniel," she whispered imploringly.

Refusing to meet her gaze, he said, "Go on up to the house and shower. I'll finish here."

She hesitated, hating to leave.

"Go on," he repeated. "You look like you've been making mud pies."

She had no choice but to do as he asked. While the touch of his body, even covered with mud, made her tremble with need, he appeared to be as unmoved by her as was the gelding he had just bathed.

She trudged up the hill, filthy, discouraged and dripping wet. All she wanted now was a tepid bath and a tall, cold drink.

By the time she got to the house, she had stopped dripping. Kicking off her muddy tennis shoes, she went into the kitchen.

"What happened to you?" Mary asked.

"We were washing the horses."

Mary's brows rose as she poured Karen a glass of lemonade. While she drank it, the housekeeper regaled her with a long story about the letter she had gotten from a relative on the Ute Mountain Reservation where she had grown up.

"Grandpa George left that old pickup right where it quit running," she concluded. "He filled the truck bed with dirt and planted vegetables." She was slicing a tomato for supper. "Everything did well except the carrots. Their ends were all bent over from hitting bottom."

Karen laughed appreciatively and finished her lemonade. "I'm going to have a shower and read for a while," she said as she set her empty glass in the dishwasher. She was still smiling at the image of Grandpa George and his crooked carrots as she walked through the master bedroom, shedding her muddy clothes, and padded into the adjoining bathroom.

When Daniel had put away the horses and taken everything else back to the tack room, he headed to the house for a shower and a beer.

"Where's Karen?" he asked Mary on his way through the kitchen.

"She said she was going to read for a while."

He went upstairs intent on his shower. As he took clean clothes into the bathroom off the hall, he remembered that he had used the last of his shampoo that morning. Jamie had taken his to Joe's house.

"Karen?" Daniel called through her closed bedroom door.

There was no answer. He listened but didn't hear anything. Maybe she had fallen asleep. He hated to wake her. She had been doing more than her share of the work since she moved in. He knocked softly but there was still no response. Quietly he opened the door to the bedroom and tiptoed inside. The wide bed was empty.

As his head jerked around, the door to the master bath flew open. Karen stepped into the bedroom, a towel wrapped around her head and another draped over her arm. The rest of her lush, wet body was totally, sinfully bare.

Karen froze in the bathroom doorway.

Daniel stared—at her breasts, beaded with droplets of water he ached to lick from her creamy skin. At her nipples, puckering under his scorching gaze. At her slightly rounded stomach and the triangle of gold between her thighs. At the legs he ached to wrap around his hips as he thrust into her.

He heard a sound, a groan. He realized it came from his own parched throat.

With hands that shook, Karen pulled the edges of the bath sheet around her body while he watched.

"Daniel."

Her husky plea snapped him back to reality. Swearing, he turned, movements jerky, and fled, slamming the bedroom door behind him.

He hurried back down the stairs, stumbling in his haste, his own shower forgotten. All he could think about was the sight of her as she stood there with nothing between them except his own tattered willpower.

Back in the master bedroom, Karen dried herself quickly, trembling all over. For one unguarded moment, she had seen the need flare in Daniel's dark eyes. Had heard the rampant hunger in his hoarse groan.

He might be denying them both what their bodies and their spirits craved, but it cost him. She sank to the mattress. The torment on his face for that one unguarded moment had shaken her to her foundation.

When he hurt, she hurt, too. When he bled, so did she. And when he fought so hard against what she ached to give him, the pain made her want to scream.

She curled into a tight little heap on the bed, the towel still wrapped around her. Had she been wrong in trying to seduce him into returning her feelings? In winning his heart, might she also destroy his soul? Was she right in thinking he needed her, or selfishly, fatally wrong?

She lay there for a long time, wondering.

"Would you run down to the barn and tell Daniel the horseshoer called?" Mary asked when Karen went downstairs. "He isn't answering the barn phone, and he needs to call the man back if he wants him to shoe those two horses today."

Karen suspected that Mary was doing her best to throw her and her new husband together as much as possible. The housekeeper knew they didn't share a bedroom, and she must wonder what was going on.

"Can't it wait until he comes up here?" Karen asked, stalling. She hadn't resolved her earlier doubts and didn't want to face him in her current state of mind.

"Not if he wants those horses shod before the buyer comes tomorrow," Mary replied.

Karen glanced at the clock. Daniel had mentioned that Hotshot had a loose shoe. She tugged on a lock of her hair indecisively, hating to cost him a possible sale because of her own inner turmoil. What harm could it do to stick her head in the barn or wherever he happened to be and give him the message? She didn't have to hang around and try to assess his state of mind.

"Okay."

Mary looked relieved. "Thanks, dear. I know he'll appreciate it."

Karen hoped she was right.

Before Karen was three feet into the shed where the baled hay was stored, she heard someone grunting with exertion. It wasn't Cully, who had left for town earlier; it had to be Daniel.

She circled the stack of bales warily. Oblivious to her presence, he was tossing one after another onto the flatbed trailer as if the heavy bales weighed no more than newborn lambs. Sweat ran down his bare back and stained the bandanna tied around his head.

She watched the muscles of his shoulders and arms flex and shift as he grabbed another bale and hefted it onto the growing pile on the trailer.

Some weird radar they shared must have alerted him to her presence. He stopped and turned.

"You," he said, eyes blazing. His chest gleamed like oiled bronze as he dragged in a deep breath.

"Mary said for you to call the horseshoer if you want him to come out today," she blurted.

"Don't need to."

Before her addled brain could send a message to her feet, directing them to leave, he stalked over to where she stood, rooted to the floor. Wordlessly he yanked her into his arms.

"You win," he growled, and then he kissed her.

His open mouth covered hers in a heated melding that allowed no less than total surrender. Helpless against the sensual assault, she parted her lips to the invasion of his marauding tongue. When he laid siege to her crumbling defenses, bending her backward over his arm, she gripped his sweat-slick shoulders to keep from falling.

The moment he sensed her capitulation, Daniel scooped her up in his arms. Her eyes fluttered open and she looked into his face. What she saw there was hardly reassuring. Unleashed desire glittered in his eyes. His dusky skin was drawn taut with passion, his nostrils flared, his mouth a grim line.

Karen knew that Daniel would never deliberately hurt her. Not physically.

Cradling her high against his chest, he shouldered open the storeroom door. Light from the high window was filtered by the dirty glass, making the interior of the room appear golden and hazy. The air was close and warm. Without pause, Daniel kicked the door shut behind him and dumped Karen unceremoniously onto the narrow cot.

"Strip," he commanded. His hands went to his belt buckle but his attention was locked on her.

Caught up in her own fiery responses to his kiss and the naked possession stamped on his face, Karen kicked off her shoes. She began to unfasten the buttons on her shirt with hands that still trembled. By the time she had them half undone, Daniel had pulled off his boots and socks and freed the snaps on his jeans.

Swearing, he brushed her hands aside and yanked her blouse open. Buttons bounced on the bare wooden floor. His gaze collided with hers as he silently removed her ruined blouse and her plain cotton bra. When he dipped his head, shifting his attention to the breasts he had bared, she plunged her fingers into his hair. His bandanna fell to the floor.

"If you want to stop, tell me now." His voice was thick, his eyes glazed. Still, he had given her a chance to say no.

Touched, Karen shook her head. "I don't want to stop."

Passion, dark and dangerous, flared in his eyes. "So be it." He lowered his head to one breast, drawing the hardened tip into his hot, wet mouth as his callused hand covered the other and his long fingers toyed with the nipple. Gasping, Karen felt a fiery response flare deep inside her as he arched her backward. Her fingers dug into his scalp as she fought to keep from crying out with the pure liquid heat that was pooling in her most secret place.

As he held her braced against his arm, his free hand glided down her body, released the snap of her shorts and slipped inside. When his fingers slid into her damp heat, she sobbed and buried her face in his bare shoulder.

"Daniel, please."

His scent, warm and musky, filled her head. His talented fingers stroked her as her legs threatened to buckle.

"Not this way," she moaned. "I want you, all of you."

"Inside you," he rasped.

"Yes!"

He peeled off the rest of her clothes and laid her on the cot. She barely noticed the rough blanket against her back as she held out her arms. He fumbled in his pocket and then shucked his jeans and undershorts.

"I guess I knew I couldn't stay away," he growled, ripping the foil and turning briefly aside while she moaned her impatience. Then he was on her, pulling her legs up around him, as he filled her with one hard thrust.

Crying out, Karen convulsed helplessly. Daniel surged into her again, deeper still. His muffled shout was guttural as his body went rigid. Karen held tight, swallowing the words of love that threatened to spill from her lips, and he gave himself up to her in total surrender.

As he collapsed upon her, utterly spent, he felt her hands on his back and her breath against his throat. Feeling safer and more secure than he had in years, he let the mindless oblivion of sleep overtake him.

For a few brief moments, Karen cradled his weight against her and gloried in the absolute trust he showed by dozing off in her arms. Then, too soon, he stirred.

"I'm crushing you." He levered himself to the side as she tried to hold on to him.

"Never," she protested. "Don't get up."

He lay beside her on the narrow cot, one powerful leg thrown over hers and one arm cradling her close.

"I should have known something like this would happen." His grumble held more resignation than resentment.

"I'm glad it did. I've missed you."

She thought she felt a chuckle working its way up from his hard chest. "I'm glad, too, I guess. It seems like I've been hard since the wedding."

Unwilling to spoil his capitulation by analyzing it too closely, Karen let happiness soar within her.

"Where do we go from here?"

He shifted again so he was above her. "I won't make you pregnant," he vowed. "But I can't leave you alone." His gaze flickered away and then back again, his eyes unreadable. "I guess we go back to Plan *A*."

Karen recalled his earlier statement that theirs would be no marriage in name only and then she reminded herself that it was still temporary. Whether or not he lost Jamie, he meant to divorce her. Yet she refused to give up.

"So," she asked, her voice a deep purr as she circled his neck with her arms. "Just how many of those little foil packets do you have in your pocket, anyway?"

"Enough," he replied. He dipped his head and covered her mouth in a kiss so tender it made her ache.

Daniel didn't say anything about moving back into the master bedroom, but that evening when Karen went to bed he walked up the stairs with her. When she switched on the light, she saw his hat on the chair. Wordlessly, heart singing, she put her arms around his waist and kissed him. Flipping the light back off, he pushed her onto the bed and followed her down.

The next morning, they showered together and then, still naked, Daniel brushed out her hair while she watched in the mirror.

"I'm calling my parents today," she told him as he worked through a tangle. His hands were gentle.

At her words, he looked into her eyes. "Do you want me with you when you make the call?"

She could imagine her parents' reaction to her news. "No, that's okay. I know you have a lot to do, but I'll wait until tonight, anyway, so they'll both be home."

"You sure?"

She nodded. "I can handle them."

He shrugged and set down the brush. She felt his breath on her neck and then he nibbled her shoulder. One hand slid around to cup her breast as they both watched their reflections.

"We'll never get downstairs," Karen gasped when his thumb rolled across the sensitive tip.

"Mmm." His eyes met hers in the glass as his hand skimmed down her belly to the tangle of curls below. As his fingers probed between her legs and her knees went weak, she shut her eyes against the erotic image before her.

Daniel carried her back to the bedroom and set her on her feet as he stripped the tangled covers off the bed. Then he pushed her gently down and his fingers began stroking her once more. Caught up in a storm of passion, Karen opened her legs helplessly as he bent over her.

What he did to her next was so intimate, so totally unselfish and wildly sensual that she thought she would surely shatter into a thousand pieces. When he had wrung every last drop of pleasure from her that she was capable of feeling, he held her close and stroked her hair. Still trembling from the aftershocks of her devastating climax, she had to bite her tongue hard to keep from telling him how very much she loved him.

Chapter Twelve

When Daniel came back into the house at midmorning and stopped by the table where Karen was snapping green beans, the heat of embarrassment stole over her cheeks. After what he had done to her earlier, she still couldn't look him in the eye.

"Hi," she said, concentrating fiercely on the beans.

"Hi," he whispered directly into her ear. "You're blushing."

"A considerate man would pretend he hadn't noticed."

"I guess I'll have to think up other ways to show you how considerate I can be," he drawled in a low voice.

Karen thanked her lucky stars that Mary had gone into town for groceries and there was no one to hear his suggestive words but her. Jamie was coming back from the Sutters' the next day and, after that, their privacy would be limited.

Gathering the shreds of her composure, she turned to face him. "I can be considerate, too." She let her gaze trail down his shirt, unbuttoned against the heat, lingering suggestively at the fly of his jeans before she returned her attention to his face.

Daniel's eyes glittered like black diamonds and his skin had drawn tight over his stark cheekbones. He hunkered down beside her and rubbed his thumb across her lips.

"I've got an idea," he said, voice husky. "When we deliver the supplies to Rudy and Marco this afternoon, let's take sleeping bags with us and camp out under the stars. We can be back in the morning before Jamie gets here. I know the perfect spot, where the river forms a hole that's great for swimming."

The thought of sleeping outside with Daniel was a tempting one.

"That sounds wonderful. I'll pack us a picnic supper."

"You really want to go, then?" he asked. Sometimes the vein of insecurity he tried to keep hidden caught her off guard.

She smiled and touched her palm to his cheek. "Absolutely. I couldn't think of anything I'd like more."

"Nothing?" He raised an inquisitive brow and she blushed hotly. No one could embarrass her the way he could.

Then she recalled what else he had said about camping. "I'm not much of a swimmer," she confessed. "And I'm not very comfortable in the water."

"That's okay." He straightened and dropped a hand to her head, stroking her hair. "There's a sandy beach right upriver from there where the water's shallow. We can go wading if you'd be more comfortable."

Karen appreciated his easy acceptance of a fear she had tried to overcome without success. It had been a parental oversight that she didn't learn to swim until after fear of the water had taken hold. By then it was too late. Her skills were still rudimentary at best and being submerged in water gave her no pleasure. Unless the experience took place in a tub with Daniel's arms around her, she remembered with a secretive smile.

The two of them spent a few more moments making plans before Daniel left. If he wanted to be gone overnight, there was a lot to do outside first.

They weren't riding the horses because they had too much to take up to the shepherds. They would drive the Jeep instead.

"When did you say you were calling your parents?" Daniel asked as he drained his coffee mug and pushed back from the kitchen table.

"I was going to call them this evening." She fiddled with her cup. "Oh, darn. I guess the news will keep until we get back."

"I don't think you want to tell them." Daniel's mouth was curved into a smile that didn't reach his eyes.

"It's not about you," Karen insisted. "I don't expect them to approve, or even to understand, but it's got nothing to do with you."

He looked unconvinced. "If you say so."

"I'll call them tomorrow night," she promised. "For sure."

After he left, she stowed the few clothes and personal items she needed in a duffel bag and started fixing the food for their own picnic supper and breakfast the next morning.

When the phone rang, she answered and identified herself.

"This is Nick Keller, Daniel's attorney." The caller had an attractive masculine voice. "Is he around? I have encouraging news I wanted to share."

"Daniel's not here, but I can tell him when he gets back," she said. "I'd like to hear any encouraging news about Jamie myself."

"Mrs. Duggan came through for us," Nick told her. "I don't know what Daniel did, but I just got a copy of her report and she was actually enthusiastic about him."

Karen took a deep breath. "I'm so glad. This case has him tied in knots."

Keller went on to say that the new hearing date had been set for a few weeks away. "I'll see Daniel before then," he added.

She promised to relay the information and thanked him for calling. Maybe the news would lessen Daniel's worries.

On the ride back to the house the next morning, Daniel was deep in thought. He knew Karen was curious, but he wasn't ready to discuss how much the night before had affected him. She was so deep under his skin; he didn't know if he would ever be able to get her out.

"Is everything okay?" she finally asked, breaking the silence.

He grasped her hand tightly and lifted it to his mouth. "Sure. I was just thinking about Nick's news, and Jamie."

They had talked to him on the phone several times while he stayed at Joe's. Daniel had been afraid he would get homesick, but it sounded as if he was having a great time. His conversations were peppered with comments about Dolly, their Irish setter, the foster children who were staying at the ranch for the summer and Joe's adopted son, Kenny, who was almost a teenager. He had been away at basketball camp when they came over for the wedding, or they might have brought him. It sounded to Daniel as if Jamie had developed a severe case of hero worship.

Besides Kenny, there was a boy Jamie's age and his older brother, who was eleven, two girls who were ten and twelve and one who was sixteen and staying at the ranch for a year.

"I've missed Jamie," Karen admitted as Daniel negotiated a pothole in the road. "I'll bet you can hardly wait to see him this afternoon."

Daniel agreed as he downshifted at the bottom of a hill. He had missed the boy more than he would have thought possible. He had offered to drive over and pick Jamie up, but Joe was delivering a cutting horse to a woman who lived outside nearby Hamilton. He had offered to drop Jamie off on the way.

When Daniel glanced at Karen, she was looking at a field of wildflowers on the side of the road.

"Aren't they beautiful? They remind me of the bouquet you brought me."

"I told you they grew around here," he said, thinking that he should bring her flowers more often.

There was no denying that the two of them had gotten closer since their unconventional marriage, despite Daniel's efforts to keep his distance. He had been right to try to stay out of her bed, he thought wryly. Not that he'd had a snowflake's chance in hell of succeeding.

The overwhelming passion she aroused in him so effortlessly—with a kiss or a touch or a stroke of her tongue—had, if possible, gotten stronger. He told himself the white-hot arousal and the mind-altering attraction were only physical. The roller-coaster ride of emotion he experienced when he drove into her liquid heat was only lust. Sooner or later it would burn itself out. For the sake of his sanity, it had to.

Otherwise, how long could he last, banking his hunger in the daylight, feeding it each night as he held her in his arms and took them both higher than he had ever dreamed possible? How much longer would he be able to convince himself that he could go back to living without her?

When Jamie climbed down from Joe's pickup, Daniel swept him into a bear hug while Karen watched the two of them with tears in her eyes.

"God, I missed you," Daniel told his nephew as they held each other tight.

Jamie clung to him like a tick on a hound dog. "I missed you, too."

Joe was in a hurry, so he stayed only long enough to use the bathroom, get his thermos refilled with coffee and shake Daniel's hand.

"Thanks for taking him."

Joe gave Karen a quick hug. "Has this guy been treating you right?" he asked. "I can beat him up for you if he gives you any trouble."

"That'll be the day," Daniel snorted. "I could whip you with one hand—"

"I don't have any regrets," Karen said softly, her arms around Jamie. She thought that Joe, with his warm brown hair and laughing, silver-gray eyes, was almost as handsome as Daniel.

The two men exchanged a couple of mock punches.

"Remember," Joe told her. "He steps out of line, you call me. I'll put ground glass in his moccasins and cut-up rubber bands in his peace pipe."

"Big talk, paleface." Daniel caught Joe in a rough hug and clapped each other's backs enthusiastically.

"Stay in touch," Joe told him.

Moments later, waving out the window of his truck, he hollered, "Come and visit us real soon."

As the three of them waved back, Joe drove down the road, pulling the two-horse trailer behind him.

For the next hour, Jamie sat at the kitchen table with Daniel and Karen, talking about the Blue Moon Ranch.

"I wish we could raise cattle," he grumbled. "They're way cooler than dumb old sheep."

Karen met Daniel's amused gaze over the top of Jamie's head and tried not to laugh at his expression.

"You'd miss the lambs," he said.

"I guess so." Jamie didn't sound totally convinced.

For supper that night, Mary fixed hamburgers and homemade french fries, with hot fudge sundaes for dessert. Afterward, Jamie went up to his room to unpack and Karen headed for Daniel's office to call her parents.

"He's a sheep rancher here in Craig," she explained to her mother, wishing she had written her parents a letter instead of calling. "Yes, it was sudden." She took a deep breath. "I'm sorry you couldn't be here, too." She sipped her ice tea as she listened to her mother's complaint that a nice wedding in Denver would have been more suitable. A wedding that would have taken six months to plan and a small fortune to execute.

"No," she exclaimed after a moment. "I'm not pregnant. We just didn't want to wait." She shifted the receiver from one ear to the other. "I'm sure he doesn't have any family in Denver. Sixkiller, that's right. Spelled just like it sounds. No, I doubt it's English."

Karen sighed and stared at the ceiling. "Mother. *Mother!* I have to go. No, you certainly don't need to tear over here and save me. I told you, I'm fine. I'll call you when things calm down around here and you can come for a nice visit, okay? Yes, give my love to Father."

She rolled her eyes as she listened to a long list of instructions and advice. "Yes, okay. Uh-huh. I'll let you know. Bye."

Karen hung up, grateful the call was over.

"Did she give you a hard time?" Daniel asked from the office doorway.

She hadn't known he was there. Trying to remember what he might have overheard, she couldn't think of anything too bad.

"They wanted to come right out and check you over," she told him with a grin as she walked up to him and touched her lips to his.

His response was gratifying. His breath caught and he deepened the kiss before letting her go with obvious reluctance.

"And are they coming to save their daughter from the savage redskin?" he asked lightly.

"No. I told Mother that the savage redskin was much too busy taking scalps to meet them right now." Her voice was dry.

Daniel chuckled and tugged on a strand of her hair. "I see one scalp I wouldn't mind hanging from my lodge pole."

Karen pulled free and looked into his face. "Seriously, they're eager to meet you, but I put them off."

"Why?"

"Because I didn't want to deal with them until after the hearing. You have enough on your mind without your new in-laws descending on you."

He looked surprised. "Why do you treat me so well?"

She flushed with pleasure. "Because you're so good in the sack."

He made a grab for her, but she dodged by him. She was running toward the stairs when Jamie appeared at the top.

"Did you get everything unpacked?" she asked him, breathing hard. For a moment, she regretted the lack of privacy, but then her deep affection for Jamie took over.

"Yeah, I'm unpacked."

"Hey, sport," Daniel said from behind her. "Come on down and we'll go see if there's any ice cream left." His arm circled Karen's waist. "We'll settle this later," he whispered in her ear as Jamie thumped noisily from step to step.

Several days later, Daniel was in the living room looking for the classified section of the newspaper, when the doorbell pealed. He knew that Mary was outside picking vegetables for a salad and Karen was upstairs, so he went to the door himself.

On the porch stood an older couple in casual but obviously expensive clothes. Behind them, a midnight blue Mercedes was parked in the driveway. The man in front of Daniel had dark hair frosted with wings of gray at the temples; the woman was a slightly more mature version of Karen.

Daniel wished he wasn't wearing his rattiest jeans and a faded plaid shirt with a button missing.

"We're here to see our daughter, Mrs. Sixkiller," the woman said in a firm voice. "Would you please get her?"

So these were Karen's parents, Daniel mused as he opened the door wider. Her father was nearly Daniel's height, but had a stockier build. Karen's mother was a small woman, almost petite, and fashionably thin. She wore her short blond hair in a sophisticated, upswept style.

"Come in." Daniel offered his hand. "I'm Karen's husband, Daniel Sixkiller."

He watched for her mother's reaction. Shock and disbelief flared in her eyes and was swiftly masked. He admired her fast recovery.

"Marcia Whitworth." Her handshake was as firm as her voice. "My husband, Karen's father, Robert."

His grip was brief as his cool gray eyes took Daniel's measure. "Karen told us she had gotten married."

Resisting the impulse to defend their decision, Daniel managed a smile instead. "That's right."

"Daniel?" Karen's voice drifted down from the top of the stairs. "Are you still here?"

"Please," he said to their guests, "come in and have a seat." He led them to the living room, noticing how worn the furniture must appear to strangers.

"Daniel?" Karen called again, and he heard her footsteps on the staircase.

Mindful of his manners, he excused himself.

"Oh, there you are," Karen said when he appeared in the hallway. "I thought you might have left already."

From his expression, she saw at once that something was wrong. "What is it?" she demanded.

He put an arm around her shoulders. "Sweetheart, we have company." If the pet name hadn't alerted her, his raised voice would have.

"Who?" she whispered.

"Your parents," he whispered back. The arm across her shoulders tightened for an instant as he steered her toward the living room. She could feel his tension. Was the pretext of a normal marriage that stressful for him to pull off? she wondered as she plastered a welcoming smile on her face.

"Darling!" As she crossed the living room, her mother stood gracefully and kissed the air by Karen's cheek. Her father gave her a self-conscious squeeze. He had never seemed to know quite how to treat her.

"You're full of surprises," he said pointedly.

"I see you've met the biggest one." She sent Daniel an adoring glance that made him blink.

Her father didn't ask if there were more surprises to come. With her choice of education over law, she had relinquished the chance to win his approval. She wondered if he were yet reconciled to having a kindergarten teacher in the family.

Daniel's hand circled her waist. "We introduced ourselves," he said pleasantly enough.

Perhaps she had been mistaken about the tension.

"How long can you stay?" she asked, knowing that being impolite would change nothing about their visit, nor would a reminder that she had asked them not to come.

They were here to see what misguided decision she had made this time, she knew, and nothing would deter them. Experience had taught her that good manners and apparent cooperation would see her through this more quickly and with less difficulty than would the tantrum she was tempted to throw. Why couldn't they have given her a little more time?

She only hoped that Daniel didn't mind too much the invasion and the interrogation that would surely follow.

"We have to leave in the morning," her father replied, "but there's no need to put us up. I'm sure we can find accommodations somewhere in town." He ended the sentence on a questioning note.

"Oh, no," Karen demurred as was expected. "You can stay here."

"That's right," Daniel agreed firmly. "After all, you're family."

She shot him an appreciative glance while she mentally cataloged what needed to be done.

"Thank you, dear," her mother said.

"Are they my family, too?" Jamie asked from the doorway.

Daniel sent Karen a challenging look as he took Jamie's hand and led him into the room.

"These are Karen's parents," he explained.

"Is this your son?" her mother asked.

"My nephew. His mother was my sister." Briefly he explained about the accident as he kept a reassuring hand on Jamie's shoulder.

"So nice of you to take him in."

Daniel's eyebrows rose but he didn't say anything more. Instead he played host and offered them a choice of either a drink or coffee. When they both chose the latter, he caught Karen's eye.

"Jamie and I will see about the coffee," he told her with a reassuring smile. "We'll just be a few minutes."

"Didn't you have to go back out and—"

"I'll give Cully a call while I'm in the kitchen," he said, cutting off her protest. "He can manage without me." His steady gaze assured her that he had no intention of deserting her.

With a jolt, Karen realized that she was absurdly grateful for his unexpected support.

"Your decision to marry must have been sudden," her mother commented.

"Yes, very sudden." Daniel's smile when he looked at Karen left her dazzled. He lifted her hand to his lips and her knees threatened to give out on her. If only he weren't acting!

"We couldn't wait, could we, sweetheart?"

Mutely unable to break away from the heat in his gaze, Karen shook her head.

The hand holding hers tightened reassuringly before he excused himself and left the room with Jamie.

"My goodness," her mother murmured when they were gone, "what an astonishingly handsome man. Is he Italian?"

"Comanche," Karen said.

"How about showing us the ranch?" Karen's father suggested after they had finished the coffee Mary brought in on a tray. "We haven't seen much of the country around here."

Daniel glanced at Karen with a show of affection. "Shall we go for a Jeep ride?"

Karen had been wondering how she was going to entertain them until dinner. "Do you have the time?"

"I'll make time." His reply earned him a smile from Karen's mother.

In the Jeep, the men rode in front, with Jamie sitting between the women in the back seat. Karen found herself bursting with pride at the beautiful scenery surrounding them, as if she had in some way been responsible for it. The extent of Daniel's knowledge about the area belied the few months he had been here. The responsibility for White Ridge seemed to rest comfortably on his broad shoulders.

"My goodness, but your ranch covers quite a bit of land, doesn't it?" Karen's mother asked Daniel, leaning over the back of the front seat as they drove toward the high summer pasture.

"Mother's a city girl, born and bred," Karen teased after he had explained the need for adequate acreage to support the sheep, whose close-cropping grazing style and sharp feet necessitated moving them to fresh pasture each day or two. "To her, a half-acre lot makes a person a land baron and an acre calls for a gardening service. Right, Mother?"

"Really, darling, you know that I spend hours selecting the color schemes for the flower beds and hanging baskets every year."

"I don't think that quite qualifies you as an expert horticulturist, dear," Karen's father commented dryly.

"Karen's been a tremendous help here at the ranch," Daniel volunteered, making her blush. "Especially with Jamie and the horses."

"It sounds like those expensive riding lessons might have finally paid off." Karen's mother gave Karen a smug look.

"She's an excellent rider," Daniel said over his shoulder.

Karen murmured her thanks, uncomfortable with being the center of attention.

"How are the arrangements for the annual soiree going?" she asked her mother. Every summer, her parents threw a huge garden party for their numerous friends and colleagues. As Karen had hoped, the question successfully shifted the conversation away from her. For the next few minutes, her mother complained about the endless details that had to be dealt with in order to pull off the event with any success.

Karen wondered what Daniel thought about the list of people who had been enlisted to help: caterers, florists, a calligrapher to do the invitations, an ice sculptor and extra gardeners to make sure the grounds were as perfect as possible. Was he impressed by the extensive preparations or disdainful of the extravagance?

"You and Daniel must come," her mother exclaimed, mentioning the date of the party. "Bring Jamie, too."

"We'll see," Karen murmured. Spending several hours with her parents' pretentious friends while they all attempted to outbrag each other wasn't her idea of a fun afternoon.

Mary had accomplished a near miracle, making up both the guest bedroom and the dining room with clean linens while the dinner she had concocted from freezer and pantry was simmering in the kitchen.

"Wouldn't your mother like to join us?" Karen's father asked Daniel as Mary served their salads.

Karen's mind went blank as Daniel's gaze met hers across the table. Then Mary's quick thinking saved either of them the necessity of making an awkward explanation.

"Thank you for asking," she replied as she passed a basket of rolls. "But my favorite game show's on in a few minutes. I'll just have a tray in my room and put my feet up."

Karen heard Daniel turn a strangled laugh into a cough. She stared down at her salad, afraid to look at either him or the housekeeper without risking an untimely chuckle of her own.

From the corner of her eye, she glimpsed Jamie's puzzled expression. How Daniel managed to keep him from blurting out the truth, she had no idea. Talk about the dinner from hell! Perhaps, by now, Daniel was thinking more along the lines of the in-laws from hell.

By the time Mary served dessert, apple pie with ice cream melting over the warm crust, it was obvious from the glint in Daniel's eyes that he was annoyed by Karen's failure to include a few pertinent facts when she'd told him about her background. Such as her parents' obvious financial success and their social prominence.

She was grateful he was still apparently willing to keep acting out the role of the devoted husband. His irritation was well hidden; only Karen knew him well enough to recognize it, simmering beneath his veneer of adoration.

Later, after her parents had turned in and Daniel went down to check the horses one last time, Karen wandered outside to the brick patio behind the house. She was leaning on the low wall, waiting for him to come back up the road, when her father joined her, carrying his pipe.

"Will this bother you?" he asked.

"No. I would rather you didn't smoke in the house, though."

"No problem." He lit it while he studied the valley and the mountains beyond, the remnants of the recent sunset glowing faintly from behind their jagged crests. "It's pretty out here," he said. "Peaceful."

Karen agreed, enjoying the few moments of companionable silence. When he cleared his throat, the sound reminiscent of childhood lectures, she wondered if he had come out for more than the mere incineration of shredded tobacco.

"If you don't mind, there's something I wanted to discuss."

"Would you like to sit down?" Ignoring her sudden attack of nerves, she indicated two redwood chairs that sat facing the house. Once they were seated, she resisted the urge to defend herself and waited, instead, for her father to initiate the conversation.

He puffed on the pipe a few times, letting out a cloud of fragrant smoke. "Daniel is an unusual man, but not the sort I would have expected you to choose," he began.

No, Mark Gresham would have been more to his taste, she suspected. Was that why she had been attracted to *him?* A chilling thought.

"You mean because Daniel's Indian?" she asked bluntly.

"Not necessarily. Because he's a rancher and because I suspect he's neither as educated nor has he had the cultural advantages you've had. I can't help but wonder what the two of you have in common."

She was aware that he was picking his words carefully. He had always been the negotiator, the reasonable one. Her mother was more volatile, quicker to show anger or, worse yet, chilly disdain.

"We have a lot in common," she spluttered. "Basic values, the important things." She was grateful for the extra attention her husband had paid her since their unexpected guests had landed on the doorstep. He must have understood how badly she wanted to make a good impression, and his actions had gone a considerable way toward salvaging her pride.

"Don't get me wrong. I'm sure that Daniel is a bright, hardworking young man."

"Yes, he is." She waited impatiently for him to get to the point.

"That isn't what concerns me."

"Then what does?" She shifted in the chair, feeling like a schoolgirl again.

"I'm concerned about the children you may decide to have," he responded, shocking her with his bluntness. "Are you planning a family?"

"I—why do you ask?" She resented his assumption that, just because he was her father, he felt justified in quizzing her on such a personal issue when their relationship was so remote.

"Have you given any thought to the problems they'll face, with you and Daniel for parents?" He took another draw on his pipe. The bowl glowed red in the darkness. Suddenly the heavy, sweet aroma of the custom-blended tobacco made Karen feel ill.

"Of course I have." She knew exactly what he was getting at.

"A child of mixed blood won't be accepted by either side. He won't fit in anywhere."

"I'm aware of the problems," she said stiffly. "We already have one half-breed child, if you have to use that term."

He looked surprised. "You mean Jamie?"

"Yes, of course."

"He's a delightful boy, but I've seen the results of this failure to fit in over and over in my courtroom. I'm only asking you to consider carefully before you bring any more such children into the world."

Suddenly Karen had heard all she could take. "Don't worry," she said in a cool voice that hid the emotions churning inside her. "I've already considered all the issues you've mentioned and I've accepted the only course of action possible, should I become pregnant."

Whether or not Daniel divorced her, she desperately wanted his baby. It was a bond the two of them would share no matter what else happened between them—and she was perfectly capable of raising the child as a single parent, if she had to. As long as she was somehow able to overcome Daniel's caution and get pregnant in the first place.

Before her father could say any more, she got to her feet. "Daniel must have been delayed down at the stable. I'm going up to bed."

Her father rose, too. "You know we only want what's best for you, don't you?"

"Yes, I know." What *they* thought was best for her, she reminded herself silently. Whatever *she* might want had never been one of their major considerations. But she wanted Daniel—and his babies.

"I'll see you in the morning, then." Her father bent to give her an awkward kiss on the cheek before he moved back to the porch railing. Still fuming, Karen slipped inside.

Hands balled into fists and stomach twisted into a hard knot of simmering rage, Daniel waited by a fat blue spruce until Robert went back in the house. He could still barely make himself believe what Karen had so coolly admitted.

She had accepted the only course of action possible. Even now, the chilling words made his blood run cold—and then begin to boil, heated by his fury.

Apparently her father's approval still meant more to her than anything Daniel might have to offer, including little black-eyed, half-breed babies. In his secret heart, he had fantasized about planting his seed deep within her, and watching her belly grow round with the child they had created together. How fortunate that he hadn't forgotten the lesson he had learned so painfully—that the image of Karen holding his child would never be any more than just that—pure fantasy.

Better to remember that she had her own reasons for entering into this unholy alliance. It was funny, but sometimes, when he was buried deep inside her and he looked into her eyes, he could swear he saw more than mere heat and hunger there. He must have been kidding himself when he thought he saw a reflection of that emotion he had tried so hard to deny in himself. And failed.

Chapter Thirteen

Karen had known Daniel might be slightly intimidated when he discovered that she had grown up the child of two well-educated, successful, socially prominent overachievers who had raised her in their own likeness. She hadn't thought, though, that he would take her failure to tell him everything so hard.

She was still awake when he climbed into bed that night. When he turned away without touching her, she figured he thought she was already asleep.

"Daniel." She whispered his name as she touched his warm, hard shoulder. Already, pinwheels of reaction were spinning inside her as her body remembered the magic the two of them made together.

He didn't answer. Lightly she traced the curve of his spine with one fingertip. He shrugged off her touch. She stroked her palm down his side to his bare hip, and then she leaned over him. Her hand drifted downward.

He rolled away. "I'm beat." His expressionless voice certainly sounded tired. "I'll see you tomorrow."

But when Karen woke in the morning, his side of the bed was empty. When she went to the kitchen, Mary told her he had eaten and gone out early.

Forcing down a few bites of Mary's scrumptious blueberry pancakes, Karen made Daniel's excuses to her parents. Neither she nor her father made any reference to their conversation of the evening before, but she was certain he had already discussed it with her mother, whose expression was faintly disapproving.

Later, as her parents were getting back into their Mercedes, Daniel came riding up on Ringo to say goodbye.

"What a handsome horse," her father exclaimed. "All you need is a spear and a warbonnet."

"My warbonnet's at the dry cleaner's," Daniel said as he dismounted.

Even Karen laughed as she bent over to explain to Jamie that he was only kidding.

After her parents said again how they hoped to see them at the garden party, there were air kisses all around and then they left. Karen breathed out a long sigh of relief.

"Are you glad they left?" Jamie asked in his straightforward way.

"Well, yes," Karen admitted. "I'm always happy to see them, and then I'm happy when they leave."

Jamie thought for a minute. "I have friends like that."

Karen had hoped that Daniel would stay with them for a little while but, before her parents' car was out of sight, he wheeled Ringo sharply around and rode back down the hill. As she watched him go, Karen worried about the way he had been acting.

That night, when the lights were out, he took her fiercely. It was only afterward, when he turned away again, his broad back as forbidding as a wall, that she realized he'd uttered not a single word.

As the days dragged by, he was chillingly aloof. Only in the darkness did he turn to her as if he could no more resist her than she could him. His hunger for her showed no sign of abating. In the daylight, he sounded the same, even looked the same. Only his eyes had changed. When Karen searched them for some sign that he was softening toward her, they were as empty as two black holes.

"We have to talk," she insisted, cornering him in an empty stall late one afternoon. She was determined to have it out with him. To apologize if necessary and to clear the air.

"Talk about what?" His eyes had iced over.

A shiver went through her. When she tried to step in front of him, he turned away. "About what's wrong."

"Nothing's wrong."

She moved and he changed direction, scooping up another shovelful of dirty straw.

Karen hesitated. Perhaps he just needed time to adjust. Maybe he was just tired. Sometimes his black eyes were difficult to read; she could have been mistaken about what she thought she saw there.

"Can't you stop that for a moment?" she demanded when the shovel almost hit her foot.

"I have a lot to do."

"Can I help?"

He shook his head.

"Are you sure?" Her voice quavered. She wanted desperately to believe him.

He didn't look up. "Yep. Would you move? You're in my way."

She watched him, indecisive. Then, when he kept working, she left him and walked back to the house, wishing he had at least looked up or said goodbye, anything to quell her fears that something was desperately, irrevocably wrong.

Ironically, the more Daniel shut her out, the more Jamie seemed to welcome her in—into his room, into his life, and into his heart.

He missed his mother and seemed willing to allow Karen, in some small way, to fill the void. As one summer day slipped into the next, the two of them spent more and more time together. If Daniel sometimes watched them with a disapproving scowl, at least he didn't try to keep them apart.

As the court date drew closer, Daniel remained in his own private hell, keeping himself closed off from Karen even though he couldn't make himself stay away from her at night. Some days, he thought the darkness would never come.

He knew she was hurting, told himself she deserved it for her deceitfulness, ignored the niggle of doubt that kept whispering to him, telling him he had to be wrong. That she wouldn't do what he had already tried and convicted her for.

He had other concerns to fill his head with painful thoughts. How was a man supposed to tell a boy who had lost his parents only months before that he might now lose the only home he had ever known as well as the uncle who had promised never to leave him? If trying to understand the battle over his custody didn't succeed in breaking Jamie's heart, it was surely bound to shatter Daniel's own.

"How did it go?" Karen asked when he finally came out of Jamie's bedroom, emotionally drained.

He would have liked nothing better than to crawl into her embrace and let her heal his pain. Instead, he beckoned her back down the hall so that Jamie wouldn't overhear them talking.

"He's hurt and confused, and he keeps asking me not to make him go and live with Ted. I don't think he understands that it isn't up to me."

"Oh, Daniel." Karen's eyes were full of tears. "Do you want me to talk to him?"

"Not now. He's worn-out from talking. I think he needs a little time to absorb what I tried to explain to him. Then perhaps Nick can get through. God knows that he's had more practice at this than I have."

"I'm sorry," she murmured, lifting a hand to touch him and then letting it drop back down to her side.

He saw the gesture and it hurt him. Perhaps she really did love Jamie as she said. Sometimes, when Daniel turned to her in the night and she welcomed him, he wondered how much longer he had until she began refusing his advances. Each time, he prayed for one more night.

"I tried not to let my feelings about Ted and his wife show," he said, raking his hand through his hair. "What if Ted wins? It will only be harder on Jamie if he hates the bastard.

"At least I think he understands how important it is for him to tell the judge how he feels and to answer his questions as honestly as possible. I just hope he finally believed me when I told him that none of this was my doing, and that I want us to stay together."

Daniel wanted to take Karen in his arms, but he knew that, if he weakened the slightest little bit, his shaky defenses would shatter like glass.

"I'm sure it will all work out," she told him. "It just has to. Jamie knows how much you love him."

Daniel searched her face, trying hard to understand how she could come across as being so sweet and sincere when he knew how deceptive she was, deep inside.

"I hope to hell you're right," he said on a long sigh.

* * *

The day of the hearing dawned hot and bright. Daniel was sweating beneath his dark suit and itchy white shirt. The hated tie Keller insisted he wear was cutting off his air supply.

Jamie, in the same outfit he wore for the wedding, walked between him and Karen, holding their hands tightly. Back at the house, he had thrown a full-blown tantrum. When he started screaming, Daniel had turned away with tears in his eyes and left Karen to calm Jamie and help him to get dressed.

"I want to go home," Jamie said again as they walked down the hallway. "I don't like this place."

Daniel stopped and squatted down while Karen waited, hands clasped together. Tenderly he pushed Jamie's hair back and looked into the eyes that were so like his sister's.

"I don't like this place much, either," he said. "And I hope that very soon this will all be over and we'll be able to go home again." He glanced up at Karen, whose lower lip was trembling. She looked like an angel in a simple pale blue dress with her hair in a neat twist.

Daniel held Jamie's head between his hands. "I love you." The words threatened to choke him. "You remember what we talked about with Nick last night?"

Jamie nodded, his expression solemn and his eyes swimming with tears. "I remember. Tell the truth. Answer the judge's questions. Don't pick my nose or belch in court."

Daniel almost chuckled despite himself. He had forgotten Nick's attempts to make Jamie laugh. Trust him to remember, though.

"I think you're going to do just fine. We're warriors, remember? We win."

"Yeah," Jamie repeated. "Warriors. We win and then I can come back home with you."

Daniel got to his feet. "I hope so, partner. I truly hope so," he muttered as they resumed their journey down the marble hallway. In a few moments, they were outside the double doors of the courtroom where they were supposed to meet Nick.

After all Daniel's anxious waiting, the hearing itself went quickly. Ted and his attorney both made statements, and the judge asked a lot of questions. Then Nick and Daniel spoke in turn.

"Jamie and I are family," Daniel told the judge. "We couldn't be any closer if he was my son. We share the same heritage, the same blood, and I love him." He wished fiercely that he could be more eloquent and find just the right words to move the judge, but Nick had told him not to worry about it. That was *his* job.

"Mr. Sixkiller, I understand you got married since you were last here," Judge Greenburg said.

"Yes, Your Honor." He did his best to ignore the butter-flies batting away in his stomach. "My wife was Jamie's teacher. We met when she called me in for a school conference."

The judge looked at Karen. "Mrs. Sixkiller?"

She got to her feet, looking lovely and relaxed as she addressed him in her clear, steady voice. Pride burst inside Daniel, despite their recent estrangement.

"How do you feel about the prospect of raising another couple's child?"

Karen chose her words carefully. She wanted to be honest but was nervous about making a mistake. "I'm fully prepared to raise Jamie as my own," she said. Then she glanced down at him beside her. A swell of emotion threatened to block her throat.

"I couldn't love him any more if he were mine," she added as her cheeks turned color. "He and Daniel are my family." She didn't look at her husband, afraid he would see everything she felt for him shining in her eyes.

Had she gone too far? Perhaps he didn't want her to care about him. It was too late for her to hide the truth, though, at least from herself.

Jamie was like a son to her, but Daniel—he was her whole life.

When the judge thanked her, she sat back down, trembling with nerves. She studied her hands, afraid to look up and see the truth on Daniel's face. Afraid he neither cared about her nor wanted her to care for him. If they survived this, what was she going to do?

When the judge addressed Jamie, he got to his feet the way Nick had instructed him.

"How do you feel about your uncle Daniel?" the judge asked after the two of them had exchanged enough small talk to put Jamie at ease.

"When he first came to the ranch, after my parents died, I wanted him to leave," Jamie admitted.

The judge looked surprised at his candor. "And how do you feel now?"

"He and Karen explained that my mommy and daddy couldn't come back, even if Uncle Dani'l went away again." He paused and scratched his arm. "Now he and Karen got married and we're a family. That's pretty cool, I guess."

After the judge had asked a couple more questions, he told Jamie he could sit back down.

"Thanks," the little boy replied with a gusty sigh. "I'm glad that's over."

Everyone smiled and Judge Greenburg actually chuckled. "I know how you feel."

As Karen tried not to fidget, he went on to mention the report from Mrs. Duggan and Joe Sutter's deposition, which he said he had read carefully as he had those of Ted Powell's friends.

"The welfare of a child is at stake here," he concluded, taking off his glasses and looking at each of the petitioners in turn. "The decision I make will affect the rest of his life. Therefore, I'm going to take the side of caution and award temporary custody, for a period of six months, to Daniel Sixkiller."

As soon as he heard his name, something inside Daniel broke loose and he felt a great lessening of the tension that had held him in its grip for so long. For a moment, he bowed his head and his eyes filled with moisture.

"Did we win?" Jamie asked as the judge left the room.

"We did for now." Daniel scooped him into a bear hug as he watched Karen wipe the tears from her eyes. He wondered how she felt about staying married to him for another half a year. If she found this new delay to be upsetting, she sure didn't let it show.

Across the aisle, Ted and Dixie were leaving. They didn't look at Daniel or at Jamie, but Ted was talking rapidly to their attorney, an angry expression on his face, as they walked out.

"Congratulations." Karen leaned across Jamie to squeeze Daniel's arm.

"It's temporary," he reminded her, searching her face for some hint of her reaction.

"It's still a victory."

"You did fine, all of you," Nick said cheerfully. "Just keep the status quo and don't rock the boat for the next six months and I'm sure you'll be awarded permanent custody."

"I hope you're right." Daniel didn't want to think about what six more months with Karen was going to do to his peace of mind. Shoving aside his mixed emotions, he thanked Nick for all he had done and grabbed Jamie's hand.

"Let's go home."

If Karen had expected the judge's ruling to have any bearing on the way Daniel had shut her out since her parents had visited, she was doomed to disappointment. He continued to keep her at arm's length during the daylight hours, but he didn't fail to turn to her in the darkness of the night. And, each time he did, he was diligent about protecting her from getting pregnant.

Even Mary noticed the new strain in their relationship.

"All married couples have arguments," she said briskly one day when she was ironing and Karen was poring over a mail-order catalog of spring flower bulbs. Jamie was watching a television movie in the living room.

"The important thing is to move past the misunderstanding, not to let it fester and get worse."

"Tell that to Daniel," Karen snorted without glancing up.

"Have you tried talking about it?" Mary asked with the easy familiarity of a woman regarded more as a member of the family than an employee.

Karen was used to the older woman's attitude. Now she looked up from the photographs of colorful tulips and daffodils without resentment.

"He refuses to discuss it. Every time I ask, he tells me that everything is fine." She rolled her eyes. "You know how stubborn he can be when he doesn't feel like talking."

"As thickheaded as a cigar-store Indian," Mary said, making Karen laugh despite her continuing worry.

"Exactly."

Mary concentrated on the collar of the cotton shirt she was pressing. "Maybe talking's not the way to get his attention," she mused.

"So," Daniel said from the open bedroom doorway, "it looks like you're stuck here with me for another six months."

Karen turned from the bureau drawer where she had been putting away clean laundry. Mary had taken Jamie to town with her and the house was silent. Karen was surprised she hadn't heard Daniel coming, except that her mind had been a million miles away, thinking about Mary's last comment.

"Stuck?" she echoed. No matter how angry he was that she had kept the truth about her background from him, how could he think she was in any hurry to leave the ranch and Jamie, if not Daniel himself? Did he think he suddenly wasn't good enough for her?

"I don't understand," she continued. "Why would you think that I feel stuck here?"

His eyes narrowed and he stepped farther into the room. "Because you can't leave now, or I'd lose Jamie for sure. Judge Greenburg wouldn't be very impressed by a marriage that failed so fast."

"I have no intentions of leaving! And I don't understand your attitude. Even temporary custody is a triumph. Why would I resent it? I *want* you to get custody, remember? That's one of the reasons I'm here."

Daniel came closer, towering over her as she searched his stormy face. "And what's the other?" he demanded.

"I beg your pardon?" When he was like this, he reminded her of something wild and untamed. Little shivers of excitement went through her at the idea of his losing control and taking her because he couldn't stop himself. The night before, she had gone to bed early and he hadn't disturbed her when he came in.

"What's the other reason?"

"Nothing I feel like discussing with you now." Tossing her head so her hair swirled around her face, she decided it was time to take a risk and break the impasse between them. Fluttering her lashes, she gave him what she hoped was a sexy smile as she moved closer.

His shirt was unbuttoned in deference to the warmth outside. His hair was damp from the heat and messed up from his running his fingers through it when he took off his hat. He was watching her warily. Keeping her eyes locked on his, she ran a hand lightly down his chest, from breastbone to navel. His sharply indrawn breath was music to her ears. Beneath her fingertips, his muscles quivered.

Encouraged by his involuntary response, she caught the buckle of his belt and pulled him toward her.

"What the hell do you think you're doing?" His voice was a low growl as he shied away, as skittish as a wild stallion. The buckle slipped from her grasp.

"What are you afraid of?" she countered, running her hand up his bare forearm and slipping it under the hem of his short sleeve. "I would never hurt you."

Beneath the bronze skin of his cheeks she could see a dark flush forming. His eyes widened at her words. "Afraid?" he jeered. "I'm not afraid of anything."

She leaned closer, so their lips were only a breath apart. "Except me," she murmured, voice husky as she pressed her breasts lightly against him.

His nostrils flared as if he were drinking in her scent. Lord, how she had missed him! Licking her lips and quelling the nervous flutter that rose inside her, she reached up to free the two top buttons of her blouse.

Daniel's gaze fastened on the shadowy cleavage she had exposed and she saw a shudder go through him.

He wanted her! The knowledge gave her the courage to go on with her seduction. Turning her back, she undid the rest of the buttons of her blouse, let it slip off her shoulders and dropped it to the floor.

"What are you doing?" His voice had thickened.

She reached behind her to undo the clasp of her bra. When she faced him again, her hands shielded her breasts.

Daniel stared.

While he watched, she slowly bared them.

"I'm trying to seduce you," she replied. "How am I doing so far?"

He didn't answer, but Karen could see the bold proof that he was hardly immune to her efforts. She raised one hand and set it lightly on the revealing bulge of his fly. When she traced his length, he groaned. A nerve jumped in his cheek. Encouraged, she began to fumble with the heavy belt buckle. Before she could free it, Daniel's hands locked around her wrists.

She thought he meant to stop her.

"Let me do that." At his urgent plea, relief flooded her, followed by a fresh surge of desire.

While he unbuckled his belt, she stripped off the rest of her clothes. When he looked at her, his breath hissed in sharply between his tightly clenched teeth.

"You better be damned sure you want what you're asking for," he said in a harsh voice. "Because you're sure as hell going to get it."

Karen sank to her knees in front of him, trailing her hands down his denim-clad legs. "In case you have any lingering doubts," she murmured. "Let me show you how very badly I do want you." Before he could react, she opened his jeans and freed his straining flesh. Then she leaned forward and stroked him with her tongue.

With a tortured groan, Daniel hauled her up by her arms and tossed her across the bed. She had awakened a sleeping dragon! Without bothering to remove his jeans or boots, he followed her down. Wedging a thigh between her legs, he parted them and drove into her welcoming warmth.

As he felt her surrounding his naked flesh and the exquisite sensations threatened to swamp his senses, the last rational part of his brain remembered the foil packets in the nightstand. He went still, but it was more than he could do to leave her. Beads of sweat broke out on his forehead as he fought for control, but it was no use.

Karen whimpered low in her throat and her eager hands pulled him closer. Any thought of stopping dissolved in the red mists of passion that swirled around them both.

Afterward, Daniel was furious with himself for his lack of responsibility. Not only had he taken her with all the finesse of an adolescent on hormone overload, but he hadn't even thought to protect her until it was too late for anything but regret. Unable to look at her face, he rolled away and began adjusting his clothing.

"Daniel," she said, sensing his dismay, but he refused to look at her. Desperately she reached up and bracketed his jaw with her hands. "Don't leave me."

"I'm sorry I was so careless." His voice was cold, chilling her.

"What do you mean?" Did he think he hadn't satisfied her? She couldn't hide the way she came apart in his arms.

"I didn't protect you!"

Now she understood what he meant. "I don't care," she cried.

"You might, if there are consequences."

"Consequences?" she echoed. How could he call the baby they might have created together "consequences"? The possibility that she might be pregnant filled her with joy.

"If there's a child," he continued, his gaze burning her with its intensity, "you'd better remember that I want it."

Was he saying that he would take a baby from her? Did he hate her that much? Her heart cried out with the pain. Crushed, she turned away and pressed her face against the pillow, hiding her bitter tears.

"I mean it," he insisted.

She didn't respond. After a few more moments, he covered her naked body with a blanket. Then she heard him take the rest of his clothes and leave the room.

Now Daniel avoided her at night as well as during the daytime. He moved back to the same room down the hall where he had slept before.

Even Jamie noticed his withdrawal. The more he avoided the house, the more time Karen had to spend with his nephew.

"Let's go on a picnic," she suggested one morning.

"Can Uncle Dani'l go with us?" Jamie asked.

Karen thought carefully before answering. "He's got a lot of work to do," she said finally. "Maybe he can go next time."

Jamie frowned and his lower lip jutted out. "You always say that."

"Tell you what," she suggested. "Let's see if we can borrow the Jeep and go down to a little beach on the riverbank that your uncle showed me. We can go wading and look for pretty rocks."

Jamie's eyes, so like Daniel's, immediately lit up. "Cool. Can I wear my swimming trunks?" He had new red ones covered with dinosaurs.

"Good idea," Karen said. "I'll ask Mary to pack us something really good to eat."

Later, watching Jamie splash around in the shallows, Karen was filled with memories of the way she and Daniel had waded in the cool water, hand in hand. It had been a mistake to come back here, she realized.

For a moment, she let the happy memories flow through her. Images from when she had thought she really had a chance to make Daniel fall in love with her. Memories—

"Karen! Help me!" came Jamie's scream.

Jumping to her feet, Karen saw that he had fallen into deeper water and the current was taking him downstream. Right toward the hole Daniel had told her was deep enough for swimming.

"Jamie!" she screamed, running along the riverbank. How could she have taken her eyes off him for even a second?

He screamed again and then he went under. With her heart in her throat, Karen kicked off her shoes and jumped in after him.

Chapter Fourteen

High on the hill above the river, Daniel sat astride Ringo, his crossed arms resting on the pommel of the saddle, and watched his wife playing with his nephew. Daniel just couldn't figure her out.

When he saw Jamie wander closer to the deeper section of the river, his hands tightened on the reins. While he was debating whether to ride down and interfere, Jamie suddenly lost his footing on the rocks and tumbled into the water.

Daniel's heart rose into his throat as he spurred Ringo into a gallop and they thundered down the long hill. Helplessly Karen ran along the bank while Jamie was carried downstream. Then Jamie's head disappeared. Knowing Karen's fear of the water, Daniel was surprised to see her go into the river. Her swimming skills were limited. Terrified for both of them, Daniel urged Ringo to go even faster.

They plunged into the water just as Karen reached Jamie in the middle of the river. Daniel shouted, but the sound of his voice was swept away. He was relieved to see Karen grab a large branch that stuck out of the water and boost Jamie up until he was sitting astride it while she continued to hold tight.

"Hang on, honey, I'm coming," Daniel muttered under his breath as he and Ringo surged through the water.

Clinging to the branch, Karen felt as if she had swallowed half the river.

"Don't let go," she shouted to Jamie, who was holding on to the limb.

He said something she couldn't hear. His face was pale, his hair dripping rivulets of water. Karen's teeth began to chatter, but she didn't know if it was from cold or fear. All she knew was that the snag had probably saved their lives.

She was wet and cold and terrified. Not only that, but it was her carelessness that had put them here. She had no idea how they were going to get back to the bank. She knew she wasn't a strong enough swimmer to get the both of them to safety and she couldn't leave Jamie here and go for help. What if she failed? How long would it be before anyone got worried and looked for them?

Above her, Jamie shouted again. When Karen looked up, he pointed toward the riverbank.

When she looked over her shoulder, she almost let go of the branch. Swimming toward them was Daniel on his pinto. Karen had never been so overjoyed to see anyone in her life.

"Are you okay?" he shouted as he got closer.

"Yes! Thank God you're here!"

He reached out an arm to pull her up behind him, but she shook her head and clung to the branch.

"Get Jamie first!"

Daniel was surprised. Karen was obviously afraid and Jamie's position was much more secure than her own.

"I'll get him, too," he shouted.

She shook her head. "Take him first."

Daniel nodded his understanding. He maneuvered Ringo as close as he could, hollered to Jamie and held out his arms. Almost immediately, Jamie let go of his safe perch, trusting Daniel to catch him, and dropped into his waiting arms.

"I've got you!" For a moment, Daniel held him tight and waited for his pounding heart to slow.

"Are you okay?"

"Yeah. Karen saved me."

"Then let's save her." Settling Jamie in front of him on Ringo and telling him to hold tight to the horn, Daniel turned back to where she was hanging on to the branch.

"Can you grab the stirrup with your hand?" he shouted.

"No." She was too scared to let go of the branch.

"Karen," he yelled again. "We aren't going to leave you here. Come on, honey, you can do it. I won't let anything happen to you."

Remembering how Jamie had trusted Daniel, she tried to overcome her own fear of the deep, swirling water. When she looked at Jamie, safe in Daniel's arms, she found the courage to try.

In order to reach the stirrup, she had to let go of the branch. All around her, the current sucked at her, and the water was cold.

"Wait a minute," Daniel shouted. Urging Ringo closer, he kicked his boot free of the stirrup. "Now!" he told her. "Come on!"

Karen took a deep breath and let go of the branch. She almost went under as she plunged toward the stirrup. Her straining fingers brushed against it, but it slipped away. Daniel's hand clamped around her wrist and he dragged her closer. Her fingers caught the stirrup.

"Good girl! Hang on tight." As she held on with both hands, he urged Ringo toward the shore.

Karen looked up at Jamie, who was clinging to the saddle horn. At least he was safe, she thought gratefully. Again, she felt like an irresponsible fool. Just because she had cautioned him about getting too close to the edge of the little beach, had she really thought an adventuresome five-year-old would obey? This was all her fault.

Daniel kept looking at her, making sure she was still hanging on. As soon as Ringo stepped into the shallows and Karen's feet touched the rocky bottom, she let go of the stirrup. While she waded ashore, Daniel rode Ringo to the grassy bank and lowered Jamie to the ground. As he dismounted, Karen collapsed onto the grass and hugged Jamie.

"I'm sorry!" she told him, flooded with guilt.

"Me, too," he cried. "I'm sorry I didn't mind."

Daniel knelt down and wrapped his arms around both of them as Ringo shook himself and spattered them with water.

"Oh, God," Daniel groaned. "Are you both okay?"

"We're safe," Karen gasped, trembling and savoring the feel of Daniel's arms. At any moment now, he would erupt into fury at her carelessness.

"I've never been so scared," he rasped instead. He kissed Jamie's cheek and then he found Karen's mouth with his. His fingers bit into her arms as he pulled her closer and kissed her possessively.

"How did you get to us so fast?" Karen asked when he let her go. "I looked up and you were right there. Where did you come from?"

"I was watching you from the top of the hill." His voice was slightly hoarse. "I saw Jamie fall in, but I never would have gotten to him in time. You're the one who saved him."

"I almost let him drown." Karen felt obliged to correct him.

Daniel bent his head. "You must have been terrified. I was scared enough for both of us when I saw you go in after him."

"I had no choice." Karen realized it was true. She loved Jamie like her own son. She couldn't have let him drown if there had been even a small chance that she could save him.

For a few more moments, they sat there, huddled together. They were soaked but the sun was quickly warming them.

"Come on," Daniel said as he was finally able to release them. "Let's go home."

"What happened to you?" Mary demanded when they came trooping through the kitchen. During the Jeep ride back, the sun had almost dried their hair and clothes, but they still looked bedraggled.

"They fell in the river," Daniel told her. "I was riding by, so I pulled them out."

Mary's mouth fell open and she stared. "Are you kidding?"

Daniel shook his head. The reminder of what might have happened still made his stomach churn with anguish. He could have lost both of them. "Would you run a tub for Jamie and get him to bed?" he asked Mary. "I think he's pretty exhausted."

"Of course," she exclaimed. "Are you all okay?"

"We're fine." Daniel fought down his impatience. All he wanted to do was to wrap his arms around Karen and never let her go. "I'll fill you in later."

As Mary guided Jamie up the stairs, he turned to Karen. "Can you walk or shall I carry you?"

She looked ready to drop. The burst of adrenaline she'd been operating on had long since drained away. "Of course I can walk."

Disregarding her protest, he scooped her into his arms and took her upstairs, through their bedroom and into the master bath. Setting her on her feet, he turned on the faucets in the shower.

"Get your clothes off." He was still shaking with all the terrible possibilities that kept crowding his mind till he wanted to scream.

"I can take a shower by myself," she argued.

Daniel looked at her and his eyes blazed. "I'm not leaving you alone. Not now. Get them off."

Karen was too exhausted to go on fighting him. Feeling self-conscious, she obeyed while he adjusted the water. He had removed his wet boots and socks in the mudroom, but he was still wearing the rest of his clothes. As soon as she was undressed, he stepped right into the shower with her.

"What are you doing?"

"Taking care of my lady." His expression was tender as he gently soaped her body and shampooed her hair. Exhausted, Karen submitted gratefully to his ministrations. Finally the deep-seated tremors of fear and reaction began to fade. Her tears joined the rivulets of water running down her face and a tiny hiccup escaped her lips.

Daniel froze. Then he bent down and peered into her averted face. Seeing her tears, he enfolded her naked body into his protective embrace.

"Don't cry, honey. It's okay," he murmured as he caressed her back. "You're safe now. You're both safe."

"I'm so sorry." Karen choked through her tears.

"It wasn't your fault!" he said fiercely. "I watched the whole thing. Jamie was only doing what any five-year-old will do. You couldn't know what would happen."

"I should have been watching him more closely," she said dully. "I should have been paying attention, instead of thinking about—" She broke off guiltily and looked away.

"Thinking about what?" he demanded, spinning her back around.

Her cheeks went pink and she hung her head. "It's not important."

"No, you're right. What's important is that you went in after him, even though you must have been terrified. You saved him."

"You saved us both," she corrected.

"That's where you're wrong. I couldn't have gotten there in time. Jamie would have gone under and I never would have found him. *You* saved him and then, when I wanted to pull you out of the river, you made me get him first. That took courage, lady. And don't you think for a moment that it didn't."

Relieved that Daniel didn't hate her, Karen cried against his shoulder as he soothed her with his low voice and gentle touch. When her tears had stopped, he released her.

"I could have lost you both." He choked.

"I'm sor—"

Daniel pressed a finger to her lips as he looked into her shimmering green eyes. "Why did you insist I get Jamie first?" he asked. "He was much safer than you were."

Karen seemed surprised by his question. "I love him," she said fiercely. "I wanted him safe."

Suddenly Daniel realized that a woman who would sacrifice her own safety for one child would not callously plan on destroying another. Somehow, he must have misunderstood her meaning when he had overheard her and her father.

He felt as if a great weight had been lifted from his shoulders. Now, however, the most important thing was that both the people he loved were okay.

Yes, he loved her! He could admit it, if only to himself.

He wanted to tell her how he felt, but he didn't dare. When she found out how weak his trust in her had been, she would hate him. Not only had he failed to believe in her, but he had punished her for what he had only thought she might do, as well. And now he would pay the price for his own stupidity, but he would never stop loving her.

Seeing the harsh need etched on his face, Karen reached up to kiss him. Immediately, his arms closed around her. Groaning low in his throat, he pulled her tightly against him.

When he finally let her go, the water was starting to run cold and his sodden clothing lay in a puddle on the bathroom floor. Fastening a towel around his hips, he wrapped her in another and laid her gently in bed.

"Get some rest," he said, covering her and kissing the tip of her nose.

"Don't leave me." She reached out to him but he shook his head regretfully.

"I have to take care of Ringo. I'll be back later." He needed to be alone, to sort out his feelings and to prepare for the devastation to his heart he knew was coming.

When Karen woke, hours later, it was dark. She sat up and turned on the bedside lamp, and was shocked to see Daniel sprawled in the chair, sound asleep.

The light must have disturbed him. He stretched and rubbed his eyes. When he saw that she, too, was awake, he gave her a crooked grin. "Are you okay?"

"I'm fine. How's Jamie?"

"Asleep, I imagine. Like you should be."

Ignoring his comment, she asked, "Why are you over there? Why didn't you come to bed?"

His gaze slid away from hers. "I wanted to make sure you were all right. Now that I know you are, I'll go in the other room so I won't disturb you."

Perplexed, Karen watched him go. After he left the room, she tossed and turned. It took her hours to go back to sleep.

* * *

As the days passed, Daniel was relieved to see that Jamie apparently harbored no lasting effects from the scare they had experienced. Karen, too, was recovering, even though he knew she still blamed herself for the near tragedy.

Sometimes, it was all he could do to keep from going to her and confessing everything. Then his courage would fail him. Once she knew why he had been treating her so badly, she would despise him. And he just wasn't ready to face that.

While he was going through the agonies of the damned, Karen realized she had to do something drastic to break through the wall he had erected. Somehow, she had to make him believe how much she wanted him. That she didn't miss the kind of life her parents had in Denver and that she had no intentions of ever going back to it. Perhaps then, he would let down his guard and begin to care for her.

She had to come up with a plan. The court might have granted her six months to win Daniel's love but, if her suspicions about her own body were correct, her time was running out.

"You want to go where?" Daniel demanded when Karen made her startling announcement over the dinner table.

"I want to go to my parents' garden party. And I want you and Jamie to go with me." Perhaps if he got a good dose of the way the other half lived, with their pretensions, ambitions and petty materialism, he would believe her when she told him that everything she had ever wanted was at White Ridge.

Now he just looked dumbfounded. "Why?"

"Because a party will be fun," she said, knowing it would probably be anything but fun. "It will be a good experience for Jamie and a chance to see my parents again. Besides, I want to show off my family. Do you have anything against that?"

Daniel looked as if he would rather eat grubs than go with her. "I guess not."

Encouraged by his easy capitulation, Karen turned to Jamie.

"A party?" he asked. "Like a birthday party, with balloons and cake and presents?"

She had to tell the truth. "There won't be any presents, but I'm sure there will be cake, and I wouldn't be surprised to see a few balloons around. And there will be other children to play with."

"Count me in," he exclaimed, bringing a dry chuckle to Daniel's lips.

"Count me in, too," he said reluctantly.

On the day of the party, the three of them left the ranch early and took the station wagon to Denver. Karen's parents had been delighted to hear they were actually coming and had invited them to stay overnight.

Now, as the road unfolded like a long, gray ribbon before them, Karen could only hope she had made the right decision. She had sneaked into town the day before and confirmed her other suspicion. The knowledge glowed inside her like a Roman candle, but she had to wait until just the right moment to tell Daniel.

When they got to the house, they greeted Karen's parents and dodged the scurrying caterers as her mother led them to a guest suite to freshen up and change. When they climbed the elegant curving staircase, Karen could see Daniel looking around and mentally comparing the lavish decor with the cozy furnishings at the ranch. She wanted to tell him how cold and empty a house like this could be, but she didn't.

"Are you ready to go downstairs?" he finally asked impatiently from the doorway of their private bath, where she had been primping. The bathroom was done in white tile, with gilt-framed mirrors on the walls and elaborate brass fixtures and towel bars. Under Karen's feet was a thick white carpet.

She pushed back the ornate, white velvet chair that sat in front of a lighted makeup mirror. When she looked at him, she was gratified to see the flare of appreciation in his eyes.

She was wearing a blue-and-lavender flowered chiffon dress with a short, tiered skirt. Her hair was loose and curly and her only jewelry was her wedding band and the delicate silver hoops that Daniel had bought her in Craig one day.

"Very nice," he murmured as he looked her over. He wore new black jeans and a white, Western-cut shirt with black stitching. With his coal black hair, he was devilishly handsome. It was all Karen could do to tear her gaze away and smile at Jamie, whose shirt and jeans matched his uncle's.

"You look pretty," he told her.

"I'm going to be with the two handsomest men at the party." She bent to kiss his cheek.

As she did, he sniffed at her neck. "You smell like the flowers at home."

"I wish we were home," Daniel muttered.

"You might as well see how the other half lives," Karen told him briskly. She took a deep breath and prayed that her bizarre plan would meet with success. If this party didn't convince Daniel that giving up this life-style was no hardship to her, nothing would. As soon as he admitted how bored and disillusioned he was, she was going to drag him to a secluded corner and tell him how much she loved him. As a great plan, it wasn't much, but it was all she had.

"Are we ready?" she asked brightly.

Ignoring his grumbled reply, she clasped Jamie's hand and led the way downstairs.

On the main floor, the party was in full swing. Jamie was most impressed by the ice sculpture and the lavish buffet. Before he could sample anything, a group of well-dressed children lured him outside to play. Daniel watched the other guests silently, but it was impossible for Karen to tell what he really thought of the lavish affair.

Determined to see her plan through, she got them something to drink and began introducing him to the people she knew. Instead of being either overwhelmed, intimidated or bored, as she had hoped, he surprised her. He was soon surrounded by lawyers, doctors and jaded wives who found a Native American sheep rancher quite fascinating.

This was not the way it was supposed to be!

While Daniel talked to a heart surgeon who bred llamas as a hobby, Karen went to refill her club soda and check on Jamie. While she was at the bar, she was shocked to run into Judge Greenburg.

"I thought that was Jamie I saw outside," he said, extending his hand. "What brings you to Denver?"

Suppressing the nervous fluttering inside her, Karen explained that the Whitworths were her parents.

"Ah, yes," he said, "I should have recognized the resemblance between you and Marcia. I thought you looked familiar when you appeared in my courtroom. Is your husband with you?"

Karen glanced around. "I think Daniel's still talking llamas with Dr. Ganz."

"Well, you may have to rescue him," Judge Greenburg told her with a smile. "Say hello for me if I don't see him first."

"I will." She excused herself and hurried back to where she had left him.

When she got there, he was talking with a small group of horse people. Standing back and listening, Karen felt a burst of pride that he was her husband. Not only was he intelligent, but he was by far the most attractive man at the party. From the expressions on the faces of the women in the group that surrounded him, she could tell she wasn't the only one who thought so.

It was clear that her plan was backfiring.

"Enough about horses," interrupted a man whose voice was slurred from too much champagne. "What I want to know is how many ponies you had to pay for that good-looking blonde you came with."

Karen saw Daniel's eyes narrow dangerously. "I beg your pardon?"

"Don't you people pay some kind of bride price when you get hitched?" the man asked with a smirk.

Several people in the group looked uncomfortable, but a few of the others were avidly curious, even amused by his remarks. Karen hadn't meant for Daniel to be humiliated and she was about to interrupt and drag him away, when he glanced up and saw her. To her surprise, he smiled and extended a hand.

Hesitantly she came forward. He pulled her close and anchored her at his side with an arm around her waist.

"This is the bride in question," he said with pride in his voice. "My wife, Karen."

She was painfully aware that her parents had stopped on their way by. This was turning into a disaster. A scene would only convince them she had married a savage, and blow Daniel's chances with Judge Greenburg.

"I'd say she was worth a few ponies," quipped the drunk. A couple of people laughed appreciatively.

Daniel cleared his throat and smiled into Karen's eyes. What she saw shining on his face made her start to tremble.

Was it real, or was he merely putting on an act for the other guests?

"Tell us, Daniel," goaded one of the women Karen had noticed watching him with interest. "How many ponies is she worth?"

Karen stiffened with embarrassment. She wished that her parents would move on.

Daniel's hand tightened on her waist. "I paid no ponies for this woman," he said, the emotion in his voice stirring an answering reaction in her. He bowed over her hand, and the feel of his lips against her skin made her weak. "There was only one bride price worthy of her," he said, raising his head so she could see the love burning in his beautiful black eyes. "The price was my heart, and I paid it gladly."

Behind her, a woman sighed. Several people applauded. Karen could only stare at him, as the love in her own heart threatened to overflow.

Daniel glanced around them. "Excuse us, won't you?"

"Oh, that's so romantic," someone gushed.

With his arm wrapped possessively around Karen, Daniel led her to a secluded spot on the patio, behind a weeping fig tree in a ceramic pot.

"I don't want to lose you," he said fiercely as he gripped her shoulders. "Please, stay with me, no matter what happens."

"Did you mean what you said out there?" she asked, hope soaring inside her.

His face was taut with strain. "I meant every word."

"Why didn't you tell me this before? You've been so distant that I didn't know what to think."

"I couldn't tell you," he said. "I was too ashamed."

Surprised, she touched his cheek. "Ashamed of what?"

He captured her hand in his and held it like a lifeline. "I overheard you talking to your father on the patio that night."

It wasn't what she had expected him to say. Puzzled, she waited for him to continue.

"You were talking about having children—my children."

She tried to remember just what had been said, but couldn't.

Daniel looked miserable. "When you told him you had accepted the only course of action possible, I thought you meant you had decided to have an abortion if you should get pregnant."

His words stunned her. How could he have believed something like that? Didn't he know her at all?

He had jumped to conclusions without giving her a chance to explain. Had coldly shut her out of his life, hurting her so badly she had thought her heart would break, and for what? Fury made Karen's blood boil.

Daniel turned slightly away and she saw his powerful shoulders droop. For a moment, she wanted to hurt him as much as he had hurt her. Then she remembered the sorrow and pain in his voice when he told her about the girl who *had* gotten rid of his child. How could Karen hurt him again after what he had already been through?

She reached out to him and he looked up, eyes filled with despair. "Later, I realized that I must have misunderstood."

"I'm sorry," she said. "I had no idea you had heard that. All I meant was that if I got pregnant I would keep the baby, no matter what else happened."

His hand tightened painfully on hers. "Why would you want my child?"

It was the time for total honesty. "Because I would love that child, just as I already love its father," she admitted.

She watched the emotions race across his normally impassive face; despair, shock, wonder, disbelief, hesitant acceptance and then, finally, blinding happiness.

"Are you sure?" His dark eyes blazed into hers.

"As sure as I've ever been about anything," she whispered. "Oh, dear! I dragged you to the party so you'd see for yourself that I don't miss this life." She made a sweeping gesture with her hand. "I thought you were upset because I hadn't told you about my parents and the kind of childhood I had."

"That's why you wanted to come today?" he demanded.

"Yes, so you'd see it all for what it really is."

His astonishment was almost comical. "I guess we were both pretty mixed up," he said tenderly.

"There's something else I need to tell you." Her hand went protectively to her stomach. "About that baby we mentioned."

Abruptly the color drained from Daniel's face as if someone had pulled a plug. "You're pregnant?"

Her smile wavered. "That's right."

"Oh, my God!" He swept her into his arms and then, just as quickly, let her go. "Did I hurt you?"

"No. No, you didn't." She had never seen him so vulnerable.

"Do you need to sit down?" he demanded.

"I don't," she told him with a gentle smile. "Do you?"

"I don't know." He still looked dazed. "Are you sure?" he croaked.

"I saw the doctor yesterday."

"And you're okay with this?" he questioned.

"Yes. Are you?"

His stunned expression began to fade, replaced by the biggest smile she had ever seen on his face.

"We're going to have a baby," he muttered, hugging her carefully. "We're going to be parents."

"We're going to be a family," she said. "You and I and Jamie and this baby. Judge Greenburg is here, at the party.

Can you believe it? I have a feeling that everything is going to work out."

"Did you talk to him?" Daniel asked.

"Yes, and he was very friendly." Suddenly a loud burst of laughter reminded Karen where they were. The crowds of people, the noise and the tinkling piano music she didn't really like were all too much for her.

"Can we take Jamie and go home now?" she asked.

"In a minute," Daniel whispered as he bent his head. "First, I want to kiss you." Right before he pulled her into his arms, she glimpsed a suspicious gleam in his black eyes. For the first time, when she looked into them, she could see all the way to his soul.

* * * * *

BABY'S CHOICE

Those mischievous matchmaking babies are back, as Marie Ferrarella's Baby's Choice series continues in August with MOTHER ON THE WING (SR #1026).

Frank Harrigan could hardly explain his sudden desire to fly to Seattle. Sure, an old friend had written to him out of the blue, but there was something else.... Then he spotted Donna McCollough, or rather, she fell right into his lap. And from that moment on, they were powerless to interfere with what angelic fate had lovingly ordained.

Continue to share in the wonder of life and love, as babies-in-waiting handpick the most perfect parents, only in

Silhouette
R O M A N C E ™

Take 4 bestselling love stories FREE

Plus get a FREE surprise gift!

Special Limited-time Offer

Mail to Silhouette Reader Service™

3010 Walden Avenue
P.O. Box 1867
Buffalo, N.Y. 14269-1867

YES! Please send me 4 free Silhouette Special Edition® novels and my free surprise gift. Then send me 6 brand-new novels every month, which I will receive months before they appear in bookstores. Bill me at the low price of $2.89 each plus 25¢ delivery and applicable sales tax, if any.* That's the complete price and—compared to the cover prices of $3.50 each—quite a bargain! I understand that accepting the books and gift places me under no obligation ever to buy any books. I can always return a shipment and cancel at any time. Even if I never buy another book from Silhouette, the 4 free books and the surprise gift are mine to keep forever.

235 BPA ANRQ

Name	(PLEASE PRINT)	
Address	Apt. No.	
City	State	Zip

This offer is limited to one order per household and not valid to present Silhouette Special Edition® subscribers. *Terms and prices are subject to change without notice. Sales tax applicable in N.Y.

USPED-94R   ©1990 Harlequin Enterprises Limited

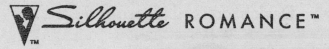

Silhouette ROMANCE™

First comes marriage.... Will love follow?
Find out this September when Silhouette Romance presents

Join six couples who marry for convenient reasons, and still find happily-ever-afters. Look for these wonderful books by some of your favorite authors:

#1030 *Timely Matrimony* by Kasey Michaels
#1031 *McCullough's Bride* by Anne Peters
#1032 *One of a Kind Marriage* by Cathie Linz
#1033 *Oh, Baby!* by Lauryn Chandler
#1034 *Temporary Groom* by Jayne Addison
#1035 *Wife in Name Only* by Carolyn Zane

HASTY

Dark secrets, dangerous desire...

Lovers DARK AND DANGEROUS

Three spine-tingling tales from the dark side of love.

This October, enter the world of shadowy romance as Silhouette presents the third in their annual tradition of thrilling love stories and chilling story lines. Written by three of Silhouette's top names:

LINDSAY McKENNA
LEE KARR
RACHEL LEE

Haunting a store near you this October.

Silhouette Books
is proud to present
our best authors, their best books...
and the best in your reading pleasure!

Throughout 1994, look for exciting books
by these top names in contemporary
romance:

DIANA PALMER
Enamored in August

HEATHER GRAHAM POZZESSERE
The Game of Love in August

FERN MICHAELS
Beyond Tomorrow in August

NORA ROBERTS
The Last Honest Woman in September

LINDA LAEL MILLER
Snowflakes on the Sea in September

*When it comes to passion,
we wrote the book.*

Silhouette®

by Christine Rimmer

Three rapscallion brothers. Their main talent: making trouble. Their only hope: three uncommon women who knew the way to heal a wounded heart! Meet them in these books:

Jared Jones

hadn't had it easy with women. Retreating to his mountain cabin, he found willful Eden Parker waiting to show him a good woman's love in MAN OF THE MOUNTAIN (May, SE #886).

Patrick Jones

was determined to show Regina Black that a wild Jones boy was *not* husband material. But that wouldn't stop her from trying to nab him in SWEETBRIAR SUMMIT (July, SE #896)!

Jack Roper

came to town looking for the wayward and beautiful Olivia Larrabee. He never suspected he'd uncover a long-buried Jones family secret in A HOME FOR THE HUNTER (September, SE #908)....

Meet these rascal men and the women who'll tame them, only from Silhouette Books and Special Edition!